The Undiscovered Archives of Sherlock Holmes

by John Lawrence

Edited by David Marcum

Hardcover ISBN 978-1-78705-954-2
Paperback ISBN 978-1-78705-955-9
ePub ISBN 978-1-78705-956-6
PDF ISBN 978-1-78705-957-3

Published by MX Publishing
335 Princess Park Manor, Royal Drive,
London, N11 3GX
www.mxpublishing.com

Cover design by Brian Belanger

Contents

1

The Case of the
Purloined Talisman

The following details an undisclosed case in the illustrious career of Sherlock Holmes, the legendary consulting detective. The existence of this remarkable document was revealed only recently by a solicitor in the firm once retained by Dr. John H. Watson. A sealed tan envelope had been entrusted to the firm by Dr. Watson shortly after it was written in 1925, and, as stipulated by Dr. Watson, had remained sealed in the firm's safe until the appointed date for its disclosure, a century after the end of the Great War. The envelope was opened recently and found to contain the following letter and manuscript, which are presented here for the first time. – J.L.

London, 14 August, 1925

To Londoners of the Twenty-first Century:

I have requested that my solicitor safeguard the accompanying document and that its existence not be disclosed until the centennial of the end of the Great War, 11 November, 2018. Following that date, the envelope and its contents may be divulged and conveyed to The Strand Magazine *or its literary successor for publication.*

Herein lies an extraordinary case undertaken by Mr. Sherlock Holmes whose nature is so delicate that it must not be publicly disclosed until long after I, and all other participants in the story, have gone to our rewards. I thank you for your willingness to conform to what must appear to be an eccentric request, but once the manuscript is revealed, the reason for a century of concealment will become evident. I only pray the world was able to avoid the grave outcome the story portends.

Very respectfully yours,
John H. Watson, M.D.
London

The Great War had ended nearly five years earlier, and yet London still maintained a discernible air of gaiety, triumph, and relief. The horror associated with the "war to end all wars" had receded, and Britons were quite convinced that nothing comparable could again be contemplated.

Having nearly reached the advanced age of seventy-one, I had long since pared down my medical practice and was content to spend my days in less strenuous activities. Upon occasion, however, I would have the opportunity to visit with my dearest companion of so many decades and adventures, Sherlock Holmes, either at his home in Sussex or on those increasingly rare occasions when he would venture to London.

It was one of those visits in late 1923 that served as the occasion of one of our most remarkable adventures, one whose impact may well be impossible to determine for years to come. I had returned only a few days earlier from a trip to Morocco during a lull in the Berber uprising and was still recovering from the fatigue of the journey when I received a wire from Holmes asking if I might meet him at Waterloo Station. I was delighted at the prospect of seeing my old friend, and was waiting on the platform when his train arrived.

"Good to see you, Watson!" Holmes called cheerily as he stepped off the train and strode across the crowded platform to greet me.

"Holmes!" I said, grasping his hand in both of mine and giving it a good shake. "It is so good to see you! I trust your journey was uneventful."

"Quite enjoyable," he assured, eying me carefully, a slight smile turning up the ends of those thin lips. "And I presume that Morocco agreed with you – except for your over-indulgence in the highly spiced foods, your lack of adequate house staff, and your constant concerns for your personal safety." I smiled patiently at yet again being the object of his astonishing deductive powers.

"Holmes, you never change, do you?" I remarked. "It is very good to be dissected by you like a cadaver on a slab." His powers of observation and deduction certainly didn't seem to have deteriorated in the months since our last visit. "All right, explain to me how you come to know so much of my recent activities in North Africa."

"Surely it's obvious," he said, flicking his long fingers towards my face. "There is white powder caked around the corner of your mouth, suggesting recent consumption of a calcium compound intended to relieve gastric distress – doubtless caused by your diet of tagines and hariras common in Morocco. Your lack of house staff is obvious by the flecks of dried food on your sleeve – perhaps some of that harira? – and by the mud you have allowed to accumulate on your boots, all of which surely would have been cleaned by any competent servant.

"As to your safety concerns, I note that you are carrying a cane of unusual heft. The elaborately carved bone handle is clearly of Tuareg origins, designed by those 'blue people' for self-protection. Certainly such a formidable instrument isn't required to assist you in walking – indeed, your gait seems quite normal – so you must have chosen the cane to serve as a club if needed against some ungrateful, feloniously-inclined urchin."

"But how did you know of my journey to Morocco?" I wondered aloud.

"Ah," said Holmes, smiling faintly. "You had sent me a note announcing your trip!"

He paused to allow me to admire his exhibition of deductive skills, and to give me an opportunity to acknowledge that he was right on every count. "Well done," I said, as he surely had expected.

He looked away, shaking his head slightly, and said over his shoulder, "Actually, it was all quite obvious – or, as you would write in one of your little stories, 'Elementary',"

He looked somewhat older than on the occasion of our last visit, but he remained whip-thin and from his grip, I could tell, as strong as ever. His hair, combed straight backwards, was thinning on the top, and his gray side-whiskers were trimmed shorter, in keeping with recent style. The lines on his thin face were more pronounced, running down from the edges of his beaked nose, past his thin mouth, towards his long, pointed chin. The hollows under his cheekbones were somewhat deeper, and there was a flap of slack skin under his chin that comes to us all, thanks to the merciless force of gravity. His eyes remained bright and sharp, but the lids above them were slightly more hooded and drooped, accentuating the hawk-like appearance that I had always perceived in his countenance.

We hailed a cab and were taken to the venerable Brown's Hotel in Mayfair, where his as-yet undisclosed client had reserved rooms for him. It always seemed odd to be in London with Holmes and not return to our former quarters at Baker Street, abandoned two decades earlier, but the warmth and elegance of Brown's compensated in nearly every respect.

"You have a reservation for me," he informed the youthful clerk at the front desk. "My name is 'Holmes'."

"Ah, yes, Mr. Sherlock Holmes," the young man said. "I believe my grandfather had mentioned your name when I was a child!"

Holmes's eyebrows arched slightly and his mouth pursed, but otherwise he displayed little in response to the clerk's remark, although I could barely suppress a smile. We deposited Holmes's luggage in his comfortable room and soon found ourselves at the nearby Goat Tavern. I quickly brought Holmes up to date with the details of my limited practice as he polished off his tea and a slice of lemon cake before reaching for his pipe and shag tobacco. "And you?" I asked. "Are you continuing to enjoy life as an apiarist?"

"I find my Sussex bees most enjoyable," he said. "I'm pleased to say that I have become great friends with Manley, whom you might know as author of *Honey Production in the British Isles*."

"Actually, no," I replied with a hint of exasperation. "I'm unfamiliar with that particular volume or its author."

"Well, never mind," Holmes said impatiently. "Watson, I've been asked to undertake a rather unique mission abroad, one in which I could very well use some expert assistance." A tiny smile spread across his normally expressionless countenance. "Perhaps something that might interest you – if you aren't too busy, of course."

Even at this late date, I almost hesitate to identify the eminent figure who had engaged Holmes, for it wasn't the Foreign Office, but rather a controversial member of Commons. We soon engaged a motorcar to carry us along the Embankment to a clandestine meeting near Whitehall. The name of Holmes's client was certainly known to me, but largely in a disparaging way, given his controversial record in government during the Great War. "Don't jump to conclusions," Holmes counseled. "The key point here is the validity of the mission, not the reputation or popularity of the man behind it."

Soon we were being escorted into an office in the shadow of the tower containing Big Ben and seated across the desk from our distinguished employer, the Honorable Winston Churchill, MP, late the wartime Lord of the Admiralty and a man in fear not only for his country's safety but his own life as well. Tensions with Ireland were at fever pitch once again – indeed, the distinguished diplomat and soldier Sir Henry Wilson had been assassinated outside his own London home by I.R.A. fanatics the previous June, and concerns about the durability of The League of Nations and The Treaty of Versailles were growing with each passing month.

"The whole map of Europe has been changed by the cataclysm that has swept the world," Churchill had recently declared. The rising menace of the Russian *Bolsheviki* threatened even greater instability for Eastern Europe, and perhaps for England as well. Mounting disruptions in India and Egypt, instigated by the calls for independence by the nationalist agitator Gandhi, jeopardized the future of the Empire itself.

Despite his thinning red hair, round form, and oddly cherubic look, no one would mistake the mercurial Churchill for anything but a gravely engaged statesman. Of course, I knew of his reputation as a hard-driving advocate for the Empire and promoter of stronger defences, but for all the world, across the table he seemed more like a frantic Puck with a cigar clenched tightly in his mouth.

"Mr. Holmes, Dr. Watson," he nodded in our direction slightly as he spoke our names, "these are grave times indeed. I recall the great service that you both provided to Britain on the eve of the Great War, apprehending that scoundrel Van Bork," Churchill said. "Now your country requires your services as never before. Were your brother Mycroft in better health," he looked at Holmes, "there would be no need for your involvement. But as it is," his shoulders involuntarily hunched, "we have no one else to whom we might turn."

"I am flattered to be of service," Holmes murmured. "May I ask to whom you allude when you reference 'we'? Are you speaking on behalf of the government – (he knew that Churchill was not a member of the government, so that was not likely) – the King – (even less so, as Churchill was not a favorite of the monarch) – or some . . . *other interest*?"

9

"I am speaking in the interest of *all* of the above, sir, whether they are aware of it or not!" Churchill replied curtly, waving his hand above his head and vaguely in the direction of the Palace of Westminster. "Your client is England itself! My honorable colleagues in the current government fail to comprehend the risks or the dangers, but I assure you, sir, the peril is grave, and becoming more so daily."

"Indeed," replied Holmes, his lips pursing slightly. "Pray explain what service I may provide to you and England."

"Germany," said Churchill decisively. "The danger is Germany. The country is coming apart at the seams, a phoenix rising from the ashes, straining to pull itself free from its moorings," he fulminated, mixing metaphors and syntax. "Few in this country appreciate the gravity of recent developments. And certainly, few in there!" he cried, pointing to Barry's massive tower with its huge clock looming over the House of Commons.

"I want you, Mr. Holmes – I *need* you – to help me to wake England out of its stupor, to encourage our countrymen to embrace rearmament, to begin preparing for the next war which is coming as surely as we are sitting here!" he declared. He slapped the tabletop with his bare hand for emphasis before sticking his fat cigar back into his rubbery mouth and hunching forward closer to Holmes's face.

Churchill described an assignment that would take Holmes into southern Germany to conduct reconnaissance of the noisy band of National Socialist extremists – or *Nazis* – who had taken root in Bavaria. Their incendiary rhetoric attributed the post-war humiliation of the German nation to treason by Jews, a group with which Churchill had developed close alliances. These fanatics, led by a cashiered army corporal who had served the Kaiser during the War, were inflaming their countrymen and denouncing the concessions made in Versailles treaty, especially the payment of millions of pounds in reparations to the allies and the hated War Guilt Clause. "He is either a maniac or the most dangerous person in the world," Churchill said of the Nazi leader, Adolf Hitler, "and perhaps both! I need you to tell me."

The portrait of life in Germany that he painted was far more insidious than that being portrayed in the British press, as was the incendiary tone of the Nazi propaganda. Between this Nazi hysteria on the right, and the rise of the Bolsheviks in Russia on the left, it seemed in the opinion of our distinguished host that, however inconceivable, another war might well be unavoidable,

"You see, Mr. Holmes," he explained, "conventional diplomacy, and even my own scholarly writings, simply fail to achieve the necessary impact. In my current diminished role. I am unable to summon the powers of our military or our intelligence services. I must turn to you, as a private consulting spy, if you will, to help expose the true nature of the Nazi plans. Only then will we wake up this naïve and pacifistic nation to the dangers looming before us."

But that was not all. Churchill was also deeply concerned with enemies that he believed were operating in England, clandestinely aiding the Germans' plans for global conquest. "They are everywhere, spinning their webs, seducing the innocents with false promises of peace," he intoned, sounding both menacing and slightly deranged "They are here in London!" he declared, lowering his voice dramatically "You have heard of Oswald Mosley? We must expose them – and *root them out*!"

He again stuck his cigar in his rubbery mouth and arched his eyebrows. His face emerged from a cloud of acrid smoke as he leaned as close to Holmes and me as possible. "Well," he asked as his exhaled smoke enveloped his bulbous head. The effect was remarkable! "Can England count on the two of you? Can *I* count on you?"

During his long career, Holmes had been no stranger to taking commissions from governments, both British and foreign alike, and on occasion they were of a distinctly clandestine nature. Few challenges, however, seemed to address a scenario as filled with diplomatic intrigue and peril as the one Churchill had outlined.

"The assignment certainly has many points of interest," remarked Holmes after we had bade *adieu* to our new client. With a report from an unimpeachable source like Sherlock Holmes, Churchill surmised, he could rouse his fellow parliamentarians from their torpor in order to begin preparations for the inevitable tempest. However, the Nazis were not to be trifled with – a slip, any intemperate comment, could easily expose Holmes's true identify and subject him to serious danger!

My immediate reaction to the proposition was negative in the extreme. "Holmes, if I may say so, you aren't the man physically that you once were," I remonstrated. In his prime, Holmes had been a formidable master of the Japanese art of *baritsu*, able to defend himself against adversaries of far greater stature. But after decades of strenuous activity and injury (and mountains of shag tobacco), Holmes didn't move as confidently as he once was able. He would have a difficult time protecting himself against an aggrieved, jack-boot-wearing brown shirt in Bavaria. He stuck out his lower lip as we rumbled along the cobbled streets, his heavy lids half-closed on his slate-gray eyes. "I believe that I can stay a step of two ahead of Corporal Hitler's thugs," he said, a slight smile crossing his lips. "And I shall have you along, Watson, if things get really sticky!"

After returning to Brown's, Holmes instructed, "Hurry home and pack for a short trip, Watson, and don't forget your service revolver. Our client will not countenance delay." Holmes passed the remainder of the day immersed in a number of books on the World War, German history, and recent political machinations in Bavaria. Returning to Brown's late in the afternoon, I found him sprawled on the floor, surrounded by open journals, newspapers, and pads of paper upon which he had been scribbling notes.

"Yes, I believe we are ready for our travels," Holmes declared. "We shall take the boat train in the morning to France. I've booked us a comfortable coach on the train to Munich and rooms in a fine hotel in that city." He turned to me. "Are you prepared for our departure?" he queried.

"I suppose so," I replied. I eyed him carefully. "Are you not a bit hesitant undertaking this mission on the instructions of Churchill? Granted, he has a fine military record, but his judgment is suspect. Remember that dreadful Gallipoli failure in Turkey!"

"True, true, not his finest hour," Holmes responded, "although he was hardly alone in bearing responsibility for the catastrophe. In any event, in this case I believe that he has a clearer eye and sounder appreciation of the threat than many who remain in high positions in the Government." We spent a relaxing evening playing whist while I recounted my recent adventures in Fez and Marrakech.

Early the next morning, I met Holmes at Victoria Station, and we boarded the train for Dover. The journey was passed in near silence with Holmes deep in thought, his head tilted back, eyes closed. But for his long fingers drumming steadily on the brim of his hat, which he held in his lap, one might have thought him asleep. We transferred to the ferry for the uneventful trip across the Channel, that magnificent moat that had keep England secure from invaders for a thousand years – although the recent innovation of hurling bombs from airplanes had seriously eroded our much-vaunted isolation from unpleasantness on the Continent.

Not until we had boarded the train at the Gare de l'Est in Paris and begun the journey across France to southern Germany did Holmes speak of his intentions. He poked his head outside the compartment to ensure that no one was lurking in the passageway and then closed the door firmly. The rumbling of the wheels over the rails provided us an additional measure of security from anyone attempting to overhear out conversation, but he still drew close to me and spoke in a measured whisper.

"Watson, this may well be our most significant case," he began, "but also our most dangerous! This Hitler must be taken very seriously, despite his ridiculous rhetoric. I doubt very much that he is the fool that some imagine. His recent speeches show him to be a formidable orator. His supporters number in the thousands, perhaps tens-of-thousands, and they are heavily armed and prone to violence. I fear, as does the Bavarian government, that he will initiate a mutinous action within weeks, perhaps days, that could destabilize all of Germany. We need not speculate about how grave a challenge that would present."

Our train pulled into the Munich station early in the morning and we proceeded to our rented rooms on the *Landwehrstraße*. Holmes quickly disappeared into the crowded streets while I made dining arrangements with the hotel-keeper. It required only a few conversations and a quick look at the newspapers – my German remained passable – to appreciate how grave the atmosphere in the city had become. A state of emergency had been declared by the Prime Minister of Bavaria in late September as fears of political violence swirled through the city. With Hitler and his armed legions threatening the fragile government, the air was thick with intrigue.

Holmes returned late in the afternoon, his face grim and his manner furtive. He turned off the lights in the room and motioned me to the window. "Watch the street, Watson," he asked. "Careful now – don't allow the curtains to move."

"What am I looking for?" I beseeched.

"Do you see anyone following me? Is anyone hiding in the shadows, looking up at these rooms?" he queried.

I could see no one, but Holmes's high state of agitation alarmed me. We had been in numerous tight situations over the years, but his manner seemed one of unusual caution.

"I don't think that you were followed," I counseled. "Or at least if you were, I don't see anyone watching the hotel." Holmes stepped towards his bedroom. "See here," I said. "I really think that it's about time that you shared with me your plan for this expedition – especially if, as it seems, I am also to be endangered by my participation."

Silently, he waved me into the darkened room and bade me sit on a chair opposite to him. Only the orange glow of the tobacco in the bowl of his pipe assured me he was present in the room at all. Soon my eyes adjusted to the dark and I could see that he was sitting quite close to me, hunched up with his chest near his knees, his left hand slowly rubbing his long jaw.

"Bad business, Watson," he remarked softly. "Bad business. I doubt very much that even Churchill is remotely aware of the state to which things have deteriorated here. He certainly was right to enlist us in this mission.

"I have been to a meeting tonight of some of the most dastardly criminals I've ever encountered," he began. "These men have no principles, no honor. They live only to intimidate, to destroy, and to dominate. They are far worse than the petty burglar or blackmailer, for their intended victim isn't a helpless widow or a confused lover, but rather an unsuspecting world!"

"Holmes!" I cried. "Do you mean the Nazi gangsters?"

15

"Precisely," he responded. "I have spent the last several hours learning of their nefarious plot, which is about to be sprung."

"But what is their objective?" I asked.

"Nothing short of revolution!" Holmes replied. "The destruction of the Weimar Government. Indeed, their initial plan was to launch their uprising in Berlin itself, but they called that off when they realized that the odds against success were too great. Now they intend to overthrow the government of Bavaria first, and then expand their anarchy and perfidy across Germany.

"Their leader, this Hitler, is a curious fellow," he mused. "A painter, of all things, and not without some talent. A minor military figure of no significance whatsoever, and yet, a master of incitement – brutally possessed, even demonic. His words seem to grab hold of the masses, who would clearly follow him into battle – as they undoubtedly will."

"But why is no one arming to prevent this uprising?" I asked.

"That is the question Churchill sent us here to uncover, for he believes – as do only a few of our countrymen – that the Nazis' appetite extends well beyond Bavaria or even Berlin. Perhaps," his voice went soft, "even to the cliffs of Dover and beyond."

"Outrageous!" I cried. But here we were in a strange city, a foreign country, with no allies. How were we to halt a revolution? I wondered. "What are we to do?"

Holmes grew thoughtful, his long chin in his hand. "As a practical matter, how do we prevent the *putsch*, which seems imminent?" Holmes mused. "How indeed?"

The following morning, Holmes was gone before I rose, so I dressed and breakfasted, and then took a walk along the Isar River before returning to my room shortly before noon.

Holmes returned soon thereafter, and his face was set with a grim look.

"I have met with von Knilling," he said, referring to the Bavarian Prime Minister. "He seems at his wits' end. The prospect of violence is growing by the hour, and his government appears nearly powerless to prevent it."

"Surely he is prepared to meet the rascals head-on," I protested.

"Yes, but the damage to his government, to the nation, may be impossible to contain," said Holmes. "I fear that our activities may not remain so secret after this evening. You must arrange for our tickets back to France and then across the Channel tomorrow. It may be too dangerous for us to remain in Munich much longer."

As the day progressed, Holmes scurried about the city while I visited the concierge to arrange our passage back to London. We shared tea and excellent cakes at a charming café at four o'clock, and we then returned to our rooms where Holmes began applying a mixture of prosthetics, beeswax, and face colorations, transforming himself into a person that even I could scarcely recognize. From several paper bags, he removed a pair of well-worn wool trousers, a shirt and a rough coat, and scuffed boots. Within minutes, he was indistinguishable from an everyday resident of the German city. We ate an early dinner in the hotel's excellent restaurant, and then Holmes slipped into the street and was swallowed up by the increasingly turbulent atmosphere of Munich.

For one of the few times in our association, I ignored Holmes's direct instructions. Given the unfamiliar city and the risk of danger, I felt my presence was warranted, as was the service revolver that I had brought on Holmes's instruction. At a careful distance, and employing the tricks of stealth that Holmes himself had taught me, I followed him through the darkening streets. Crossing the *Ludwingsbrüke*, Holmes hurried to the *Au-Haidhausen* district where loomed his destination, the enormous *Bürgerbräukeller* beer hall.

The hall was well populated and the sounds of music and merriment floated out despite the doors and windows that were closed against the November chill. Far more bracing than the air, however, were the dozens, perhaps hundreds, of Nazis in their characteristic brown shirts menacingly milling about outside the *Bürgerbräukeller*.

I watched from a distance as Holmes maneuvered through their ranks and quickly slipped inside. After waiting a few minutes, I followed him into the cavernous room that reeked of beer and hummed with the laughter and arguments of thousands of inebriated Bavarians and the dreadful *"oom-pah"* orchestra that no civilized ear could find pleasing.

I was weaving through the crowd when I suddenly felt someone drawing me close. "Watson!" hissed Holmes into my ear. "You shouldn't have come! The danger is too great!"

"Balderdash," I whispered back, although whispering was hardly required in the raucous room. "I cannot abandon you to such risk! Did you not see the small army of brown shirts outside?"

"And the members of the local government inside!" Holmes responded, pointing to a large table where Kahr, Seisser, and Lossow were huddled over their steins of beer, clearly evaluating the deepening sense of crisis. "They are at enormous jeopardy if – "

Holmes's words were cut off as the doors to the *Bürgerbräukeller* crashed open and a band of the brown shirted agitators burst into the chamber. At the head of the intruders was the now-familiar visage of Adolf Hitler, a lock of dark hair falling over his forehead and a small moustache giving him a distinct if slightly ridiculous appearance. He was accompanied by his chief lieutenants, the heavily scarred

Ernst Roehm, the bloated Hermann Göring, and the bushy-browed Rudolph Hess.

Suddenly Hitler shouted, "The national revolution has broken out! Nobody is allowed to leave!" He punctuated his declaration by pulling a revolver from inside his shirt and firing a single shot into the *Bürgerbräukeller*'s ceiling. The effect was electric: The music and laughter halted, replaced by expressions of shock and outrage. The shot was the signal for sympathizers inside the hall to spring into action, as well they did, seizing the Bavarian leaders and hustling them to a grim fate.

"Holmes!" I cried in the direction of my friend. "This could be the beginning of the collapse of Weimer!" But he was gone, having vanished into the teeming crowd. In the confusion, I decided to follow his instructions, easing my way outdoors and making my way back to our hotel. For a long while, I sat up waiting for him, but I unwillingly drifted off to sleep in the stuffed chair.

"Wake up, Watson," I heard murmured roughly in my ear. It was Holmes, and his appearance was alarming, He remained in the costume and make-up, but now he was dirty and haggard, with a ragged cut that ran down his left cheek, just missing his eye. The knuckles on one hand were red and torn, and a bandage on his left hand was stained with dark red blood. His shirt was ripped, as was one knee of his trousers. I noted the cuckoo clock on the mantel read two o'clock in the morning, just as its little door flew open and a carved bird popped out uttering a double chirp.

"Good Lord!" I exclaimed. "What has happened to you?"

"Oh, nothing too serious," he calmly replied. "I couldn't have hoped for a better seat to the evening's very consequential activities. But I should say that the storm clouds gathering in Munich have every likelihood of darkening all of the continent in the not-too-distant future, and very likely our island as well."

While I ministered to his wounds – washing and bandaging the cuts with sterile gauze that I had fortunately packed – Holmes filled me in on the events that had transpired after I had retreated from the *Bürgerbräukeller*.

"The Nazis presumed to declare an end to the current government of Bavaria," Holmes explained. "The three officials in the beer hall were taken into custody, and a call went out for other bands of Nazis to seize government buildings throughout the city. Hitler whipped the mob into a terrifying frenzy. His closing words were – 'Either the German revolution begins tonight, or we will all be dead by dawn!' Very theatrical!"

An involuntary shudder shook his thin shoulders as he pulled his woolen scarf up tighter around his neck. "It was quite alarming, Watson," he muttered. "Even preposterous. This ridiculous megalomaniac! And yet, I fear what we have witnessed is far more the prologue to a long and tragic nightmare than the denouement of a low-brow melodrama."

He quickly stood and gathered his coat and hat. "I must return to the agitation," he declared, although it was still hours before sunrise. "I will be cautious, but whether I return or not, Watson, you must be on the train to France in the morning." I opened my mouth to protest, but Holmes was out the door before I could reach him.

Holmes's fears of growing violence were more than prescient. In the pre-dawn hours, a band of the Nazis attempted to lay siege to the *Reichswehr* barracks and then the Defence Ministry, where a cordon of police blocked their way. From my hotel, I could hear a furious gun battle between the two groups. When it was over, I soon learned that four officers lay dead in the street along with sixteen members of Hitler's legions. Hitler himself, along with other leaders in the abortive *putsch*, had been rounded up and sent off to prison where, one could only hope, they would soon hang for their acts of treason.

Fortunately, the disorder did not disrupt the travel plans that I'd made. I anxiously waited for Holmes to appear at the train station. Just a few minutes before the scheduled departure, he rushed onto the platform where I was waiting with our tickets. We clambered aboard as the train began to depart the station.

"I've sent a wire to Churchill advising him we're returning to London," he reported. "I promised him a full report within a few days of our return."

I looked at his battered face and injured hand. "You certainly will require assistance preparing such a report so quickly," I said as the train picked up momentum and we mercifully began speeding towards the French frontier. "I'm afraid I must check on several patients upon my return," I added, hoping he would understand my time was not entirely at his disposal.

"Not a problem on either account," he assured. "Churchill has extended my stay at Brown's Hotel and has thoughtfully engaged a temporary assistant to help me. She will meet me at Brown's, and you may take whatever time that you require attending to your patients."

We quickly found our compartment where we sat in silence for most of the trip, reflecting on how close we had come to being trapped in the spreading political conflagration. I didn't draw a relaxed breath until we were safely on board the ferry back to Dover.

Ensconced once again in great comfort at Brown's, Holmes quickly prepared to draft his report to Churchill, who eagerly awaited our bird's eye account of the Munich uprising. The assistant arranged by Churchill was a Miss Edwena Hunt, a most attractive and efficient young woman, with blonde hair, a slight limp, and exquisite taste in clothing. She arrived promptly in the morning and proved a devoted aide to the famous detective.

As we sat drinking our morning coffee and reading *The Times* a few days later, there was a knock on the door. Holmes was poring over his draft report and showed little signs of rising to open it, and so I strode across the room. There, once again, was the ever-attentive Miss Hunt, along with an unfamiliar young man holding a well-wrapped box.

"Mr. Holmes," she said, as they stepped into the room. "I encountered this fellow in the lobby. He claims that you've been expecting this."

Holmes seemed excited by the young man's arrival and quickly strode to the door, not even pausing when he knocked some papers and a pencil off his desk. Miss Hunt quickly stooped to pick them up and then carefully straightened up the pages strewn over the desk.

The messenger was casually dressed, the growth of a few days covering his chin. He extended the package to Holmes and stepped backward, his soft cap in hand.

"Ah! Franz, good!" Holmes said, taking the box. "Watson, you remember Franz, one of the 'Irregulars'?" he said, referencing the young urchins who had run errands and provided intelligence to Holmes during the hey-day of his career.

"Guv'nor," said Franz, tipping his head towards Holmes, his crooked smile revealing broken and yellowed teeth. "A real pleasure to see you again!" Somewhere in that grizzled face was the young boy who had scampered up and down the stairs at Baker Street all those years past, but I couldn't recognize him. Holmes handed him a few coins and, with a tip of his hat, he clambered down the stairs and back into the bustle of Albemarle Street.

"Well, it is a relief that this package has arrived safely," said Holmes, as he tore at the tape and string sealing the brown paper wrapping. In a moment, he lifted a plain, brown cardboard box perhaps two-feet square. I could see the excitement in his eyes as he set it on a low table and lifted the lid, allowing a bright red cloth to partially spill onto the floor. Pulling the rest of the material out of the box, Holmes revealed to my horror a white circle in the middle of the red banner, and in the center of the white patch, the horrid black swastika of the Bavarian Nazis.

"Holmes!" I cried, "I am appalled! I'm horrified! A Nazi flag? In Brown's Hotel?"

It was clear Miss Hunt shared my surprise at the contents of the box, which she regarded with keen attention. Holmes stuffed the flag back into the box, thanked Miss Hunt for her assistance, and escorted her from the room, instructing her not to mention the contents of the package to anyone. Once she had departed, he again withdrew the despicable banner and held it out in front of him, a smile of deep satisfaction spreading across his face. He examined the flag carefully, holding it close to his face and grunting a satisfied recognition. Finally, he turned back to me and saw the look of horror on my face.

"Ah, Watson," he said, carefully laying the object on the table. "You see, this isn't just any flag. You see this?" he pointed a long finger at dark red splotches that flicked across the white portion of the flag. "This is the *Blutfahne*." I remained perplexed. "The 'Blood Flag', certain to become a priceless talisman to the Nazi leaders," Holmes continued. "Especially Hitler.

"I saw this flag carried into battle the other night by the Nazis in Munch. When the police fired on them near the Defence Ministry, unwisely creating sixteen undeserved martyrs, the flag bearer was among the gravely wounded. He collapsed on top of this flag, staining the cloth with his blood, here – " he pointed to a red spot and then to others " – and here, and here. Hitler, I have heard, has let it be known from his prison cell that he prizes this flag more than any relic of the *putsch*. I have no doubt that madman will do anything to recover it."

"But how did you come by the . . . *Blut*-whatever?" I asked.

"All in good time," Holmes soothingly purred. "All in good time. Meanwhile, I have here in my hands a most valued artifact of the lunatic Nazis, and their mustachioed leader is sitting in a Bavarian jail wondering what became of it! I shall keep it here," he motioned towards a trunk near the fireplace, "for safekeeping until I deliver it to our friends at the Defence Ministry." He quickly folded the flag, returned it to its cardboard box, and locked it inside the trunk.

The next morning, Holmes was still triumphant when I arrived for breakfast, which soon appeared along with Miss Hunt.

"You seem in an excellent mood, Mr. Holmes," she cheerfully said as we sat down to steaming plates of eggs, bangers, and toast. "Are you so enthused over the arrival of yesterday's package?"

"Oh yes, Miss Hunt," he replied. "I'm afraid I cannot speak about it too much, even to you," he added, this latter comment spoken in a theatrical *sotto voce*, although no one else was in the room. "I must visit Whitehall later today to describe it to some members of the government. It may seem an inconsequential souvenir, but I assure you, the contents of that box may well involve questions of war!"

"*War!*" she cried with great alarm as she stood up, her hand flying up to her mouth. "But no one believes there is a risk of war, do they? Why, we just ended such a terrible conflict! I – I am distressed just at the thought of another one!"

She buried her attractive face in her hands, and as her knees buckled slightly, I sprang forward to steady her.

"There, there," Holmes comforted. "I'm sure that I spoke too dramatically. There has been a slight ripple of agitation on the Continent, but the likelihood of conflict is quite minimal. League of Nations and all. But I must hurry. The sooner I speak with these officials, the better our country will be served." He disappeared into his bedchamber and re-emerged carrying his satchel, bade us farewell, and disappeared out the door.

My mind was hardly on my patients that morning – one with the croup, another with symptoms of measles – as I kept an eye on the clock. At one-thirty, I closed the office and headed back to Brown's as planned, arriving ahead of Holmes. I was alarmed to find the door to his room slightly ajar, and when I entered, I immediately drew in my breath.

The sitting room seemed as though a typhoon had blown through it, with papers and other items strewn haphazardly around. Boxes and drawers had been opened, their contents tossed indifferently on the floor and the furniture upended. Lying on the floor was the distraught Miss Hunt, surrounded by papers and the contents of the desk, the bureau, and even her own handbag.

"Good Lord!" I shouted and rushed to her assistance, tearing the gag from her face and pulling on the cords that bound her wrists. As I did so, I noticed as well a nasty bruise upon her forehead from which a small amount of blood was still flowing, evidently the result of a blow from a blunt instrument. Fortunately, she seemed more terrified than badly injured as I knelt by her side, frantically untying the knots that bound her.

"Oh, Dr. Watson, thank goodness you have come!" she cried, big tears running down her soft cheeks and her shoulders heaving. "This is all my fault!"

"Don't be silly," I counseled, fetching her a glass of water, although she might well have appreciated something considerably stronger. "What happened here? And are you alright?"

"Oh, yes, I am now," she gasped as she sat on the sofa. "I had come by early to straighten up Mr. Holmes's rooms a bit. You know, with his injured hand, he really cannot do so himself. They arrived soon afterwards, pushing their way into the room when I answered their knock. As I attempted to call the concierge, one hit me here – " she pointed to the abrasion on her forehead " – and they bound me with these ropes. They refused to believe that I didn't know what they were asking about, and they proceeded to create this unfortunate mess."

Just then, Holmes burst into the room and quickly surveyed the disorder that only hours before had been his comfortable quarters. We quickly filled him in on Miss Hunt's terrifying account of the past several hours.

"Hmm, do you have the ropes that they used to bind you?" he asked. Miss Hunt handed them over and Holmes scrutinized their length, their material, and the remaining knots.

"How many men?" he asked.

"Three, I think," she responded, "and they talked to someone in the hall, so at least four. They went through everything. It took over an hour! Oh, Mr. Holmes, do you know what they were searching for!"

"I have no doubt," he declared. "I pray they didn't injure you." He held her hands tenderly and closely examined her hands and wrists where the intruders had bound her. "No damage, thank goodness," he said, shifting his examination to the bruise on her forehead. "And this bruise is superficial – no concussion. Don't you agree, Watson? What a relief that you weren't injured more seriously!"

"Indeed!" I added.

"Well, they were out of luck because I had the object of their burglary with me," he explained, patting his satchel. "I'm delivering it this very evening to the Defence Ministry. I fear these hooligans are to be disappointed should they return tomorrow.

"I am deeply sorry for your troubles," he smiled at Miss Hunt as he gathered up the contents of her handbag and handed it to her. Reaching into his satchel, he withdrew a small box wrapped in blue paper with a red silk bow "Perhaps this small gift will compensate you for your very unnerving day," he said, handing it to her. "A souvenir of our recent journey to the Continent. I hope it helps soothe you following this most disgraceful assault."

"Why, Mr. Holmes!" she cried, pulling at the ribbon and tearing the paper. As she opened the box, she uttered a tiny gasp and lifted out a glittering crystal bottle.

"It is the newest perfume in France," he declared, watching her face eagerly for her reaction. "Chanel No. 5. I don't know whether there was a 1, 2, 3, or 4, but No. 5 is 'the rave' in Paris. I do hope that you will accept it in appreciation for the devoted care you've extended to me over these past days."

"Mr. Holmes, your thoughtfulness and generosity are remarkable," she replied. "I'm sure it is an extraordinary fragrance. Do you mind if I try some now?"

"I should be deeply disappointed, indeed, if you did not!" he answered reaching for the bottle. His pocketknife cut loose the sealing tape and then he extended his hand to the lady. "Allow me." She gave her hand to him and as he gently pulled it towards him, dousing her forearm with a generous dollop of Chanel No 5.

"Oh! Perhaps a bit more than required," he laughed. "But a truly remarkable fragrance, don't you think?"

"Oh, yes, Mr. Holmes, I cannot possibly thank you enough," she said as she wiped off the excess perfume with her forearm. She flashed him a sweet smile that, given my own experience with women, I took as an indication that the young lady was indeed a bit smitten with the world's most famous detective.

"Now you should take your leave for the evening. I must complete some work before delivering this wretched flag to Whitehall. After this outrageous intrusion, I shall be relieved to be done with it," he declared.

"But I must help you clean the room," she protested. "I feel the mess is in part my fault, as I unwittingly provided the intruders their entry."

"Certainly not!" he proclaimed. "You bear no responsibility for this intrusion at all." He helped her to her feet, gathered her coat and hat for her, and gently eased her towards the door. "As they say, 'Störe dich nicht!'"

Miss Hunt smiled wanly. "Thank you, Mr. Holmes," she said, "but I am afraid I do not understand that language."

"Hah! Of course not," Holmes responded. "A remnant of my recent trip. In German, it means 'Don't disturb yourself'." He ushered her out the door with a self-satisfied smile, which told me he was pleased with the response his gift had received.

"Remarkable, indeed!" I exclaimed after Miss Hunt had left. "What an extraordinary gift!"

"Now, now, surely Miss Hunt is deserving of a special thanks for her many services, not to mention her terrible ordeal," Holmes replied. "I don't think one small bottle of perfume is a terrible extravagance. Besides – " he suddenly became quite serious " – the game, as you would say, is afoot, and we must prepare for the resolution!"

"What 'game'?" I exclaimed. "What 'resolution'? Have you devised a plan to apprehend Miss Hunt's attackers without even knowing their identity?"

"The 'plan,' dear chap, is in that bag," he said, drawing the Nazi flag from the satchel. "You didn't think that I would be so foolish as to leave it unguarded in this room! The key to resolving this case should arrive within minutes. In the meanwhile, let me close my eyes for a time, and when our guests arrive, please show them in."

What guests? I wondered. What role were they to play? Why did Holmes still have that flag, which I thought he would already have delivered to the Defence Ministry or Churchill? As he sat motionless in the stuffed chair, his eyes closed and his eyelids occasionally fluttering, I tried to reconstruct the chaotic journey of the past few days – from Whitehall to a beer hall in Munich, to barely escaping the growing violence in Bavaria, to a purloined, blood-stained Nazi flag in the sitting room at Brown's and now, the terrible assault on Miss Hunt. I welcomed the knock on the door that signaled the arrival of our guest.

Holmes bounded out of the chair with an alacrity for which I would scarcely have given him credit, given his age and recent injuries. He was at the door in an instant and threw it open.

"Ah, thank you, thank you, Carruthers," he called to the slender man who appeared in the doorway. "And welcome to you as well," he said to a tan-and-white dog of impressive size that bounded into the room. In an instant, the dog's massive paws were on Holmes's chest as it lapped at the detective's face, which he turned away to avoid its enthused slobbering.

"He's Ollie, he is," said Carruthers, introducing the hound. "That's short for 'Olfactory'. That means 'smell', you know."

Holmes murmured his familiarity with the term.

"I tell you, Mr. Holmes, this dog has a nose on him like no dog I've ever trained," Carruthers continued. "Blood, sweat, a scent on a glove or shoe – nothing gets past that nose, it don't."

"Well, Ollie, we shall put your nose to the test today," declared Holmes once Carruthers had departed. "He will assure that our little souvenir from Munich remains secure. Later this evening, we shall depart with my memento, which will never return to this room. I certainly don't want to risk another intrusion by whomever was searching my room and tying up our poor Miss Hunt like a Christmas goose!"

Ollie's arrival did little to dispel my utter confusion. For the next half-hour or so, with the dog curled up at his feet, Holmes and I sat by the glowing fireplace as he reviewed the text of his final report for Churchill. He finished his study, stuffed the papers into his bag, and sat back in his chair, his long fingers were supporting his nose while his thumbs hooked under his pointed chin, the thumbs and forefingers forming a diamond and his lids closed. The only sound in the room was the ticking of the mantel clock.

The late afternoon light outside had begun to grow dusky when Holmes declared softly, "I think that will do. Ollie, come here my friend." In a louder voice he said, "Come, Watson. Let us prepare to deliver this dastardly flag to the proper authorities. The sooner it is out of these rooms for good, the better."

The hound had stood up and lazily walked to the chair where Holmes sat. Holmes reached across to the small desk, opened a drawer, and withdrew a small vial. Removing the top, he held it out for Ollie to sniff. "Here you go, Ollie," he offered as the dog wandered over to investigate the contents. When he got close, his head started and Holmes withdrew the vial and replaced its cap.

"Now, Ollie," he said, intently staring at the hound. "Show me!"

Ollie stood immobile for a few moments, and then turned to a door on the far wall of the room that had been locked shut since we had first arrived. He froze, not moving a hair whilst Holmes followed his gaze to the door.

Suddenly Holmes pulled a silver police whistle from his pocket and blew it three times, emitting a piercing shriek that chilled my bones. At the same moment, he grabbed my Moroccan walking stick from where it rested next to my chair and strode to the door on which Ollie remained fixated. Without warning, Holmes raised the heavy end of the cane above his head and brought it down forcefully on the doorknob, smashing the glass handle and the lock attached to it. Seizing the door, he yanked it open.

He swiftly reached into the dark recess and pulled through the doorway a flustered and angry Edwena Hunt, writhing against his steel-like grip and with a shocked look on her face. She shrieked and swung at Holmes with her free hand, pummeling him again and again, but he held her tightly and kept pulling until she tumbled onto the floor.

"There we are, Miss Hunt!" Holmes cried, brandishing my stick like a club over the enraged woman. "You are unmasked!"

The door of the hotel room flew open and several young men in police uniforms rapidly filed in, led by a tall young man with sandy hair and trim moustache who bent down next to Miss Hunt, grasped her by her left arm, and forcing her to stand. "Edwena Hunt," he declared, "I am Inspector Trilling of Scotland Yard. You are under arrest."

"On what charge?" she angrily demanded, trying to twist out of his grip.

"On the charge of espionage against the Crown!"

"Espionage?" she cried, forcing a sharp laugh. "On behalf of whom?"

"On behalf of the Nazi fanatic, Hitler," Holmes interjected. "It will do you no good to feign ignorance."

"We have the incontrovertible facts, thanks to Mr. Holmes here – and our colleague, Ollie," Trilling added, nodding to the hound. He forced handcuffs on her wrists as she struggled vainly.

My head was spinning with the gravity of what had just occurred. "Wait," I pleaded, sitting down in one of the chairs. "Miss Hunt is . . . a spy . . . *for the Nazis?*"

"She is not Miss Hunt," Holmes seethed. "She is Anna Stanzhofler, a disciple of the Nazi rabble, sent to spy on me in hopes of thwarting my services to those in the British government who recognize Nazism as a venal and dangerous ideology."

"But it is inconceivable Churchill would send a spy to assist you!" I protested.

"Churchill did arrange through an agency for Miss Edwena Hunt to assist me during my stay in London," he explained, "but apparently a Mosley agent in Whitehall must have learned of the arrangement and arranged for her to be absconded-with on her way to Brown's. I fear that Miss Hunt's current whereabouts remain unknown, although we must hope for the best. Miss Stanzhofler was then substituted to impersonate her while conducting nefarious spying activities."

Holmes looked over at the furious German agent. "I was hardly likely to grant an unknown person – even an attractive young lady – unfettered access to my room without a far more thorough background check than Miss Stanzhofler had evidently anticipated.

"The Nazis had learned of our recent trip to Bavaria," he said, holding up the stained flag. "They dispatched the ersatz Miss Hunt to see what they could learn of my activities and my report to Churchill. It was, I confess, a deception I perceived quite readily. However, when the flag arrived and I saw Miss Hunt's reaction, I realized that it would serve as the bait I needed to lure the spy network here in London into exposing itself!

"Some consultation ensued with our friends at Scotland Yard, who were able to confirm my suspicions. Have I got it about right, Miss Stanzhofler?" he asked the seething woman, holding the bloodstained flag where she could see it clearly.

"The *Blutfahne!*" the fake Miss Hunt hissed, her eyes flashing. "Give it to me!" She lunged for the flag, but the police held her tightly and Holmes moved the flag away from her grasp. "You do not deserve even to touch it!" she shrieked.

"I have a good mind to toss it into the fire and be done with it," he responded, "but Whitehall has uses for it. Not that you will be in any position to inform your colleagues. Ah, your colleagues!" Holmes strode to the window and opened the sash. "Have you got them?" he called out to those in the street below.

"Yes, Mr. Holmes," came a voice from the street. "Four of them came running out of the hotel when you blew the whistle, and we got them all, three by the front door and one by the rear."

"I had Twilling here station several Scotland Yard men outside the front and back entrances of the hotel," he smiled, "knowing that the conspirators would flee when they heard the police whistle and the commotion caused by your apprehension." He pointed his long finger down to the group of officers gathered on the street who were holding the angry prisoners in their clutches.

"Should you find yourself free and again engaged in the business of espionage," Holmes said to the spy, "which I very much doubt will be the fate that awaits you, I suggest that you pay greater attention to details, for your amateurish blunders quickly alerted me to your little masquerade.

"The ropes your associates used to bind you were too loosely tied to be credible restraints," he explained. "When I examined your wrists and applied the perfume, I saw no signs of chafing that would surely have been expected had you made a genuine effort to free yourself. And that bump on your forehead . . . ." He shook his head disapprovingly. "I'm afraid it was far too gentle a knock, probably self-inflicted, which is why it raised only a superficial welt.

"In addition, the cut was still oozing blood when I examined you, which indicated that the attack had occurred only minutes before Watson and I arrived. Had it been an hour or so since you had been assaulted, as you reported, the blood surely would have coagulated by the time I examined you. Tsk, tsk, not at all convincing." Holmes turned to me and I nodded my agreement about the freshness of the wound although, in the excitement of discovering her predicament, I confess to having ignored the implication.

Trilling's' men grasped the spy by her arm and escorted her out of the room. Holmes carefully folded the Nazi talisman and placed it back in the box and handed it to the inspector. "Now this is your responsibility," he declared, "and I would appreciate your delivering it to the Defence Ministry at your earliest opportunity. I prefer never to see it again." I watched Trilling and his prisoner depart, then glanced at Holmes, at the smashed door to the adjacent room, at my ruined walking stick, and finally at Ollie, who was happily chewing on one of Holmes silk slippers.

"I must be getting too old for such adventures," I admitted to Holmes. "At a minimum, I would have thought I might have suspected some part of this bizarre case, but I must admit, she had me utterly fooled. I am as confused and surprised as I was during the earliest days of our association."

"Don't be hard on yourself, Watson," Holmes counseled, carefully clapping me gently on my good shoulder. "A pretty face can easily interfere with rational thought, I understand. Come, let us venture off to The Globe for an early dinner, and I shall lay the entire case out for you."

Soon, bolstered by a fine *pinot grigio* and *primo plato* of grilled fish, Holmes began to clear away the fog that still swirled about the case.

"Churchill has been desperate to raise the alarm of the rising German threat," he said, "but the resistance within the government has been ferocious. They are tired of war, of death, of fear itself. They seek tranquility at any cost, he fears, and are prepared to embrace false hopes to avoid the trauma of rearmament and conflict."

Our journey fortuitously had coincided with the beer hall *putsch*, providing us with incontrovertible evidence of the capacity of Hitler and his thugs to rally thousands of frustrated Bavarians. Upon our return to London, Holmes had spent a morning dropping hints of his escapade at clubs frequented by known German sympathizers, including the young parliamentarian Churchill had mentioned, Oswald Mosley. In effect, Holmes used himself as bait to expose an underground cell of British devotees of the fascist cause. A day later, Miss Hunt had appeared at our door, ready to care for the wounded detective.

"I was instantaneously skeptical of Miss Hunt when she appeared," he said as our lamb chops arrived, along with a fine claret, and he began slashing through them. "I have an instinctive suspicion about anyone who conveniently arrives in my presence as a case is afoot. Churchill had arranged for a young lady to assist me whilst in London, but of course he had never actually met Miss Hunt. So I had no reason to accept that she was who she presented herself to be without some checking.

"My motto, as you know, Watson, is to 'assume *nothing*'," he said, spearing a juicy cube of lamb and taking a long drink of wine. "It wasn't difficult to find holes in her story, especially when I took the liberty of visiting the placement agency that had referred the young lady. The manager was pleased to hear that she was proving satisfactory for my needs, especially given the car accident that had left her with a slight limp.

"Miss Stanzhofler's masquerade was quite thorough in that respect, as you noticed, but I noted that the wear on her shoe heels was even. The differently worn heels of anyone with a genuine limp undoubtedly would have been quite distinguishable.

"She also struck me as too well informed about my habits – my . . . 'quirks,' if you will – for someone that I had never met," he said, adding slyly, "and she remarkably claimed *not* to have read your little stories. She made a few mistakes that revealed her as a fraud.

"For example, I took the liberty of checking the contents of her purse when I picked it up after the assault and discovered several pamphlets printed in German. When this imposter claimed not to understand the fragmentary words I spoke to her in German, my suspicions were further aroused. Surely a young woman who read German pamphlets would have understood such simple terms. And yet this woman implausibly denied all understanding of the language."

He took a deep swallow of the claret and continued. "She spent far too much time examining my rooms on those occasions when she was announcing the arrival of a guest. Remember when she picked up those papers and pencil that had fallen on the floor the other day?" he asked. "She stole a few moments to read over the papers as she was rearranging them on my desk. If she was so curious, might she not also have sought to overhear the conversations that occurred after she had departed? After a good deal of searching, I discovered that my suspicions were correct.

"I was very curious about that door in my suite that evidently was locked from the other side. Where did it go? Clearly into a communicating room, because there would be little reason to lock a closet that opened only to this suite. My suspicion was confirmed in a discussion with the hotel manager, who reported the door led to a small room with its own access to the corridor, typically used by servants accompanying a guest staying in the suite that I'm occupying. Anyone wishing to overhear my conversations need only enter that room silently from the corridor and listen at the door to hear our conversations as clearly as if she had been standing next to us. Of course, it was difficult to know if, or when, Miss Stanzhofler might sequester herself in the room to learn of our plans to deliver the flag to the authorities. So a plan was needed.

"Even before our departure for the Continent, I had been contemplating how to maneuver the Nazis in London into revealing themselves, and the *Blutfahne* unexpectedly provided me the perfect means. When I saw the wounded demonstrator, Heinrich Trambauer, fall bleeding on this Nazi banner in Munich, an idea immediately struck me. Hitler, who reportedly holds a fanatic's obsession with the occult, likely would regard such a talisman as having incalculable value and go to great lengths to retrieve it. I believe it is fair to say the entire strategy had occurred to me even before the flag had fallen to the ground in front of the *Feldherrnhalle*."

"So, you made arrangements to secure the flag in Bavaria and have it sent to you here in London?" I inquired. "How?"

"I saw the crowd's angry reaction when a police officer grabbed it from the Nazis," he explained. "I hurried to the local police headquarters to speak with a high-ranking officer, an old friend whom I had assisted some years ago on a case involving a prominent nobleman in Bavaria and a certain – ahem, '*singer*' – in a local club.

"'I should be greatly indebted to you if this flag were to find its way to me,' I told him. 'I must have it, even if only briefly. It may well provide us an essential opportunity against these zealots who threaten your country as well as mine!" He readily agreed, and when the flag, bloodied as it was, appeared in his office later in the day, he immediately boxed it and sent it to me here in London, where it was delivered by the one-time Irregular, Franz, with whom you were recently reacquainted."

"But if you knew that Miss Hunt, or whatever her name is, was a spy, why didn't you just arrest her?" I asked.

"I needed proof, and I needed her to lure her henchmen to reveal themselves, which is why I loudly proclaimed my intention to deliver the flag to the Defence Ministry tonight. I had to force her hand. Such a disclosure, I was quite certain, would lead her to enlist her own crew of musclemen to intercept me and ensure that the flag didn't make it to my intended destination."

"Well, if you suspected she was a spy, why did you give such expensive perfume to her?"

"No young lady can say 'no' to perfume, Watson, of that I was quite confident," Holmes declared. "Yet if she was fond of it, so, too, was my loyal friend Ollie, whose perceptive nose could detect it easily through the locked door leading to the anteroom. I needed to be certain that Miss Stanzhofler was in place to overhear my loud announcement that we were departing. I had little doubt she would signal her compatriots to prepare to subdue me and abscond with the flag.

"By the way," he added, "I must apologize for damaging your walking stick, which proved quite effective in exposing her hiding place."

He speared another piece of lamb and smiled.

"I think that Churchill will be pleased to learn that we've rounded up the most dangerous band of German spies operating in London, and all because they risked their necks to recover a stained flag," Holmes said with an air of satisfaction.

We concluded our dinner and took a cab back to the hotel for a nightcap. "England and the world are a bit safer tonight, Watson," Holmes declared. "A deadly team of maniacal Nazis is safely under lock and key at the Old Bailey, Hitler and his group of fanatics are in jail in Munich, the flag is safely in the hands of Scotland Yard and on its way to the Defence Ministry, and Europe is on notice that the menace of German nationalism far from extinguished. I certainly hope that the government will at last heed Mr. Churchill's call for a bigger navy, a new air force, and rearmament now that the intentions of the Nazis are so unmistakable. Of one thing we can be almost certain: no British statesman will advocate appeasement with so unstable a tyrant as Hitler!"

Several weeks later, after Holmes had returned to his bees and I to my patients, we heard disturbing news. Evidently a Mosley sympathizer in the Foreign Office, perhaps the same one who had likely tipped off the Nazi saboteurs about Miss Hunt, had pinched the *Blutfahne* and returned it to the Nazis in hopes of appeasing their maniacal hostility towards England. The icon indeed soon resurfaced in the hands of Nazi officials in Bavaria, where it was being revered as symbol of fanatical nationalism. Even more inexplicably, a few months later, Hitler was surprisingly released after just nine months in Landsberg prison, during which he produced his monstrous autobiography published just weeks ago. Undoubtedly, he has now resumed his struggle to revitalize German militarism, which I fear will not end well for Europe.

"This loss disheartens me more than I can say," Holmes bitterly admitted. "I fear Whitehall's sloppy security cost England an item of great symbolic value that will be exploited by very dangerous extremists. And I'm gravely concerned that we have, within our own government, those who still fail to appreciate the grave danger these Nazi hooligans pose to our security."

The conclusion of the case, however was not without one bright spot. In return for a promise of leniency in sentencing, Miss Stanzhofler agreed to intercede to secure the release of the real Miss Edwena Hunt, who had been held in a dank basement at the Isle of Dogs in the East End. The young woman was shaken but unhurt by her alarming experience and quickly departed London for the quiet of her parents' home in Berwick-upon-Tweed.

"Holmes, your service has been invaluable," I assured him. "Surely the culpability lies entirely with Whitehall. One can only hope that your work has raised sufficient concern to prepare for any dangers the flag and its fanatical followers will unleash."

Given the continuing instability in Continental politics as I write this account in 1925, I have decided to sequester this report on our adventure in Bavaria. I very much hope the readers of the Twenty-First Century will recognize the great debt they owe to the prowess of Sherlock Holmes for identifying the dangers at grave risk to his own safety. Most fervently, I pray that they proved able to avoid the terrible conflagration that this adventure seems to foreshadow.

The Case of the
Consulting Physician

This story was written by Dr. John Watson in 1927, some 25 years after the events recorded in the account occurred. It is published here for the first time. – Editor

It hardly seemed possible, in mid-June of 1902, that more than two decades had passed since New Year's Day of 1881 when I had first met Sherlock Holmes and agreed to share rooms at 221B Baker Street in London. I had just returned then from the Battle at Maiwand following my shoulder injury at the Afghan campaign, when I was fortuitously introduced to Holmes by my medical school colleague Stamford. Now, on this particular morning, I watched Holmes as he undertook one of his periodic efforts to organize the clutter that overwhelmed our sitting room – just the latest attempt in all those years that I had known him.

Holmes was examining the souvenirs of dozens of cases and packing them into several wooden boxes. I sat in my old comfortable chair, ruminating about the years of our collaboration as my eyes ran across the many scientific journals and theses stacked on the bookshelves awaiting sorting.

"Yes, Watson, you are right," Holmes said. "I have been most fortunate to have a medical man as my compatriot and friend all these years."

I couldn't help but agree with him. "Yes, my thoughts exactly," I responded, but then stopped abruptly. "See here!" I cried. "Once again, this mischief of breaking into my thoughts and voicing my own opinions! There is a time not that long ago that you surely would have been burned at the stake as a witch for such deviltry!"

Holmes laughed heartily. "It is a trick that never seems to lose its impact on you, my friend," he responded.

"All right, tell me how you guessed my innermost thoughts," I insisted, regretting the use of the work "guessed" as soon as it emerged from my lips.

"You know that I never guess," Holmes remonstrated. He picked up his pipe and packed it with some of the shag tobacco he had crammed into the Persian slipper. Lighting his pipe, he blew a stream of blue smoke into the air, and a smile crossed his face.

"I could see that you were looking intently at my collection of medical articles and monographs," he began. "Naturally, consideration of medical matters led you to think of your own history as a physician and then the grave injury that nearly cost you your life in Afghanistan. Your hand involuntarily moved to clasp the injury and you even winced slightly, recalling the pain. But then you glanced in my direction and a smile crossed your face, suggesting to me a recognition that – however unpleasant the injury had been – by a strange fortune it had enabled us to meet and begin our long and productive partnership. At which point, I made my comment about my good fortune in having a medical man as my associate."

"It always seems very simple when you describe it thusly," I admitted.

Holmes continued puttering about the room, picking up a book or folder and dropping it into a box. He paused as he passed by a part of the wall pocked with several indentation and lingered briefly.

I couldn't help myself. "Yes, Holmes, Her Majesty Queen Victoria is deeply missed by her grieving subjects." Holmes turned to me with knowing smile on his face.

"Watson, you are a delight!" he cried.

"Well, I saw you pause as you passed the 'V' which you had shot into the wall to honor the Sovereign," I explained, "and that must have led you to consider the great loss we all felt at her passing." Little more need be said about the death of the great queen, an inauspicious way for Great Britain to begin the new century. For the vast majority of Britons then living, she had been the only sovereign they had known. For nearly sixty-four years, from the age of steam engines through the rise of great powers and trading pacts, wars and the expansion of the Empire, Victoria had ruled: dour, imperial, and always dressed in black as perpetual mourning for her late Albert.

"An incomparable loss," Holmes agreed. "Now, our unqualified loyalty must be pledged to Albert Edward," the son who had waited longer to inherit the crown than any Prince of Wales in British history.

"He will be challenged to live up to the legend that his mother became," I noted. The new king, who was widely known as "Bertie" but would rule as Edward VII, had led a spirited life as a young prince. As a result, his relations with his mother, a reserved, proper ruler, had been strained. Indeed, some believed Victoria had blamed a scandal involving the young Albert Edward for exposing his father to the typhus that had killed him. Rumors quoted the queen as having confessed, "I never can or shall look at him without a shudder." Like any mother, Victoria had worried about Bertie's many escapades and indiscretions that damaged his own reputation and drove the monarchy itself to the brink of public disapproval. Rumor had it that as Prince of Wales, he had engaged in sordid and immoral activities with a virtual galaxy of women, married and unmarried, of the highest social position and of no position at all, both before and since his marriage to Princess Alexandra of Denmark.

Although Victoria had departed this Earth in January 1901, the coronation of her successor had been delayed a year-and-a-half and now was scheduled for June 26th. All England – indeed, the entire British Empire and much of the rest of the world – awaited the grand event for which feverish planning had been underway since the late Queen's funeral. Since Holmes had provided assistance to the government (and perhaps the Royal Family as well) over the years, I fully anticipated he would be attending the festivities.

"I suspect his mother kept a tight grasp on life to spare the nation from Bertie's reign as long as she could," Holmes mused. "You know, of course, she would not even share the most confidential of state papers with him for fear his lack of discretion would lead him to misuse the information they contained."

"I had no idea," I responded. "After all, he is the most well-educated monarch in our history, at both Oxford and Cambridge."

"True, but as you are surely aware, there is a significant distinction between 'education' and 'wisdom'," he stated. "It remains to be seen how much of the latter King Edward VII will display."

Uncomfortable with questioning the intellect of the man who ruled the Empire, I elected to change the subject. "I presume you will be an honoured guest at the coronation?" I inquired.

"Not unless I wish to strong-arm my way into Westminster Abbey," Holmes replied. "I am amongst the millions of our countrymen without an invitation."

I was shocked by this oversight. "After your many services to the government?" I responded, but Holmes waved off my outrage.

"It is a minor issue, I assure you," he said, "if it is any issue at all. Neither the King's life nor my own is likely to much influenced by my attendance. I wish him well and would gratefully serve him at any time." He grew pensive for a moment, doubtless considering his ambivalence for the new monarch. "And for almost any purpose, I would think."

It was clear that I was far more indignant at the oversight than Holmes himself, which made what occurred next even more curious. As I was preparing to offer another opinion about the thanklessness of the royal family, there was a sudden knock on the door.

"Come in, Mrs. Hudson," Holmes called out.

Our landlady opened the door, holding a silver tray on which an envelope was resting.

"Excuse me, but I believe you need to see this letter without delay," she said, eyeing the disorganization of the room. "It is from Buckingham Palace!" – the London residence of none other than the King of whom we had just been speaking so unceremoniously.

Holmes strode to her and reached out for the envelope.

"Oh, no, Mr. Holmes!" she said, involuntarily pulling the tray away and looking in my direction. "It is for Dr. Watson!"

"Well," Holmes said, smiling, "it seems one of us has gained Royal attention!"

"For me?" I asked, reaching for the envelope. "Why, I cannot imagine what it might be."

I carried the thin, tan envelope over to the writing table and sat down. Both Holmes and Mrs. Hudson hovered, anxious to learn the reason for such a missive. I tore open the letter and began to read out loud the typewritten message:

Mr. Dear Dr. Watson,

I am writing to you seeking a professional opinion on a most confidential matter.

I looked upon and spoke to Mrs. Hudson. "If you do not mind, Mrs. Hudson, I am afraid I must ask for privacy, given the request of this correspondent," I said. "Medical information, you can understand."

Our housekeeper quickly gathered up her things and hurried from the room. After she had firmly closed the door, I resumed my reading.

Perhaps you are aware of my own standing as a physician and surgeon, (the letter continued).

Here, I glanced at the signature, which read "*Frederick Treves*".

"Well, of course I am well aware of Dr. Treves!" I exclaimed to Holmes. "He is the author of *Surgically Applied Anatomy* and *A Student's Handbook of Surgical Operations*, both first rate texts." I could see that Holmes had no familiarity either with Treves or his publications. He moved to his medical reference book and quickly turned the pages until he found Treves' name.

"Quite a distinguished surgeon," Holmes declared. "He gained some notoriety treating that pathetically deformed man, Merrick, the one that they called 'The Elephant Man', and then became a surgeon to the late Queen. Quite a spectacular ascendency in the profession."

"Yes, and now he serves as one of the Serjeants Surgeons to His Majesty, the King," I added, continuing to read aloud:

A matter of some importance requires the greatest surgical adroitness. Unfortunately, the circumstances also happen to have grave political overtones and perhaps some intrigue. Such matters as these lie entirely outside my skills as a physician. It occurs to me that you, given your own

46

professional training and your collaborations with Mr. Holmes, might be in a unique position to provide me the peace of mind and confidentiality I desperately require. I am therefore hopeful that you will be willing to receive me at 11 o'clock this morning at your Baker Street rooms.

Sincerely yours,
Frederick Treves
Surgeon

I turned to Holmes with what must have been a look of pure puzzlement on my face.

"What possible assistance might I provide to a physician as distinguished as Treves?" I wondered aloud.

Holmes came over and requested to be allowed a look at the letter, which I was only too pleased to hand to him.

"Well, quite impressive stationery," he said. "Heavy quality and expensive engraving." He peered closely at the text. "Typed on an Underwood, I have no doubt, likely a Number Two. I have, you know, been working on an article on the typescripts of various typing devices. Quite a good machine. Yes, this certainly bears the stamp of authenticity. But I think we need only wait briefly for a more complete explanation, as it is nearly eleven o'clock now and I hear a carriage outside that is likely to be delivering our visitor."

I went to the window and looked out. Indeed, a fine carriage was drawing up before the house. There was no heraldry on the door, indicating a desire to maintain the confidentiality of the occupant, but without question, he was a man of means and standing.

Holmes quickly straightened up the very worst of the clutter in the room as we heard footsteps on the stairs followed by a knock on the door, which opened to admit Mrs. Hudson.

"Dr. Treves," she announced. Holmes nodded his approval and she admitted our visitor and departed herself.

Our guest was a man of perhaps fifty or so, with thinning hair and a graying mustache. He was dressed in well-tailored clothes, including a cutaway jacket and waistcoat, and a pair of golden pince-nez glass was perched on his nose. He turned to be certain the door had been firmly closed behind Mrs. Hudson, and then walked towards Holmes and myself, extending his hand to me.

"I am pleased to make your acquaintance, Dr. Watson," he said. "I am Dr. Treves. I hope you have received my letter. Ah, yes, I see it in your hand, Mr. Holmes. A pleasure to meet you as well."

Holmes nodded, unaccustomed to being recognized second – although I must say that for once, I enjoyed being the object of a visitor's primary attention. "Please, Doctor, be seated," I offered. "Some tea?"

"No, nothing, thank you," he said. "I very much appreciate your agreeing to see me and request that you honour the necessity for absolute confidentiality." Holmes and I nodded our agreement. "As you know, the King's coronation is supposed to occur in just two weeks," he began.

"'Supposed to occur'?" Holmes interrupted.

"Yes, Mr. Holmes, it is on that point that I have come to consult with you this morning."

"Is there a problem with the health of a member of the Royal Family?" I asked.

Treves said nothing, but looked back and forth at Holmes and me, clearly straining to utter the words.

"It is the King himself," he declared in hushed tones. "He is ill, in great distress and, I fear, at tremendous risk of a catastrophic infection that, quite frankly, a man of his age and overall health – typhoid fever, a heavy smoker, more alcohol than is advisable – is extremely unlikely to survive."

His words fell like a thunderclap to my ears. Just the previous year, the Queen had succumbed at the age of 81. Now her successor, a generation younger, lay at death's door, if the learned physician was correct.

"What do you suspect?" I asked. "Peritonitis? Diverticulitis?"

"I am nearly certain of **perityphlitis**," he replied. Glancing at Holmes, he added, "A severe inflammation of the caecum, undoubtedly related to infection that could result in sepsis and – "

"I understand completely," I declared, turning to Holmes who had an uncharacteristically quizzical look on his face. "The King is almost certainly experiencing what is commonly referred to as 'appendicitis', a serious infection of the small appendage to the colon. But surely this is good news," I said to Treves. "You are widely regarded as the most knowledgeable surgeon in the successful treatment of patients with this diagnosis!"

The renowned physician's face turned gray. "Not expert enough to save my own daughter, Hetty" he said softly. "I lost her to this very disease a year-and-a-half ago. She was just eighteen years old."

The room was quiet for several moments, and then, Treves began to speak once again.

"I believe the medical course is clear," the doctor said. "I cannot, of course, guarantee the success of the outcome, but if we act swiftly, I believe we have a good chance to save the King. If there is delay, then I can make no assurances."

"Then why should there be any delay?" Holmes asked brusquely.

"Why, indeed," Treves repeated. "Absent drainage and irrigation of the belly, the King will not live to have the crown placed upon his head. Of that I am certain! Yet he is being obstinate, believing so radical an invasion is unnecessary. 'I have a coronation on hand,' he insisted to me."

"How did you respond to him?" I inquired.

"I told him, 'With the greatest respect, sir, it will be a funeral if you don't have the operation.'

"Unfortunately, there are those in the Court who appear to be encouraging his erroneous belief. They prefer more traditional approaches – liquids, rest, purgatives – but these will unquestionably result in the King's death, I have no doubt. Here is the chart the doctors have written on our patient for the past week," he said, handing a folder to me. "You can see the notations of the various attending physicians – each has their initials by their notes – and to a man they concur with the symptoms exactly as I have described them. And yet, they obstinately refuse to authorize the proper treatment."

I reviewed the charts for a few moments before handing them to Holmes, who studied them and handed them back to Treves.

"What role can I possibly play?" I asked. "I don't share the medical skills that you possess. Indeed, few do! Why should His Majesty give credence to anything I would say since he, however unwisely, doubts your advice?"

"It is true I am a Serjeants Surgeon to His Majesty, but I'm not the only one," Treves began. "For reasons unclear to me, there is disagreement that is unnecessarily threatening the King's life, in my opinion. You, sir, are universally well-regarded in medical circles, and you are far removed from the Royal Court," he continued. "You would bring a knowledgeable opinion free from the intrigue that influences every aspect of life at the palace."

"Even treating the health of the King?" asked Holmes.

"Oh, yes, Mr. Holmes," he replied. "But I fear something other than medical opinion might well be playing a role in this dispute, and that is where I thought you might assist while Dr.

Watson and I attend to the King's medical crisis. You can see why. You are a pair of experts, each in your own right, are so invaluable to me in this matter."

Treves asked that we accompany him to Buckingham Palace at once, as the King's condition might weaken at any moment and put him beyond even his medical skills. Within an hour, we had arrived at the magnificent palace and been admitted. We quickly walked upstairs to the audience chamber on the second floor. "I expect we'll be visited by some of the other medical staff once they learn of our arrival," he said as we settled into comfortable chairs.

"Who are these other physicians?" Holmes asked.

"There are several who have attended the King for some time – in some cases decades," Treves replied. "Frankly, some are less skilled in surgery than one would like. Some haven't kept up on the latest medical journals. In my view, the King would be better served were the physicians attending to him of a higher quality, but he has his favorites."

As expected, we didn't wait long before several grave-looking men appeared in the doorway. They greeted Treves with varying degrees of enthusiasm and cast doubtful looks towards Holmes and myself.

"Gentlemen, I am pleased to introduce you to the distinguished physician, Dr. John Watson," he said, extending his arm in my direction. "You may have read some of his very fine articles on battlefield surgery which described new techniques for treating abdominal injuries while minimizing the chances for opportunistic infections."

I considered Treves' comments thoughtfully as I have never published any such articles. While a surgeon in combat must be inventive when operating under inhospitable conditions, little of the surgeries I performed in Afghanistan had any applicability to the circumstances of a gravely ill King lying in his palace bed. Still, Treves' introduction brought forth murmurs of "Yes, of course," and "An honor for you to join us," and so I was not inclined to correct him about his misplaced representation of my innovative surgical techniques. Holmes, for the moment, went unintroduced as Treves and the other physicians began to discuss the patient's condition, and I was drawn into their circle to participate.

"Little change in condition, Treves," said an older man, clearly a senior member of the team. "Extreme abdominal sensitivity, fever, and a pronounced swelling in the lower right quadrant of the belly."

"All quite consistent with appendicitis," I noted. "And what treatments have been provided in the last eight hours?"

Here the physicians looked at each other and at Treves before a younger member of the medical team replied. "We are continuing with non-invasive treatment," he said. "Fluids, rest, purgatives, icing of the abdomen."

"But you have seen no improvement?" I asked.

"No, nothing to speak of," the young physician admitted. "Frankly, I'm concerned about the possibility of rupture and peritonitis if we don't see significant change fairly soon. These conditions can deteriorate quite rapidly, as you may know."

"I am well aware of the prognosis," Treves interjected. Certainly, everyone in the room knew of the loss of his daughter two years earlier from just such an infection, and the men all grew respectfully silent.

"Why has no drain inserted to determine whether a rupture has occurred and to remove fluids if it has?" I asked forthrightly.

Here there was some stirring amongst the physicians before the older gentleman again spoke up. "We think that very unwise," he responded, looking at Treves. "At least, most of us do. The technique is highly dangerous for a patient of the King's age and physical condition. The treatment may well be worse than the condition."

"With all due respect, Sir Jeffrey, the outcome of the current course will most certainly be worse than any other possible outcome, I assure you," Treves declared. "My surgical plan is well-established, as years of experience have proven."

"Treves, as we know, your methods are far from assured of success," Sir Jeffrey responded. The words seemed especially cruel given Treves' own reference to his late daughter. "I believe more traditional treatments will prove of great success if we but give them several days to take effect."

"If we wait several days," Treves responded, "we will be preparing for the coronation of a very different king, I assure you!"

He walked past his colleagues towards the door and bade me follow him down the hall into the King's bed chamber. The monarch was reclined in a large wooden bed, the bedclothes pulled up around his chest. His eyes were closed and his breathing seemed somewhat laboured. Nearby, Queen Alexandra sat with an expression of the greatest disquiet on her face, although she brightened slightly when she saw Treves enter the room.

"Your Majesty," Treves said, bowing slightly as he approached her. "May I present Dr. John Watson of London, whom I have asked to consult with us on the King's treatment?"

The Queen nodded towards us, and he and I bowed. "And may I present – " I began, looking for Holmes, but realizing he hadn't followed us into the sickroom. "Your Majesty, I will do everything I may to assure the full recovery of His Majesty. If you don't mind, I will conduct a brief examination."

The Queen discreetly walked to another part of the room while Treves and I removed some of the bedclothes covering the King's corpulent abdomen. The sight of his lower belly was certainly disturbing, to say the least. There was obvious swelling – even beyond its normal considerable girth – that was quite warm to the touch. The King groaned slightly when I applied gentle pressure. After a few additional moments of examination, I replaced the blanket over his prostrate figure and motioned Treves to join me outside the room.

"Treves, there is no question that this is a most serious case!" I began. "The inflammation extends considerably towards the umbilicus, which suggests infection. Water and rest will have no benefit whatsoever. Frankly, I cannot imagine why surgery hasn't been the unanimous recommendation of the medical staff."

"We have until the morning to make that decision, I have concluded, but after that, I fear it will be too late," he responded. "Let us return to your rooms with Holmes and determine how to proceed."

We walked back to collect Holmes, but he was nowhere to be seen. Treves called over one of the palace staff who was straightening up the room. "Have you seen the gentleman who arrived with us – the tall man in the overcoat?" he asked.

"Yes, sir," the response came. "He has departed already."

"Departed?" Treves said.

"Yes. After receiving a note, he asked for a carriage and he departed."

"What note?" I inquired.

"A note that arrived with instructions to be delivered to a 'Mr. Holmes' who had just arrived at the palace," the man said. "I asked him whether that was his name, and he acknowledged it was, so I handed him the note. He opened and read it, and quickly left."

"Who gave you the note?" I asked.

"Dr. Jeffrey handed it to me," he replied. "He said, 'Here is an envelope I have found on the table over there,'" he explained, pointing to the far side of the room. "Attached to the envelope was a note asking that it be delivered to '*Mr. Holmes*'."

"How peculiar!" Treves said.

"I must leave right now and try to find him," I said.

"You don't suspect something evil is afoot, do you?" Terves asked.

"Holmes is more than able to defend himself," I assured him. "He is in pursuit."

"In pursuit?" Treves asked in a perplexed tone. "In pursuit of *what*?"

"I understand your confusion, Dr. Treves," I explained. "I spend much of my life asking the very same question. Holmes is on the scent, I have no doubt."

We rushed out of the palace to a waiting carriage and flew back to Baker Street, but he hadn't returned. It was drawing close to dinner time and I asked Treves to join me for a meal. We left word for Holmes with Mrs. Hudson and walked to one of our favorite restaurants a few blocks away.

"In my judgment, we can wait until morning to conduct the surgery, but no later," he repeated. "But for the disagreement amongst the physicians, I would recommend we initiate the procedure tonight."

"How will you proceed if the disagreement persists?" I inquired.

"I will have no alternative but to go to the Queen and explain to her that without surgical intervention, her husband is doomed," he answered. "Frankly, I'm hopeful that you and Mr. Holmes may be of assistance if that step is required."

"I presume the Queen is familiar with my extensive scholarship on treating abdominal wounds on the battlefield?" I asked with a smile.

We waited more than an hour, and finally, Holmes arrived and joined us at the table. Unlike Treves and myself, he had a jaunty air about him that seemed ill-suited to gravity of the situation. After ordering a dinner of hearty roasted beef and vegetables, he took a drink of his beer and sat back.

"Progress, Treves and Watson, progress!" he said with satisfaction.

"Holmes, one of the staff at Buckingham Palace said you received a note while we were examining the King," I said.

"Yes," he replied with satisfaction. "And here it is." He produced a piece of the Royal stationery much like the one Treves had used for his own note to us, but this message – obviously written with pencil in great haste – was barely legible and far more ominous.

Holmes –

You have no role *here.* Do not interfere *with medical business.* Leave immediately *or prepare to suffer* grave embarrassment.

Despite the abysmal penmanship, the author had taken care to emphasize certain words with great vigor. There was no signature. On the envelope was scrawled "*Sherlock Holmes*".

"I will never understand why some people insist upon providing me with clues!" Holmes said merrily. "I was perfectly content to remain in the library and await the report of your examination. Instead, I am presented with this most instructional message, the untangling of which consumed the entire remainder of the afternoon and some of the evening as well."

"And what can you tell me, Mr. Holmes?" Treves inquired.

"Oh, prepare to operate, Doctor," Holmes replied, "as early in the morning as you can."

"And the resistance from my colleagues?"

"I think you will find it has quite melted away," Holmes said with confidence.

I was up very early the next morning and, by arrangement, a carriage collected me at Baker Street at eight a.m. for the short ride to Buckingham Palace, where I was whisked through the guard house and shown up to the sickroom. The King remained in great distress but had been informed that there was no alternative to surgery and no time to delay. A nearby room had already been outfitted as a surgical theatre.

Treves led me into an adjoining room where we could speak privately. "I have been here half the night," Treves said upon greeting me. "I don't know by what magic Mr. Holmes achieved this complete reversal, but at nine o'clock last evening, I was sent a note that informed me of the unanimous agreement by the other physicians that the surgery should proceed at once. I'm deeply grateful to him, and to you for joining me in this operation."

"Join you?" I cried. I lowered my voice. "Treves, you know that I'm no surgeon of your skill!"

"You are a reliable partner," he said, placing his hand on my arm. "That is what I need right now, every bit as much as a surgical assistant." Quickly we changed into our surgical gowns. "Come, let us get to this business without delay!" Treves urged.

He disappeared into the sickroom, and then returned with a number of other gentlemen, some of whom I recognized from our earlier visit to the King's bedside. "Dr. Watson will be assisting me today with the surgery," he informed his colleagues, including Dr. Frederick Hewitt, who would serve as the anesthesiologist, Alfred Fripp, who had been the King's personal surgeon for several years, and Dr. Francis Laking, who had been treating the King for several days along with Treves.

"Watson, Watson," Hewitt muttered. "I seem to recall a John Watson when I was a medical student." Hewitt peered towards me but as his eyesight was extremely poor. He failed to recognize me and the conversation quickly moved to more immediate concerns.

Treves explained the procedure for every step of the operation. Shortly after noon, we gathered in the operating suite. A door opened and the King walked laboriously into the room, assisted by Dr. Jeffrey, greeting each of the physicians whom he recognized. He paused for a moment when he saw my unfamiliar face and stared at me closely.

"This is Dr. John Watson," Treves announced, "the renowned Army surgeon who has consented to assist me in this matter."

The King gave a sharp nod of his head. "Of course, of course," he said. "I am fortunate to have you, Doctor!"

With that, he hoisted himself onto the surgical table with some difficulty owing to his discomfort and his significant portliness. Dr. Hewitt spoke with the King to calm his evident nervousness and then began to administer the anesthesia to render him unconscious so the surgery could begin. Almost immediately, the King began to choke and his face turned purple as the other physicians watched in alarm. Hewitt was unperturbed and responded by grasping the King's beard and pulling it quite sharply. The King's jaw pulled forward, clearing his windpipe, and after a moment, he took a deep breath and his color returned to normal.

"An obstructive apnea," Hewitt explained, "undoubtedly due to the weight on his diaphragm." He examined the King's breathing again. "I think you should be alright to proceed now," he said to Treves, amid audible sighs of relief from the other physicians.

I moved to stand next to Treves as he exposed the King's very sizeable abdomen before liberally applying an antiseptic wash according to explicit directions provided by Dr. Lister, the pioneering surgeon. Treves picked up a scalpel and deftly began to cut into the inflamed portion of the lower abdomen as I administered sterilized cloths to staunch the bleeding.

"This is going to be slightly more complicated than the typical case," Treves said to me in an aside. He pulled apart the incision slightly to expose several inches of yellowish fat girdling the King's mid-section. "I would say there is four inches or more to cut through before we reach the abdominal wall!" Once he did so and inserted the rubber tubing, it quickly became clear that the King's appendix had indeed ruptured and the great swelling and pain he had been enduring was due to an abscess that had formed. I will spare the further graphic details of the surgery to readers whose tastes may not run to descriptions of abdominal drainage. Suffice it to say that the operation occurred not a moment too soon, as further reliance on the disproven treatments would surely have led to sepsis and certain death within days.

Within an hour-and-a-half, the surgery was complete. Treves had elected not to attempt to remove the appendix itself, which would have required a much larger wound and greatly expanded the possibility of infection. Instead, the abdomen had been drained and the wound packed with sterile gauze. A tube had been left in place to allow the drainage to continue. Now, it would simply require careful observation to ensure the infection dissipated and the wound healed cleanly.

"My congratulations, Treves," I declared as we pulled off our surgical gowns. "You have a deft and practiced hand in the operating theatre."

"Thank you, Watson," he responded. "I was fortunate to have your assistance today. There were several moments when your experience in cauterizing gave me great confidence."

The other physicians, having paused to look at Treves' handwork, now filed into the room and clapped him on the back. "Bravo!" and "Well done!" they called out as they filed past, nodding their heads to me in acknowledgement even though, I imagine, they fully recognized that the credit properly belonged to the colleague they had so recently maligned and dismissed.

"We will need to watch him carefully over the next several days, but I'm hopeful," Treves said. "I'll personally monitor the drainage and repacking of the wound periodically until I'm certain there is no evidence of further infection."

We washed our hands carefully before stepping back into the makeshift operating room to check on our patient. He remained snoring comfortably with no further signs of the apnea that had come close to ending the surgery before it had even begun.

"Come," Treves said, "let us go find Mr. Holmes and tell him of today's success."

After leaving explicit instructions as to his whereabouts with the nursing staff, Treves and I departed the palace.

A carriage ride returned us to Baker Street, where we were greeted by Mrs. Hudson who, like virtually everyone in our busy city, had no idea of the great danger from which their King had been rescued by the expert ministrations of my companion.

"Mr. Holmes is awaiting your arrival," she pleasantly said. "He was certain you would be arriving very soon." We climbed the familiar stairs and opened the door to reveal him sitting in his comfortable chair, smoking one of his favorite briars.

"Ah Watson. Treves," he said expectantly. "I presume from your demeanor that you achieved a successful outcome."

"Most definitely," I replied. Gesturing to my medical colleague, I added, "Treves is a skilled and fearless surgeon. There are not many men who might have been as decisive in cutting into the considerable abdomen of our King, but he did so without hesitation and with great dexterity."

"Thank you, Watson," the object of my comments replied. "It was an interesting case, and I was most fortunate to have your colleague assisting me." He made a little bow in my direction, to which I reciprocated. "And I certainly want to acknowledge your own considerable contribution to the successful surgery, Holmes."

"*My* contribution?" Holmes responded. "Whatever do you mean? I was nowhere near the surgery, and good fortune I was not, for my skills with a scalpel and retractor are vastly inferior to Watson's prowess."

"Come, come, Holmes, I think you know what I mean," Treves replied. "Last evening, the King lay near death, and I was unable to secure the consensus amongst my fellow medical men to take the one action with a chance of saving his life. Several hours later, I'm summoned to the palace and ushered into the sickroom with instructions to prepare for surgery – orders I had been anxiously awaiting for two weeks. Surely there is a great deal to tell about how this fortunate change in circumstances came about."

Holmes regarded the physician and puffed on his pipe. "Well, why don't we just say, as did the Bard himself, '*All's well that ends well*'. I think you'll find the King most generous in his response to you for your services, and that your role as Sergeant Surgeon to the King remains most secure."

"Yes, yes, but how did all this come about?"

"As Watson will tell you, Doctor," Holmes replied. "I'm not always at liberty to discuss my methods, but I can assure you no further challenges to your authority. I have no doubt that the King will live as long and healthy a life as your ministrations enable him."

Treves clearly wasn't pleased with Holmes's unwillingness to share more information, but he was reconciled to honouring the detective's discretion. "Then I will thank you again, both of you, for your inestimable assistance," he said.

"And one more thing, if I may," said Holmes. "My name was not prominently mentioned in connection with this affair and I should prefer to keep it that way. Let the plaudits fall where they ought: On the medical men and their impressive skills."

"Of course, Mr. Holmes," Treves answered.

After we had heard him descend the stairs and close the front door, I turned to Holmes. "Come now, surely you cannot keep the answer to the mystery from me!" I implored.

"Well, we do have our secrets," he said smiling, "and some of those with respect to this case must remain secret even from you, Watson. Even from you."

Holmes sat in one of the comfortable chairs, lit his briar, and stretched out his long legs.

"In many ways, not a very remarkable story," he began, "except for affecting the survival of the King and the future of the monarchy.

"The key to the case, in my view, was that Dr. Treves alone served as the advocate for immediate surgery," Holmes said. "True, one might discount his fervent advocacy of such a course, given his specialization in appendix removal and his great sensitivity over having lost his own daughter. But I was struck by the reluctance of the other consulting physicians who seemed to dismiss Treves' greater experience in dealing with this particular condition."

"I must say I agree with you," I interjected. "While undoubtedly the King is anything but a fit physical specimen

– those four inches or so of fat could lead to no other conclusion – I couldn't make sense of the resistance of the other physicians. Clearly, there was but one suitable course which was removal of the appendix or drainage of the abdomen!"

"Yes, precisely," Holmes answered. "There seemed to be no logical medical rationale for delay, particularly since the leading practitioner of appendectomies was standing by the King's bedside urging just such a course.

"I think you know my methods well enough to recognize why I began to reach a very dark conclusion," he continued. "What lay behind their opposition to the surgery? No alternative treatment was available and clearly, the regimen they followed had produced nothing but a worsening of the King's condition. Inaction, as you explained to me, could only ensure a rupture of the appendix, sepsis throughout the King's body, and certain death.

"Now assuming that no one wished the King ill, the only rationale seemed to me misplaced medical judgment. Perhaps the medical men were fearful that the chances of surgical success were so miniscule that they wished to avoid encouraging a procedure that could result in their incurring culpability for the King's death."

"Yes, that seems possible," I responded. "But these are distinguished physicians, men at the very top of the profession. Surely they could explain to the Queen and others that the King's condition left them no alternative but to undertake such a risky procedure."

"I agree," said Holmes. "If they were prepared to make that argument, who in England has sufficient credibility to dispute their recommendation? Which is why I rejected that explanation for their inaction."

"But what other explanation can there be?" I wondered aloud. "If they didn't believe their current treatments effective and they weren't reluctant to recommend a precarious procedure, what other motive might there be?"

"Ah, Watson, how many times have you heard me say when confronted with just such a conundrum, 'When you have eliminated the impossible – '"

"' – Whatever remains, however improbable, must be the truth'," I completed. "But what remains in this case?" I wracked my brain for whatever option remained that might explain the obstinance of the medical experts, with the exception of Treves. Suddenly, a black thought entered my mind.

"No, Holmes!" I cried. "You cannot be serious! It is impossible!"

"*Whatever* remains," Holmes replied, looking at me with the gravest expression I have ever seen on his face. "*Whatever*."

I sat back in my chair to fully comprehend the implications of my friend's deduction. Holmes was not inclined to idle speculation or fancy. If he believed what he was saying, he must not only be convinced of its accuracy, but also have corroborated his theory through his investigations.

"Who would have such a motivation?" I asked. "Who could possibly wish such an outcome?"

"Oh, that is the least problematical issue," Holmes said. "There are any number of influential people and powerful interests that Edward may have offended. It is always a sound rule to ask '*Cui bono?*' Who benefits should Edward never be coronated and the Crown passes instead to the Prince of Wales? '*Uneasy lies the head that wears a crown*' – yet another of Shakespeare's observations that might have some applicability in this affair.

"Clearly I lacked the time to investigate everyone with a grievance against the King, which might well be a lengthy list given his decades of – let us say – *rambunctious* behavior,"

Holmes said. "But I certainly could focus on those who, despite convincing testimony to the contrary, seemed adamant to deny the King his one chance for a recovery.

"And so, that is what I did. I spent much of yesterday deep in the newspaper records and other sources examining the backgrounds of the men who now hovered over our critically ill monarch, trying to find a cause that might explain their reticence in following Treves' persuasive diagnosis.

"Watson," he continued, "I cannot reveal the details of those inquiries, even to you – even if you promise me, as I am hoping you will, that the details of this story remain undisclosed for some time. Indeed, I think this a perfect example of a case that belongs in your box at Cox and Company, rather than in the pages of *The Strand* or any other publication.

"What I found was deeply disturbing, it goes without saying. One of the attending physicians – and here, Watson, I will not reveal the identity, even to you – possesses a motive against the King that he dared not reveal, but that unquestionably provided him more than a little rationale for denying Edward the only treatment that would save his life.

"Treves, it turns out, was not the only father to lose a cherished daughter, as it turns out. So did at least two of the other attending physicians treating the King, and another lost a son to disease in the army. I need not tell you that the loss of a child profoundly affects any parent beyond any anguish those of us without issue might imagine – the psychologists have been quite clear on this point.

"The connection of two of those lost children to Edward, or the Crown, seem tangential at best. One daughter died after an accident at the father's estate while he was attending to one of the King's earlier illnesses. He deeply blamed himself for being absent when his daughter desperately needed medical care, but the King certainly bore no plausible responsibility for the loss of the child.

"The second case, that of the son, might have produced a grievance against Edward since the son had been in military service to the Crown at the time of his death, the result of an attack in India."

"But surely no educated person would blame the monarch because a child dies in military service!" I responded. "Such decisions are made by the government, not the Crown!"

"I agree. The likelihood of seeking revenge for such a loss did not strike me as plausible either, and I dismissed that suspect as well. But the third case – ah, there seemed more promise, since the death of the daughter was shrouded in secrecy. It was only reported in *The Times* that she had taken ill quite suddenly and passed away, with no discussion of the details of her illness.

"However, *The Times* isn't the only source of news. I delved in the back issues of the penny weeklies that cover the seamier side of life in our city to see whether this particular death had occasioned any coverage."

"And did it?" I asked expectantly. "Did you find something?"

Holmes leaned forward in his chair, drawing his head close to mine and spoke in a hushed tone.

"Yes, Watson, I most certainly did find something," Holmes said. "Something so grievous and contemptible that it left no doubt in my mind that it was the answer to this entire case.

"The daughter was just nineteen years old and had a most independent nature. Although her father preferred that she engage in university study, she preferred to flirt with society and became engaged as a lady's assistant to Miss Alice Keppel."

"I have heard the salacious rumors about Miss Keppel and the King, of course," I said. Holmes looked at me with surprise. "Well, you aren't the only one who dabbles with the penny weeklies, you know!"

Alice Keppel was only half the King's age, but well-founded rumors had swirled around her indiscreet relationship to the King. It was said that she had become his mistress two or three years earlier and enjoyed an unusually close friendship with Edward, one that could hardly escape public attention, including that of the Queen who, for whatever reason, chose to overlook his improper behavior.

"This young woman accompanied Miss Keppel almost everywhere," Holmes continued, "and in doing so, she inevitably became known to the Prince. Despite the relationship with Miss Keppel, it appears the Prince had sufficient time and energy to also strike up a brief relationship with this young woman.

"Trouble quickly arose, rumor had it, when word of the Prince's unfaithfulness to his mistress, if that is an appropriate concept, the young lady was discharged from service. Shortly thereafter, the young lady became quite ill with a medical condition. Given her father's prominence and association with the Royal Family, she concealed the condition from him, seeking treatments from unreliable quacks whose ministrations were utterly ineffective."

I considered Holmes's story thus far and was naturally appalled. "How did you proceed?" I inquired.

"There was little I could do but confront the father directly with my findings," Holmes said, "and this I did last night in a surreptitious visit to his home in Mayfair. I sent a message to him early in the evening, explaining that I would be arriving at six o'clock and that it would be to his distinct advantage to see me. Frankly, I assumed that someone of his station would recognize that the arrival of Sherlock Holmes at his door was not something to be trifled with.

"I arrived promptly and used the heavy brass knocker to announce my arrival. I gave my name to the butler who answered the door, and was promptly escorted into the library. After a few moments, the door swung open and Doctor – well, let me not use names – entered the room and walked directly up to me. He conveyed an unmistakable attitude of superiority.

"'I am not used to visits from the police,' he haughtily declared.

"'That is just as well,' I replied, 'since the police might have a far more extensive list of questions if they, rather than I, were knocking at your door. However, I am a private consulting detective, with little interest in involving the police in the matter which brings me to your library this evening.'

"'I know of your reputation, of course,' he began. 'I would ask you to sit down, Mr. Holmes, but I first would like to know the explanation for your unsolicited arrival. What can a – what did you say, a *private consulting detective?* – possibly want from me? And on whose behalf are you consulting, if you don't mind my asking?'

"'Actually, I *do* mind,' I responded, settling into a comfortable chair beside the large fireplace and gesturing for the doctor to sit as well, an invitation which he ignored. I recognized the effrontery of my action, but I felt I held the upper hand in the conversation, and besides, I was offended by his aristocratic air.

"'I am here to insist that you discontinue your opposition to the King's surgery,' I boldly stated. 'I believe that you are well aware that Treves' surgical option alone can save the King's life, and yet you have rallied your colleagues, except for Treves, in opposition to an appendectomy. If you persist in your unreasonable opposition for simply another day, you surely know that England will soon conduct a funeral rather than a coronation.'

"I have seen men become distraught and agitated when I have confronted them with their misdeeds, Watson, but I must say I have never seen the kind of reaction my words elicited on this distinguished physician. I do believe that had he had a scalpel or other dangerous tool of his profession at hand, he would have assaulted me right there in his magnificent library.

"'Have you lost your mind?' he thundered. 'How *dare* you come to my home and make such unfounded and conspiratorial accusations against me! I do not care a whit for your reputation or connections. I shall summon the police and have you hauled off to the Old Bailey!'

"'I would counsel against such an action,' I replied.

"'And give me one reason why I should listen to a word that comes from your impertinent mouth!' he insisted.

"'Well, first, because I would have very little trouble connecting you to the threatening note left for me at the Palace, despite your crude attempt to disguise your handwriting, which I saw clearly displayed on the King's medical chart yesterday. You may not be aware of the papers that I have authored precisely on the topic of efforts to conceal one's telltale penmanship.

"'Second, because the memory of your daughter would be sullied if all of the details of this matter to be publicly discussed, as they surely would be, were I subjected to police examination.'

"He stopped moving towards the door and stood motionless. 'What do you know of my daughter?' he asked.

"'Doctor, I know nearly everything, and what I do not yet know for certain, I have no doubt I can hypothesize – though that is not in my nature – and you could confirm. For example, I know that your daughter, against your wishes, left your home to become an assistant to Miss Keppel, that through the arrangement she was introduced to Edward when he was still Prince Albert. I have no doubt that, as was the case with apparently innumerable other attractive young women, the Prince was able to entice her into sordid behavior.'

"'By now, the doctor's face had returned to its normal hue and his arrogant air had been utterly deflated. Instead, his head hung and he reached to his eyes to wipe away tears.

"'Of course, it became worse,' I continued. 'She developed a condition quite common amongst those engaged in such indiscriminate behavior, a condition that she concealed from you, even though she must have known you were aware that the Prince's own case of this disease was under expert treatment. By the time her physical condition became serious enough to convince her of the fruitlessness of the quackery she was receiving, it was too late. She told you of her plight, and your examination revealed the infections had progressed too far. Within weeks, she had fallen gravely ill and – '

"'Stop!' he said, holding up his hand. 'Stop. I cannot relive the awfulness.' He turned to face me and the tears continued to stream down his cheeks. 'Yes, Mr. Holmes. Yes. She was terribly ill, far beyond treatment by the time she confessed her behavior to me. She refused to identify from whom she had contracted the infection, but given her position with Miss Keppel and my own knowledge of the Prince's medical condition, it was hardly a difficult diagnosis to make. Within weeks, she was gone.' His voice choked. 'And I was unable to do anything to help her, despite my degrees and diplomas. And I was unable to do anything in retribution against the person who had brought such a disgrace upon her and upon me as well.

"'But I am a professional physician, and my job is not to judge my patients,' he continued. 'I had a responsibility to the Prince, who shortly thereafter succeeded to the throne, and I could not allow my personal antagonism to mutate into thoughts of revenge, although I had innumerable opportunities to provide the King with something other than the medicines he required.

"'And then this new illness appeared several weeks ago, and something changed in my outlook,' he continued. 'Surely, I could never take any action to administer a dangerous drug to the Sovereign, but withholding medical assistance did not seem to me to fall into the same category.' His face grew grave as looked up at me and spoke. 'This . . . *man* – this egotistical, indulgent dilettante! He has left a trail of ruined women behind him like a dog abandons bones it has chewed and tired of, with no concern for his own immorality or their disgrace. He does not deserve to wear the Crown! And suddenly, because of my position and stature in the Court, I had a means to ensure that he never would.'

"He sat down at last into a chair and stared blankly ahead. 'Yes, I knew Treves was right,' he admitted. 'I knew an appendectomy was called for, or at least drainage of the abdomen. I knew that time was running out, that the appendix would burst and that afterwards, the chances of sepsis were beyond doubt. A man in that condition had virtually no chance of surviving such a turn of events.

"'The King himself had deep reservations about proceeding with an operation, even under the supervision of so skilled a surgeon as Treves. It wasn't difficult to alarm him sufficiently that he allowed me to continue a non-surgical course which I convinced him had a greater likelihood of success than an invasive procedure. Yes, I knew that my prognosis was flawed and that following my recommendations means that it would be George, not Edward, who will be coronated as King. I considered that outcome the appropriate one for the nation.'

Holmes completed this recitation and remained silent for a few moments.

"Even in my long career of exposure to the vilest criminals that the sewers of London have dredged up, I've never had the revulsion and loathing I felt for this celebrated medical professional," he said. "I could barely believe what was being confessed to me. But I also knew there was little time to act if we were to avoid precisely the outcome this medical malcontent desired.

"I walked to where he sat and handed him a piece of paper from the desk. 'You must send a note at once to Treves,' I instructed, 'informing him of the change in your opinion, and that the surgery must take place as early tomorrow as feasible.'

"Without a word, he rose to sit at desk, where he quickly wrote the note I had dictated. He summoned his butler and directed the letter be carried immediately to Treves, and that a confirmation of its receipt be brought back to him.

"'Now, we are going to the Palace, where you will inform the King and Queen of your change in opinion, and that they must prepare for tomorrow's procedure.'

"We were soon passing through the gates of Buckingham Palace and, upon entering, were escorted to the King's bedchamber where he lay moaning and only semi-conscious. In a few moments, Queen Alexandra arrived. Although I had little doubt the doctor would obey my precise instructions, I determined to remain in the room to be certain, which naturally necessitated an introduction.

"'Your Majesties, I have the honour to present to you Mr. Holmes,' he said.

"The King stirred, lifting his head slightly from the pillows and looking in my direction.

"'Mycroft, is that you?' he asked.

"'No, Your Majesty,' I replied, 'Mycroft is my older brother. I know of his long service to the Foreign Ministry. I am his brother, Sherlock.'

"'A physician?' he responded.

"'No,' the doctor interjected, 'but Mr. Holmes has made,' he searched for the words, 'invaluable contributions to our efforts on your behalf.'

"'Ah, very well,' replied Edward, resting his great head on the pillow again. 'I shall knight you, too, as well as all these physicians who are endeavoring to save my life.'

"'That is very kind of you, but let us focus first on your recovery,' I replied. 'I believe the doctor has some thoughts about the next course of treatment.'

"The doctor cleared his throat. 'Yes, Your Majesties, we have determined that despite our best efforts, it will be necessary for Dr. Treves to conduct a surgery tomorrow to remove the infected appendix,' he said. This remark was not well received by Edward or the Queen, but as it was coming from so authoritative a source, they offered no resistance. 'I will be speaking with Dr. Treves later this evening to put all of the plans in place,' he continued. 'I think that by tomorrow evening this time, you will be feeling considerably better and assured of a healthy recovery.'

"We exchanged some comments all around and then took our leave of the sickroom. I told the doctor I would monitor each step of the process and would speak with Treves myself to ensure the directions were clearly conveyed. If there was any deviation from our agreement, I promised, my call would not be to him or to the palace, but to Scotland Yard."

And that is precisely what transpired prior to the surgery taking place the next day just after noon. I was among the physicians who visited with the King the following day, and was surprised to find him alert, sitting up in his bed, reading the newspapers and, I am sorry to say, smoking a cigar. It was soon clear the treatment had been effective and within a couple of weeks, the drainage had ceased and the infection was gone. On 9ᵗʰ August, the King was formally crowned Edward VII, beginning what would be a tragically brief although surprisingly distinguished era in British history. The King made good on his pledge of knighthoods for all of the physicians who participated in his successful treatment including, of course, Treves. One day in the summer, a visitor to Baker Street arrived in a carriage from the Palace and ascended the stairs to our rooms. He brought with him two oversized envelopes which we opened to reveal formal announcements from the King that he was conferring knighthoods on Holmes and myself in appreciation for our endeavors in saving his life.

After the courier had departed, Holmes sat at his desk and drafted a letter in his own hand, which I replicate here.

Your Majesty,

I am in receipt of your gracious announcement of your desire to confer upon me a knighthood in connection with my service to you during your recent illness. While I am grateful beyond words for your extreme kindness and recognition, such an honour as this is far beyond any contribution I could possibly have made in the successful outcome of your treatment, and I am unable in good conscience to accept your munificent gesture.

I hope that you appreciate both my gratefulness and my desire to ensure that knighthoods are reserved to those for whom public recognition is a benefit. In my occupation, however, such an acknowledgement might complicate certain activities I am called upon to perform. Therefore, with the greatest respect and wishes for a long reign, I choose to decline this generous offer.

With respect,
Sherlock Holmes

I fully understood Holmes's desire for anonymity and agreed a knighthood could complicate the conduct of the unconventional occupation he relished. Moreover, accepting such a recognition would invariably raise questions as to exactly what role he played in the King's treatment and recovery, and he had no desire for such speculation.

On my part, while a knighthood was certainly something to which most men aspire, I felt my own trivial contributions to the successful treatment of Edward VII were similarly undeserving of so great an honour, and so I also declined. Besides, how could I subject Holmes to future collaborations with a knight of the realm at his side!

Alas, Edward's tenure proved all too short, lasting less than a decade before his many health problems proved too debilitating. And yet, considering the five decades he had waited to actually become King, his reign was not without some significant achievements that brought honour to his name and the nation.

As for the mysterious medical saboteur, his name remains unknown to me. While I certainly could have followed Holmes's clues (some of which I have not included in this account), I chose to honour his request that I not do so. Presumably the physician who conspired to cut short the brief reign of Edward VII was among those the King honored with a knighthood, and he may well have continued to provide medical care to the King and his successor for years to come.

The one physician I can be sure was not implicated in the dastardly plan was Treves himself, with whom I remained friendly for many years. Tragically, even incomprehensively, the celebrated surgeon himself died at the age of seventy as a result of a burst appendix.

I remember the date very well, for it was in the same month that Holmes refused a knighthood for services which may perhaps someday be described.

– Dr. John H. Watson
"The Three Garridebs"

The Case of the
Norwegian Daredevil

As I review the many adventures in which I was engaged with Sherlock Holmes, I note that I have never before related the strange case of Larsen the Poisoner. The adventure, which occurred in April of 1898, appears in my files under the heading of *"Poison"* between "The Case of the Poisoned Scones" and the misplaced *"Poisson Frêche* Caper", and had several intriguing features which make it a most remarkable example of Holmes's skills.

A cold and blustery winter had left London longing for the gentle rains and bursting gardens of the springtime. Holmes and I sat at breakfast in our rooms at 221B Baker Street. He was deeply immersed in *The Times*, alternatingly sipping his coffee and taking long draws from his new briar pipe, and then filling the air with a stream of acrid smoke. As he threw down sections of the paper, I would pick them up and peruse them for interesting tidbits and potential cases.

"Ah," I said, holding up the newspaper, "do you see here there is some controversy brewing over the treaty that Sir Rennell Rodd signed with Menelik II?" Holmes put down his paper and took a long draw on the pipe.

"No, I wasn't aware of that fact," he archly replied. "Nor is it likely to influence significantly my plans for the remainder of the day."

"Quite significant, I should think," I added. "You realize, of course, that England has joined France in recognizing him. A blow to Italy, I should think."

Holmes put down his pipe and settled his arms onto the tabletop. "Pray explain why you believe I should care about Emperor Menelik," he asked.

"The *second*," I corrected. Holmes raised his hand to his mouth and slowly shook his head in disapproval.

"Or the *fifth*, for all I care!" he exclaimed in a theatrically exasperated voice.

"The Emperor of all the Abyssinians," I explained. "The treaty helps to clarify the border with Somaliland."

"Watson," Holmes began with a fatigued voice, although it was only 8:30 in the morning, "with all deference to Sir Rennell and the Abyssinians, what difference does this triumphant development mean to me? Menelik – the second – the Somalis, and Abyssinians will surely continue to conduct their affairs with no attention from me."

He pushed away the plate containing the crumbs from his breakfast and stretched his long legs under the dining table. He gazed out the slightly opened window to Baker Street, where the carriages were bustling along, their wheels click-clacking on the paving stones.

"Spring is finally upon us," he began.

"And '*a young man's fancy lightly turns to thoughts of love*'," I said, finishing Tennyson's quotation.

Holmes looked disapprovingly at me. "I was going to say, 'and still no problem of interest has crossed our entry way in days.'"

"I suppose one can always hope some heinous crime will make its appearance," I offered hopefully.

"Just so," Holmes replied, missing my sarcasm entirely while continuing to stare out the window.

A sharp rap on the door broke our reverie, followed by the entry of Mrs. Hudson who poked in her head, surveyed that all was well, and then slipped inside, leaving the door slightly ajar behind her.

"There's an officer of some sort here, Mr. Holmes," she said in a hushed tone, looking back over her shoulder towards the staircase. "He is most desirous of seeing you immediately." She looked to Holmes and then back again over her shoulder again. "I must say, he seems greatly agitated!"

Holmes drew in a deep breath and waved towards the door.

"Show him in, Mrs. Hudson," he called. "Show him in, by all means."

She opened the door and beckoned in an officer of perhaps thirty, dressed in civilian clothing and wearing a look of great concern.

"Mr. Holmes, I'm so grateful that you've agreed to see me," he said, extending his hand to Holmes. "I'm Waters, Inspector Roger Waters, of Scotland Yard. A detective," adding tentatively, "like you."

Holmes considered the description for a moment, and then swept his hand towards the basket chair instead of grasping the stranger's outstretched offering. "Please sit down and explain your urgent mission."

"Inspector Lestrade suggested that I come to see you about a most peculiar incident that occurred last night," he began, removing his overcoat and throwing it over a chair before seating himself.

"And yet Lestrade hasn't come himself," Holmes noted. "Indisposed?"

"On holiday," Inspector Waters explained. "He left this morning for Inverness. But he did have a chance before departing to help me with the initial inspection of the premises where the crime occurred."

"How fortunate to know the clues were treated with as much care and attention as Lestrade invariably provides," Holmes murmured. His deprecation was utterly lost on the young detective.

"I scarcely know where to begin," the man said. "Such a peculiar matter."

"Start at the beginning," Holmes urged. "It is invariably the most instructive place." We all sat around the table,

79

Holmes's elbows resting on the surface, his hands folded with his long fingers interlacing each other.

"There has been a most peculiar death at the Great Eastern Hotel," the young man began. "A guest has been found dead in his room, with terrible injuries, but what exactly occurred remains a confounding mystery."

"Certainly you must have learned the man's identity," Holmes said.

"Oh, yes. He was Mr. Meriwether Flicker, an American salesman. And just arrived yesterday."

"An elderly man?" Holmes inquired.

"No, not at all," said Waters. "Rather about twenty-nine or thirty, I would say. He arrived on a ship from New York. My men were summoned this morning when he failed to respond to repeated knocks from the cleaning staff of the hotel. I don't mind telling you they were quite startled when they were finally able to enter the room."

"You say 'finally'," Holmes noted. "I presume, therefore, that access was difficult?"

"Oh, yes, Mr. Holmes, that is one of the mysteries," replied the young officer. "The door was locked from the inside, with a bolt."

"Of course it was," Holmes responded with evident exasperation. "Are there no communicating rooms?" I asked.

"None," answered Waters, shaking his head. "There is but one way in and out of the room, and that is via the door through which the police entered after breaking it down."

"And what did they find?" inquired Holmes.

Waters gave a small shudder. "Mr. Holmes, it was quite horrible. Mr. Flicker was lying on the floor in the middle of the room with terrible cuts on his hands and wrists. The mirror in the lavatory had been smashed to pieces. That was evidently the cause of the lacerations, and there was blood everywhere. It seemed an obvious case – for some reason, the man had shattered the glass, perhaps intentionally, mortally injuring himself."

"And yet," Holmes replied, "you have come to me."

Waters shook his head slowly. "Something doesn't feel right. I find it difficult to understand why Mr. Flicker should travel all the way to London from New York, only to go mad the first night after his arrival, let alone purposefully kill himself by smashing a mirror. And yet, we can find no alternative explanation as to what transpired."

"Might there have been an altercation?" asked Holmes. "Could someone else have entered the room?"

"And locked the bolt behind them? I think not," Waters insisted.

"A window?" asked Holmes.

"Oh, yes, of course, there is a window," agreed Waters. "But Mr. Flicker's room was on the second floor, and there is no fire escape or other way anyone might climb up the sheer wall to enter that window. Quite impossible, I assure you."

"And yet," Holmes replied. I could hear the familiar remark coming even before it escaped his lips. "When you have excluded the impossible, whatever remains, however improbable, must be the truth," he declared for the hundredth time in our association.

"Whatever do you mean?" asked Waters. "Are you suggesting an intruder might've entered through a window located on the second story, accessible only by climbing a sheer wall?"

"Since I don't have all the facts as yet, I cannot say that is what happened," Sherlock Holmes declared. "Never allow theory to run ahead of the facts, Inspector. I'm saying it isn't improbable that it happened as you describe. Why don't we visit the scene of this tragedy and see what clues might still remain that would help clear up this matter?"

"I've given an order that nothing be disturbed," Waters assured. "My cab is downstairs."

We grabbed our coats and hats and descended into busy Baker Street where the police wagon was awaiting us, and soon we were clattering along to the Great Eastern Hotel.

We were met outside the hotel by a distraught gentleman who hurried to our carriage as it came to a stop. "Please, please, I beg of you, keep a low profile!" he urged.

"And you are?" Waters asked.

"Gilleston. The hotel manager," the worried man declared. "Oh, please, can't we keep this as quiet as possible? The scandal!" He looked apprehensively over his shoulder towards the lobby.

"May I remind you that a man is dead in your hotel, Gilleston?" Waters rebuked him. The manager uttered a whimpered groan. "We will have to conduct a thorough inquiry." The remaining color drained from the manager's distressed face.

Holmes stepped forward and put his hand on Gilleston's shoulder. "Rest assured, we will do everything possible to avoid disturbing your remaining, living guests." Gilleston uttered another soft groan.

The hotel was a well-known London landmark built in the previous decade on the former site of the mental hospital known as "Bedlam". It was tastefully furnished with plush sofas and chairs arranged around the lobby, flickering gas lamps and muted rugs covering much of the wooden floor. People were gathered reading newspapers and otherwise going about quite normal business, seemingly unaware of what had transpired above them during the night.

"What is the dead man's room number?"

"214."

"May I see the registration materials for that room?" Holmes asked Gilleston, who nodded and handed him a card.

"*Meriwether Flicker*'," Holmes read. "What can you tell me about his movements since his arrival? Think carefully!"

"Well, he arrived shortly after two in the afternoon," Gilleston responded. "He went to his room and remained there until about five-thirty, I believe, when he came down the stairs to have an early supper at our restaurant."

"Did he seem suspicious or wary in any way?" Holmes asked

"Not at all," Gilleston replied. "He was quite calm and polite. He remarked that this was his first visit to London and that he was looking forward to a good night's rest before beginning his sales meetings."

"Did anyone visit with him" Holmes asked. "Did anyone stop to speak with him, or perhaps visit his table? Might a guest have visited him in his room after his dinner?"

"No, no one went to his room, of that I'm quite sure. He seemed a quiet, solitary young man."

"And yet," Holmes mused, turning the registration card over and over in his hand. "And yet."

He slipped the card into his pocket and strode off in the direction of the staircases. None of the patrons in the lobby gave our group much notice at all with the exception of a large older man who moved to block our path.

"Hey, what's going on here anyhow?" he insisted to Waters and Holmes, who led our little delegation. He wore a slightly frayed shirt and inexpensive woolen pants, and he had a small cap sitting back on his head, despite being indoors. The man spoke loudly and his brusque manner clearly identified him an American.

"You guys the cops?" he inquired, employing the curious vocabulary of the States.

Waters regarded the man for a moment and then took his shoulder in his hand and pushed him out of our path.

"Hey! Whatsa big idea?" the man called after us, before breaking into a phlegmatic cough. Holmes had already evaded the intruder and bounded up two floors, heading to the room of the unfortunate Mr. Flicker, and I was in close pursuit. A groan escaped Holmes's mouth as we arrived at No. 214. Several policemen were gathered in the hallway and the door to the room was wide open with additional police inside. I didn't have to ask why Holmes was distraught. Certainly, they had already trampled many of the clues that he might have been able to glean from an untouched location.

Holmes pulled Waters by his arm. "Please ask these men to leave," he urged. "They are doing little here but eradicating any hope of my determining what has happened."

"But they are from Scotland Yard!" Waters protested.

"Precisely," answered Holmes as he eased past the battery of departing police and cautiously stepped into the room. Knowing Holmes's attention to footprints, I carefully placed my feet only where his had already landed and followed him in.

In the middle of the room lay Mr. Flicker, dressed in his sleepwear and soaked in blood. Holmes avoided the corpse as he knelt upon the floor, carefully examining the carpeting, but his dismay was immediately evident. "There might as well have been a herd of cattle through this doorway!" he protested. "Any clues as to who entered or left have been obliterated!"

"But what difference does it make?" responded Waters. "No one could've entered through the locked doorway."

Holmes drew himself up to the detective, looking down his long nose several inches to the shorter man's face. A long, bony finger emerged from his fist and he poked the young man soundly in the chest.

"That is merely your supposition, Inspector Waters," he said sharply. "It isn't a fact. We don't yet know the facts, and thanks to the trampling of this carpeting, we may never know them." He turned and knelt again beside the unfortunate Meriwether Flicker.

"Is this the man who registered as Flicker?" he asked Gilleston. The horrified man couldn't stop staring at the gory scene laid out before him. Rapidly, the manager shook his head up and down to confirm the identification and quickly turned away.

Holmes began to examine the area around the body, again searching for identifiable footprints. Finally, clearly exasperated, he turned his attention to Flicker's corpse.

The dead man lay on his back, his eyes were wide open, the pupils fully dilated, and his mouth hung open. Altogether, his visage was one of utter horror. His hands and wrists were a mass of deep cuts that had bled liberally. Where he had fallen, thick puddles of coagulated blood had pooled under his lifeless arms, which lay stretched out to his sides.

Holmes peered into the man's vacant eyes and placed his nose near the gaping mouth and took a deep sniff. He held each hand, considered the wounds, and examined the blood saturating the carpet. "Look here, Watson," he called, pointing to the injuries on the wrists.

"Yes, I see," I answered. "Severe damage to the ulnar and radial arteries," I affirmed. "He would've bled most profusely without treatment. Unconsciousness would've occurred within a fairly short period, I should say, with death inevitable, absent immediate medical attention."

Holmes nodded his head in agreement. He turned his attention to the dead man's bare feet, which were also a mass of lacerations. Using a pen knife, Holmes dislodged a number of shards of glass from the bloody soles which he held in his palm, regarding them for a moment. Then he stood and walked briskly to the lavatory where a scene of similar carnage greeted him.

Above the sink, the mirror had been shattered into thousands of pieces that now lay on the floor, along with the remnants of a drinking glass. Clearly great force had been used. The effect was obvious: Razor sharp glass had sliced through Flicker's hands and wrists. Prodigious amounts of blood had streamed onto the sink and were flecked around on the walls, and the floor had a path of bloody footprints, streaking back towards the chamber where Flicker had collapsed as his blood gushed from the multiple injuries.

After several moments regarding the pattern of the blood spatters, Holmes returned to the bedchamber and surveyed the room, taking in the doors, the furniture, and the fixtures. Satisfied, he walked over to a small table where there were several small boards with bits of brightly coloured ribbon attached to them, as well as a schedule of appointments in London. The dead man had evidently been reviewing the materials, and his ribbon samples, before going to bed.

"Have you this gentleman's wallet?" Holmes inquired. Waters handed it over and Holmes rifled through it, pulling out some papers and cards. "Mr. Flicker of Paterson, New Jersey seems to have been a seller of silk bows and ribbons," he declared. "Paterson is a manufacturing center known, if I recall correctly, as 'The Silk City of America'. Hardly an occupation one would associate with such business as this."

Holmes poked among the scattered items on the cluttered desk and looked in the trash pail next to it, and then pointed to a small blue bottle, which was next to an empty glass. Beside it rested a note on which had been roughly handwritten *"Welcome to the Great Eastern Hotel!"* and a small envelope in which the note had been enclosed. He picked up the bottle and sniffed it, closing his eyes to blot out other sensory distractions.

"Is this a bottle of spirits which your hotel routinely provides to guests?" inquired Holmes?

Gilleston regarded the bottle curiously. "Why, I have never seen such a thing before," he declared. "We provide no such gift to our guests!"

"And there is no chance someone in the hotel might've come to his room to provide this bottle?"

"Absolutely not. No peddlers or others except registered guests are permitted above the ground floor."

Holmes moved towards the window, taking time to examine the carpeting in that area as well, and then briefly studied the sill with his magnifying glass. Planting his gloved hands on the sash, he pushed it up and stuck his head through the open window, looking up and down the outside of the building and then at the alley that ran around the back of the hotel. Bringing his head back inside, he pulled down the sash and turned triumphantly to face us.

"Well, we have one answer," he announced triumphantly, "and two remaining questions."

"What are the questions?" asked the inspector.

"The questions are 'Why', and 'By whom'," Holmes responded.

"And the answer?" Waters inquired.

"Oh, I would've thought that was obvious," answered Sherlock Holmes. "The answer is that this man was murdered."

A look of astonishment froze the faces of those in the room, myself included. "Murdered?" repeated Waters incredulously.

"Indisputably," replied Holmes.

"Holmes!" I said. "Did the murderer walk into the room, murder Mr. Flicker, then walk out and bolt lock the door behind him? Or perhaps he just scaled the outside wall like Poe's orangutan and came in through the window."

"Yes, Watson," Holmes said. "That is precisely what he did. Obviously neither the murderer nor Flicker could've possibly locked the door from the inside *after* such grievous wounds were administered. Therefore the only remaining possibility must be that the murderer entered here," he said, pointing towards the window. "When we catch him, I must thank him for wearing shoes having such a characteristic sole. By the way," he said to Waters, drawing his finger across the sill and producing a small residue, "here is some dirt that scraped from his very distinct shoe when he climbed through the window."

"How did you find those footmarks?" asked Waters, squinting to see the faint impressions on the carpeting.

"I *looked* for them," Holmes replied. He pointed to the carpeting. "There are impressions – faint, I grant you, but unquestionable – that lead from the window to the desk and back again. Since our unwelcome visitor is unlikely to have walked through the walls, he must have opened the sash from the outside and entered the room."

"But why would he do that?" asked Waters.

"Presumably for the same reason you would do so," said Holmes, "to avoid being observed leaving this room or walking through the hotel." He moved carefully to the window to avoid trampling the barely visible footprints that he'd detected. "For someone to possess the required skill, however, I image it was no more challenging to scale the building and enter the window than for you or I to turn the knob and enter by the door."

"But murder!" Waters persisted. "How do you know Flicker was murdered? Clearly these injuries are self-inflicted as a result of smashing the mirror. Might it not even have been suicide?"

"Well, it is consistent with someone wanting us to *believe* it was an accident or suicide," said Holmes, "but I rather doubt it. The evidence is quite to the contrary." He pointed to the empty bottle on the desk. "Waters, I suggest that the remaining contents of that bottle be analyzed. I would be quite surprised if it doesn't contain a very heavy dose of some drug that can induce the most erratic behavior. I've made a study of such drugs," he added. "Perhaps you recall the paper I published last year on the disturbing effect of mood-altering drugs, in excessive quantities.

"I suspect Mr. Flicker was deceived into drinking the spirits that were in this bottle," he said, pointing to the blue bottle. "No! Don't touch it!" he cried as a policeman who had remained in the room reached for the vial.

"Undoubtedly," Holmes then continued, "he became highly disoriented and erratic after imbibing the mixture and went to the lavatory for water, but became utterly distraught and smashed the looking glass. Whether that was the intended outcome of whoever supplied this concoction, of course, I cannot say. He walked around disoriented and waving his arms, smearing blood from his lacerated feet – that accounts for the splattering of blood and the bloody footprints. Yes, indubitably, there has been bad business here in the night, and it has ended with this man unintentionally taking his own life."

Every mouth in the small room except for Holmes's hung open in astonishment. Finally, Waters spoke. "How can you *possibly* guess such a horrible act?" he incredulously asked.

Holmes stared hard at him and narrowed his eyes. "I *never* guess," Holmes sharply responded. "Facts! The facts lead to the escapable conclusion that a person unknown to us scaled the exterior wall of this hotel, opened that window, and gained access to this room."

Waters and the other policemen looked at Holmes with expressions of mystification on their faces. "And why didn't the murderer simply leave by way of the door, which surely would've been a far easier means of egress?" asked Waters skeptically.

"He might well have been seen," Holmes said, "which would have precluded this crime being dismissed as a suicide or accidental overmedication." Then he added, somewhat ungraciously, "As it evidently *was* before I arrived on the scene. No, no, far safer to depart the way he arrived, by the window, down to the alley, from whence he made good his escape. It cannot have been much more of a challenge for him to descend than it had been to climb up in the first place."

The room grew quiet as the observers contemplated Holmes's words. Finally, Waters spoke up. "But why, Mr. Holmes? Why would anyone commit this terrible crime?"

"That is precisely what I intend to discover," replied Holmes.

We reconvened in the small office of the hotel manager on the ground floor, joined by the housekeeping supervisor, Mrs. McSorley, who had first raised the alarm. "You saw and heard nothing from Mr. Flicker after he had returned to his room for the evening, after dinner?" Holmes pressed. "Not a request, not a call of any kind?"

Mrs. McSorley paused thoughtfully. "No," she said. Then, just as Holmes was about to speak again, she suddenly perked up. "Well, there was one curious thing. Last night, I would say perhaps around ten o'clock, one of the chambermaids was walking on the second floor. She said she heard very loud voices from one of the rooms down in this part of the floor, but she couldn't say which one. By the time she came down to this area, the voice had died down, so she didn't bother to report it."

"Doubtless the effects of the hallucinogen," Holmes declared. "And had Mr. Flicker left his order for his breakfast?"

"Oh yes!" Mrs. McSorley exclaimed, relieved to abandon the earlier topic. "A good breakfast, with eggs and bangers and toast and jelly," she described. She began to weep as she considered the man never had had an opportunity to eat it. "We thought he'd decided to sleep in, and so we returned the breakfast to the kitchen."

The body had been discovered about two hours later, when Flicker had failed to respond to the repeated inquiries from the hotel's cleaning staff.

"And what did you do after making the discovery?" Holmes asked the manager. "Where did you go? To whom did you tell of this unfortunate tragedy?"

"Why, I went to the desk downstairs to alert the police," Gilleston replied. "Of course I didn't want to alarm the other guests and I spoke only to Rufus, the boy who runs messages. 'Go get a constable, on the double!' I told him," the nervous manager recalled. "'There's been a murder in No. 214!' I assumed it was murder. There he is now," he added, pointing to a boy of perhaps twelve or thirteen who had suddenly appeared in the office door, the scruff of his neck firmly in the hand of a policeman.

"I caught this hooligan hanging about," the officer announced. Holmes regarded the boy and then walked over. He then guided him to a nearby sofa.

"Now, then, I'm Sherlock Holmes," he began. "Perhaps you've heard of me."

At the mention of the detective's name, the boy brightened considerably. "Oh, yes, sir," he said, bowing slightly his chair. "I know who you are. A pleasure. My name is Rufus," he offered. "Rufus Janney."

"Now, Rufus, what was the message you received from Mr. Gilleston this morning?" Holmes calmly asked.

"Well, sir," the boy said hurriedly, "he – Mr. Gilleston – said there was an awful bloody mess in No. 214, and that a man was dead, and I needed to go fetch the police right quick

"And what did you do?" asked Holmes.

"Well, I ran down the street to fetch the police," Rufus declared, "just like he asked me."

"And did you encounter anyone on the way?" asked Holmes. "Did anyone accost you and ask about your mission?"

The boy looked wary, his eyes darting. "I – I didn't tell nobody, Mr. Holmes," he said rather unconvincingly. "Really I didn't!"

"Come, come," Holmes said soothingly. "No harm done! We were all once boys, Rufus. I'm sure that with such a juicy bit of information as a bloody corpse in the room, you must have shared it with someone between here and the police station, and perhaps have a shilling to show for it."

The boy chewed his bottom lip for a moment or two and ruminated about the question.

"Well, I did tell one person," Rufus admitted. "An older American who was hanging about in the lobby of the hotel."

"That is the same older gentleman who just inquired about the goings on when we entered the hotel!" Gilleston declared

"I bumped into him as I was running off to get the police," Rufus said. "I bumped into him just outside the front door."

"Did you?" asked Holmes. "And pray, what did he say?"

"Well, he asked what all the commotion was about, and offered me a shilling," Rufus explained. "I couldn't see where there was any harm in letting him in on it, so I said that a man had been killed in No. 214 and I had been deputized to bring the police."

"And what did your new friend say in response?" Holmes inquired.

"He got quite alarmed," the boy said. "'What's that you say? A body in No. 214? Did you say No. 214?' That's what he said. 'Are you positive?' I just answered 'Yes, that was it.' And off I went."

"Is that man a guest at the hotel?" asked Holmes asked, turning to Gilleston again.

The manager licked briefly at the corner of his mouth. "No," he said slowly, "I can't say as he is." He thought a little more, then added more confidently, "No. No, sir. He most certainly isn't a guest. He's just passing time in the lobby, watching the stairs. I presumed he was waiting for a guest to come down."

"Have you seen him otherwise?" Holmes asked.

"Well, I first saw him in the lobby, after the alarm had been given," he offered. "There was quite a bit of agitation as the word spread, as you can imagine. We even had one guest who very abruptly appeared, bags in hand, and declared to me he was leaving the hotel immediately."

"Do you recall who that guest was," asked Holmes.

"Oh, yes, it was Mr. Lewis Ullman, from No. 314."

"Room No. *314?*" Holmes repeated. "Are you quite certain?"

"Oh, yes," said the manager. "He arrived from the U.S. yesterday as well." The coincidence suddenly struck him. "Why, his room was right above the room where . . . ." His voice drifted off. "I wonder if he might've been disturbed by the loud noise during the night."

"So might I," added Holmes. "What else do you know of our late friend in room No. 214? You say he arrived just yesterday. Do you know from where? Did he have kith or kin here in London? Or was he passing through to another destination?"

"He arrived yesterday, on the *Isle of Wight* from New York," said Gilleston.

"Yes, of that much I'm aware," said Holmes. He noticed the curious looks on the faces of the men surrounding him. "The remains of a ship's receipt in the waste can," he quickly explained.

Holmes turned briskly and abruptly walked out the front door of the hotel. I followed as he went around to the alley running behind the building. Locating the window of the unfortunate man's room, Holmes fell on the ground, carefully examining a number of footprints while picking up bits of paper and other detritus on the ground, some of which he slipped into his pocket.

"Very interesting," he murmured, standing up and casting a look the nearly sheer wall. "A most formidable climbing achievement, wouldn't you say, Watson?" He picked up a small amount of the dirt and examined it under his hand glass, and then rolled it thoughtfully between his thumb and middle finger.

"The mud on the sill in Flicker's room most certainly originated here," he said assuredly, "in this very path behind this building. And here are more of those marks left by that peculiar shoe."

Back inside the hotel, he asked Gilleston for a copy of the London *Directory*, and the manager soon returned with the thick volume. Holmes sat at a desk in the small room, pouring over the contents. For the life of me, I couldn't imagine for what he was searching, but within a few moments he smiled. He quickly wrote down an address and stood to leave.

"Watson, please do me the favour of conducting some research this afternoon," he requested. "Can you check with the steamship office and secure a list of the passengers who had accompanied the late Mr. Flicker on board the *Isle of Wight*? Let us compare that list with the guest list here at the Great Eastern Hotel. I will meet you at Baker Street by four o'clock with information of my own."

"And where will you be looking for clues?" I asked.

"Oh, I think I *have* the clues," he replied cheerily. "What I'm looking for is a Norwegian daredevil." He gathered up his coat and hat and hurried out the door and into the street.

Waters looked at me with a face filled with puzzlement. "A what?" he repeated incredulously.

"Of course!" I responded, although I was quite as mystified as the detective.

"He seems quite sure of himself based on rather sketchy evidence, if I say so!" the inspector declared as we strode back into the hotel. Accepting a list of the hotel guests from Gilleston, I bid *adieu* to Waters and sped off to the shipping office to secure the list of passengers that Holmes had requested. Acquiring the manifest proved no difficult matter and I returned to our rooms in Baker Street to compare the hotel and ship lists while awaiting Holmes's arrival.

At the appointed hour, Holmes strode through the door to the sitting room. "You were quite right," I called out as I greeted him. "There are several people from the *Isle of Wight* who spent last evening at the hotel."

Holmes took the list from my hand and looked over the names from the Great Eastern Hotel register that I'd circled with a red pencil. "Let me see," Holmes mused. "Mr. and Mrs. Cecil Gladnow of Philadelphia, in room No. 223. No, of no interest," he said, crossing off the Gladnows' names. "Miss Catherine McCliff of Newport, Rhode Island, and Mrs. Emma Staansfield – undoubtedly a young woman of means and her chaperone," he commented, again crossing off the names next to room No. 308. "There is the recently deceased Mr. Flicker in No. 214, and Mr. Lewis Ullman," he read, his eyes narrowing, "who this morning departed room No. 314. Let us go speak with our friend Gilleston back at the Great Eastern."

We rattled along the streets in our hansom as Holmes explained that he'd made several inquiries of his own that had been proven suggestive. The intervening hours had done little to calm Gilleston, who had spent his day explaining to alarmed guests that "Everything is just fine. Please don't feel it necessary to interrupt your stay." He seemed relieved when we strode into the lobby and motioned us into his office.

"Have you found the murderer?" he anxiously inquired.

"Patience," replied Holmes in a soothing voice. He produced the list of names that I'd acquired from the shipping office and pointed to that of the former inhabitant of No. 314. "Let me ask you about this gentleman, who departed the hotel this morning in something of a hurry," Holmes said. "What can you tell me of Mr. Lewis Ullman?"

"Ah, the *other* American gentleman who checked in yesterday," he said. "He arrived somewhat earlier than Mr. Flicker, and wanted a room for just a single night, but he had no reservation. Mr. Flicker had booked a room for three nights," he added approvingly. Holmes's face noticeably brightened at hearing this piece of news.

"He fairly flew out of the hotel once news of the murder was disclosed!" Gilleston added. "He didn't even wait to pay his bill. He just put two pounds down on the counter and walked out quite briskly. Do you think he might've been involved in the murder?"

"What of the loiterer in the lobby?" asked Holmes instead of answering.

"He stood up when Mr. Ullman came down the stairs, now that I think of it," Gilleston said. "He had a hard look on his face, and he followed Mr. Ullman out the door. I followed to look outside, Mr. Ullman was already quite far down the street and the big man was hurrying to catch up to him." The manager looked mournful and then brightened. "Perhaps they were it in together!" Gilleston suggested hopefully.

"No," said Holmes, "I rather doubt that was the case. Ullman and the stout gentleman certainly are connected, but not associates, I suspect."

"What relationship do you presume?" I asked.

"I think rather hunter and prey," Sherlock Holmes replied.

"But surely Mr. *Flicker* was the prey," I protested.

"I wonder," Holmes replied. "Thank you for your cooperation, Gilleston. Come, Watson, we have a trip to make and it's getting late."

Soon we were rambling in a cab towards East London, where a rougher element made their homes and workplaces. Thirty minutes later, the cab pulled up outside a nondescript stone building. A weathered sign hung over the doorway: "*Saylor's Mountaineering and Expeditionary Club*". We disembarked and went inside, where we met a tall and lean man, quite as weathered in the face as the sign hanging outside.

"Can I help you gents?" he agreeably asked.

"Thank you, some information, please," said Holmes. "I'm interested in finding out about a hiking trip I'm planning in Kjeragbolten." The man behind the counter looked blankly at him. "In Norway," Holmes explained.

"Of course!" the proprietor exclaimed.

"Perhaps you might know of someone knowledgeable about that region," Holmes continued. "I know I could make arrangements once I arrived there, but I would so much rather do so before my departure. And there is a fat fee for identifying someone who could assist me."

"Well, now, I believe that I can help," the man responded. "It just so happens I know a man from Norway himself, and he's one of the best climbers I've ever known."

"Is he available?" Holmes asked.

"Well, there was another man round here yesterday who went to talk with him," the shop manager recalled. "Asked if we hire any foreigners." He lowered his voice. "Sometimes they're the best, you know. Now, for that fee, of course, I could give you his address and you could go around and see if he might be available for the job."

Holmes quickly produced a five-pound note and laid in on the counter while the man consulted a list of names he kept under his desk, and then dashed up a quick note on a scrap of paper. "There you go," he said. "You go 'round to that address and see if you can find Mr. Dag Larsen."

Holmes thanked his informant and we strode back to our waiting cab, handing the paper with Larsen's address to the driver. "Quick now," he said, "not a moment to lose!"

Ten minutes later we stopped before a row of shambled mews off a main street. Holmes hopped out, checked the address, and walked to the door. I followed. He knocked heavily, but there was no response. Again, he knocked and this time, there was a gruff voice from behind the door, which remained close.

"*Ja?*" came the response from inside.

"*Unnskyld meg, er det Dag?*" [1] Holmes said loudly.

"*Ja! Dette er Dag,*" came the reply. "*Hvem ringer?* [2]

I looked at Holmes amazed. How was he carrying on a conversation in Norwegian with this unseen person, and why?

"*Jeg er så glad for å endelig finne deg!*" Holmes responded. "*Jeg har søkt etter deg så lenge. La meg se på ansiktet ditt, min gamle venn!*" [3]

Behind the door, I could hear the lock being opened and in a moment the door swung open to reveal a man of perhaps thirty, of medium height and muscular build. Seeing Holmes and myself, he quickly tried to shut the door, but Holmes had wedged his walking stick into the jamb and prevented it from closing. With a grunt, Holmes shoved, but the door barely moved.

"Watson! Together now!" he called, and breaking from my astonishment, I leaned my good shoulder into the door as well. Larsen was strong, but not strong enough to resist the two of us, and the door was flung open as he fled back into the small house. Holmes was on him in an instant, however, and the two rolled together in the corridor trading blows until I was able to bring my service revolver down on the man's head with an authoritative "crack". He slid unconscious to the ground and Holmes, pushing the man off him, stood up and clapped me on the arm.

"Good job, Watson! You likely saved me from a much worse altercation with this very strapping young man," he remarked. "Let's get him revived. But first –" Holmes reached into his pocket and withdrew a pair of steel handcuffs. Slipping them on to the inert man's wrists, he leaned him against the wall and brusquely slapped his face.

"Larsen! Larsen! *Våkn opp!*" [4] Holmes said next to the man's ear. "Perhaps some water."

I returned with water in a filthy glass I found in the kitchen. "I'm not sure how good that would be to drink," I admonished Holmes, but he simply looked at me before splashing the water in the face of the mountain climber, who shook his head and slowly came back to life.

"*Hven er du?*" [5] he said, but then, realizing he had been tricked into believing Holmes was one of his countrymen, switched into understandable English. "Who are you, and why have you broken into my room?" he inquired. He looked down at his manacled hands. "Are you the police?"

"No, but we could arrange for them to come and arrest you if you prefer," Holmes responded. "We would like to discuss your recent climbing feat at the Great Eastern Hotel."

His eyes grew wide and he looked from Holmes to me, and then back at Holmes. Then a look of terror crossed his face. "No! No!" he cried. "I did no wrong. I did no wrong! It was the American! I did no wrong!"

Holmes laid his hand on the man's shoulder. "Calm yourself," he said. "I believe that I can be of some help with the police." The man looked horrified but Holmes patted his shoulder and continued. "But I cannot help you if you don't make a clean breast of it. Shall I begin for you?"

The man looked confused, but Holmes's hand on his shoulder seemed to provide him genuine calm, and he nodded his head.

"I believe I'm not the first person to be seeking your services as a climber of late, am I right?" Holmes asked. The man mournfully shook his head affirmatively. "I expect a rather large American recently found his way to the shop to engage your services."

"Yes, that is right," the Norwegian said. "He said, 'Just call me Smith,' but I don't think that is his real name."

"Yes, I have no doubt," Holmes responded drily. And he asked you to deliver a package for him – to a friend in a room at the Great Eastern Hotel, correct?"

"Yes, a bottle and envelope, exactly, to the man staying there," he answered.

"And did you ask why he engaged you to climb that outside wall instead of simply delivering the package by the more conventional way, such as the door?" asked Holmes.

"Oh yes, he said it was a surprise, a joke, and he didn't want his friend to know where the package had come from. He offered me five pounds, and when I'm offered so much money, no questions. He was afraid someone might be seen entering the room by the door," he explained. "He thought it would be a good joke, and it wasn't a difficult climb at all, just three stories."

"Because he told you the man was in room No. 314, is that correct?" Holmes asked.

"*Ja*, I waited behind the hotel for a while for Smith to signal the man had left his room to go to dinner," he continued.

"And you ate a chocolate bar while you waited," Holmes added.

Larsen stared at Holmes. "*Ja.* Then about six o'clock, Smith signaled that the man had gone to dinner. I climbed up to his room and opened the window. The room was empty," he explained, "so I left the bottle."

"On the small desk?" Holmes asked.

"*Ja*, that was what Mr. Smith said to do," he agreed. "Then I climbed back out the window, closed it, and climbed back down."

"Are you aware that the man in that room was found dead this morning?" Holmes asked sharply.

Larsen physically started, and his chin trembled. "Dead!" he cried, rising to his feet. "Dead? No, no, no. This was a joke," Larsen said. "A present for his friend. How is he dead?"

"That isn't important right now," Holmes explained. "What is important is for whom you were working, and what has become of him." Holmes looked intensely into the man's face as the Norwegian pondered his options.

"If you know, Larsen, I cannot implore you too strongly to come clean, " Holmes said, "I might be persuaded to appeal to Scotland Yard and save you from the gallows."

Larsen turned as white as a sheet, and I truly believed that he was about to collapse. I reached into my bag and brought forth my flask of brandy, which I held to his lips as he took a long swallow and then shook involuntarily

"*Herregud!*" the terrified man exclaimed. "*Dette er forferdelig!*" [6]

"Yes, quite terrible," Holmes translated. "Come, there is no time to lose. The whereabouts of the portly Mr. Smith who hired you."

"I'm to meet him tonight, at ten at The Prancing Horse to get the rest of my pay," he said, identifying a local pub. "He would only pay me half before the job was done. I told him I needed to be sure he'd show up, so I demanded to hold his pocket watch." Larsen displayed a cheap watch on a chain.

"He didn't care for that," he said, "because it belonged to his dead son, but he say all right, and now, I have to be there to get my money and return it."

"Yes," said Holmes. "You will show, but so shall Dr. Watson and myself. We will take you, but if you give him a signal or otherwise double cross us, I give you my word you will not hang because I will instruct Watson to blow your brains out on the spot!"

Although I knew it was false, I was startled to hear such a belligerent tone come from Holmes's mouth, not to mention the idea that I would do such a thing.

At 9:30, Holmes and I were racing with Larsen in a four-wheeler to The Prancing Horse pub, after first stopping to send a message to Inspector Waters. "Now remember, engage in conversation for as long as you're able, and we will handle the rest," he told the Norwegian, who soon disappeared behind the grimy painted windows that sheathed the front of the building. We waited together across the street for a few moments before ambling up to the door.

"Watson, remain here and stay alert," he explained. "I'm going to lock the rear door, and then we'll attempt to apprehend our prey. Should he bolt, it will be through this door, and therefore it's upon you to apprehend him. Do not fail me!"

With that he was gone into a dark alley that ran alongside the pub. I waited for several minutes, occasionally peering through the glass where the paint had worn away. Excitedly, I saw that Larsen had quickly met up with the large American from the hotel lobby. They were sitting at a small table, glasses of some concoction between them, and the heavy man was speaking in an excited manner.

The large man held up his hand to summon the waiter who was meandering through the dimly lit room, and the tall, thin man ambled over to the table. They spoke briefly and then suddenly, the large man jumped bolt upright and pushed the waiter hard on the chest, knocking him backward over some tables, before disappearing into the rear of the pub. The patrons were all on their feet and talking excitedly when the large man came running back into the room and headed for the door near which I was standing. As he ran past me, I stuck my walking stick out and he fell head over heels into the street. Holmes quickly appeared, still dressed in the costume of the waiter the he'd donned inside the pub.

"Nicely done, Watson!" Holmes said standing over the fallen man, who was already attempting to stand. Holmes grabbed his arm, on which already dangled the formidable handcuff that earlier in the evening had been affixed to Larsen. Locking it to the man's wrist, he led the manacled prisoner back inside where he attached the open half of the device to a heavy chair and then pushed the man onto the seat. Momentarily, none other than Inspector Waters came running into the pub and addressed Holmes.

"Move away, move away," he instructed the patrons who were gathering around us with growing curiosity. "Scotland Yard!" The crowd took several steps backward. "See here, Mr. Holmes, what is this message I received to meet you here to take possession of the murderer?" he questioned. The inspector looked down at the groggy man handcuffed to, the chair. "And who might *this* be?" he asked.

"Based on the information from the ship's records, this must be Mr. Drago Szabó of Hazelton, Pennsylvania, who arrived yesterday on the *Isle of Wight* along with the late Mr. Flicker," Holmes declared. "He is responsible for the tragic events at the Great Eastern Hotel last evening." The man stirred further and began a heavy cough that shook his large frame violently.

Holmes turned to Larsen. "Is this the man who hired you?" he inquired.

"*Ja! Ja!* That is the man!" the Norwegian said excitedly as Szabó glared at him.

"And who's *this?*" exclaimed the perplexed Waters, jabbing his thumb towards Larsen.

"This is the Norwegian daredevil that I was seeking!" Holmes said.

"The Norwegian . . . I'm so confused!" Waters admitted, putting his hand to his forehead. "Who *are* all these people?" He sat down in a chair next to Szabó who continued to rub his head with his free hand.

"I believe it is quite clear. Szabó hired Larsen to poison Ullman, but the concoction was mistakenly delivered to the wrong room. Mr. Flicker mistook it to be a complimentary welcome gift from the hotel management and drank it, with tragic results. Szabó had arranged to meet Larsen here at The Prancing Horse to finish paying him off before escaping back to New York tomorrow," Holmes explained. Waters' face was a mask of total puzzlement.

"I suggest you gather up these two and take them back to Scotland Yard," Holmes offered. "I will come by in the morning to clear up this entire case for you, which you can then present to Lestrade as your great success."

Waters' face brightened at that suggestion and two officers were summoned to escort Szabó and Larsen to the waiting police wagons. Waters offered his appreciation to Holmes, and then accompanied his prisoners back to central London.

"Holmes, I must say, I'm not much clearer on all this than Waters appears to be," I admitted. "Can you untangle the skein for me and make sense of who hired who to kill whom and why?"

"Good old Watson! Of course, it's admittedly a complex matter," Holmes agreeably said. "What do you say we return to Baker Street and I'll tell you everything over a generous glass of brandy and some shag.

"The key to the case was, as always, answering the question 'Why?'" Holmes began as we settled into our familiar chairs at 221B. A small fire crackled and hissed against the chill in the early spring air, and the brandy proved an excellent relaxant for the day's hectic and confusing events.

"Why, I wondered, would Mr. Flicker – an unassuming New Jersey ribbon salesman who had booked a three-day hotel stay, scheduled a number of business appointments, and ordered a good English breakfast – suddenly go mad, smash the mirror, and cause his own death, probably quite unintentionally? That was the initial question I asked myself. It didn't seem possible that this was the entire set of facts.

"My examination of the room clearly indicated that someone had entered his room via the window and left a bottle of tainted spirits, complete with a counterfeit welcoming note, where Flicker couldn't possibly fail to imbibe its contents."

"But do you know it was tainted?" I inquired.

"We will know more when we see the results of the autopsy and the analysis of the bottle's contents," he answered, "but I have no doubt an ingredient was added to the spirits to ensure the victim had a very unpleasant experience. Probably a hallucinogen of some type, perhaps mescaline or psilocin. Driven mad by the drug – that would account for the cries heard by the maid in the hallway – Flicker became highly unnerved and doubtless smashed the glass in the lavatory, badly cutting his wrists in the process."

"How horrible!" I replied. "Do you think the intention wasn't to kill him, but rather to have some fun at his expense with the drug?"

"No, I imagine the expectation was that he might throw himself out the window or otherwise do severe damage to himself," Holmes replied.

"But why drug him at all," I asked, "if he was an unassuming ribbon salesman on a business trip to London?"

"Ah, the motive," Holmes repeated, stretching his long legs towards the fireplace. "The motive was to accomplish exactly what occurred. To cause the death of the young American who arrived at the Great Eastern yesterday from the *Isle of Wight.* The problem, in this case, is that the wrong man drank the drug that cost him his life."

"The wrong man!" I cried. "How could you know that to be the case?"

"Well, it is really as simple as *1-2-3,*" said Holmes with a slight grin crossing his face.

I threw up my hands in utter vexation. "What on Earth are you saying?" I responded.

"The fact that the entry to the room was through the window was absolutely fundamental to understanding the case," Holmes began. "Once I determined there was an American implicated in the matter – the bellicose gentleman in the lobby who turned out to be Mr. Szabó – I had no doubt that I'd hit on the explanation, which was only confirmed when we learned of the hasty exit of Mr. Lewis Ullman from Hazelton, Pennsylvania from the Great Eastern Hotel.

"Suppose, I thought, the intended victim wasn't Mr. Flicker at all, who seemed to present no reason whatsoever to be murdered, but rather the American in the room directly *above* his, Mr. Ullman, who had arrived the same day and on the same ship," Holmes reasoned. "I imagine Szabó had followed Ullman from the wharf to the hotel and discovered that his intended prey was in room No. 314. The window to that room would've been easily accessible from the alley by a proficient climber.

"But Szabó himself was far too large to ascend such a sheer wall. He must have had an accomplice, someone with considerable climbing skills. There were only tiny irregularities in the stone wall, and the ascent would've been quite challenging for anyone but an experienced mountaineer. That fact was confirmed by my examination of the ground below the window which yielded footprints made by the climbing shoe whose prints I discovered inside the victim's room, including one set particularly deeper than the others."

"And what was the significance of that set of prints?" I asked.

"They were the prints left when the climber jumped down the last several feet whilst descending, of course," Holmes explained. "The prints were familiar to me – I've written several monographs on the soles of various shoes and boots, as you well know – as being typical of a type of climbing shoe manufactured in Scandinavia.

"My suspicions were confirmed by this scrap of paper I discovered not far from the prints," he said, handing me a wrapper with the word "*Freia*" and a picture of a small boy. "Apparently our climber was a Norwegian who enjoyed a chocolate bar while waiting for the signal that it was safe to begin his ascent.

"Where better to find a Norwegian climber than through a climbing club?" he asked. "Thus, our visit to East London."

"But the mistake in the rooms?" I asked.

"Forgive me," Holmes answered. "Yes, a most calamitous error, particularly for poor Mr. Flicker. Having managed to examine the hotel's registration book, Szabó knew his target was in No. 314. He instructed the Norwegian climber Larsen to climb up to the third story, enter the window, and leave the bottle of poisoned spirits.

"But they both made a mistake, and one with tragic consequences for our ribbon salesman. Americans describe the entry floor of a building as the first floor, whereas we in England call the entry the *ground* floor. So, too, does nearly everyone else on this side of the Atlantic. The *first* floor for *us* is the *second* floor for an American, and so on.

"When Szabó told the Norwegian to enter the window of room No. 314 and leave the bottle, Larsen naturally assumed that meant the third floor from the street level, as it would in the U.S. But the intended victim, Mr. Ullman, was really one floor *above,* on the American *fourth* floor," Holmes explained. "The mistake would have been immediately obvious if the bottle were brought in through the entry door, which is marked with the correct room number, but from the alley, a climber would've no way of knowing he had entered the wrong room!"

"But surely the Norwegian climber would have instinctively gone to the correct floor," I reasoned. "After all, Norway is a European nation. Even if Szabo's instructions were flawed, any European would've automatically selected the correct window."

"True, if that European were from any country but Norway," Holmes said. "I learned a good deal about that country during my sojourn, after my escape from the Reichenbach Falls, as the Norwegian explorer Sigerson. Remarkably, Norway alone among all European nations counts the floors of a building in the same manner as Americans!

"When the clerk at the climbing store confirmed that he had recommended a Norwegian climber to Szabó, I had no doubt I was on the right track," he continued. "My passing mastery of Norwegian was helpful in tricking Larsen into believing I was a countryman of his, and the pieces began to fall into place."

"Remarkable!" I exclaimed. "Szabó must have realized the mistake when he was informed by that ragamuffin that the murdered man had been in No. 214 rather than No. 314, as he had intended."

"Precisely, Watson, well done!" Holmes congratulated me.

"Well, we know 'how' the murder was committed, but there remains the important question of 'why'," I added.

"We can confirm that in a conversation in the morning with Szabó and Larsen, who are fortunately now in the reliable custody of Scotland Yard," Holmes said. "By the time we meet with them, I will have received the information I'm awaiting by wire which, I've no doubt, will clear away the remaining fog of the matter."

Holmes was gone by the time I awoke in the morning, but returned as I was finishing my breakfast and perusing *The Times*.

"Have you the information you were seeking?" I asked.

"Yes, yes!" he excitedly replied. "Right here." He patted his breast pocket and withdrew a sheath of papers that he threw on the table. After pouring himself a cup of coffee, he picked up the papers and leaned back in his chair.

"The key to the case lies in the bad business in Lattimer, Pennsylvania last year," he began. "The cast of characters had left little doubt in my mind that the origins of this messy business lay on the other side of the Atlantic. When I determined that the intended victim, Ullman, as well as Drago, were from eastern Pennsylvania, it remained only to uncover what might have recently transpired there that would merit such a trans-Atlantic pursuit. These responses to my wires confirm my suppositions."

"And what were those suppositions?" I inquired.

"Doubtless you've heard of the recent labor dispute involving the anthracite miners in Hazelton?" he asked. I shook my head as this topic was totally unfamiliar to me. "A most unfortunate incident. Twenty-five unarmed miners, mainly immigrants from East European countries, were gunned down by police during a strike at the Lehigh and

Wilkes-Barre Coal Company last September. Many more were wounded. There was a report of police shooting wounded strikers as they lay helpless on the ground!"

"Shocking!" I exclaimed.

"Yes," he said, reading aloud the headlines. "'*Dead in Heaps*'. '*The Slaughter Was Terrific*'. And the tragedy continued last month," Holmes recounted. "The sheriff and his officers were acquitted on all charges, despite many eyewitnesses who confirmed their role in the unwarranted massacre.

"A check of the court records confirmed that Mr. Ullman was one of those officers who had been acquitted," Holmes said. "A quick review of the victims also revealed the name of Lukas Szabó, a miner just nineteen years old. I wouldn't be surprised if, following the unsatisfactory end of the trial, the victim's father swore to track down Ullman to seek revenge. Perhaps he even informed the deputy of his intentions, and Ullman wisely decided it was advisable to flee Pennsylvania and even America."

Holmes further perused the wires from America, and we were soon on our way to Scotland Yard, where Waters and several officers were waiting with Drago Szabó, who glowered menacingly at Larsen, the mournful Norwegian climber.

"Good morning to you all," Holmes said with seriousness to the prisoners. "I believe I understand what has transpired here, and I need only a few additional pieces of information from both of you to conclude this investigation."

"Go to the Devil!" spit out Szabó, followed by the same hacking cough we had heard the night before. As a physician, I couldn't help but conclude the man suffered from some serious pulmonary disorder, but for the moment, the focus was on his criminal activities.

"Gracious!" replied Holmes. "I rather suspect it is you rather than I who shall be meeting Lucifer in the near future! But let us clear up the details first, which will explain your actions following the trial in Hazelton."

At the mention of the Pennsylvania mining town, Szabó sat upright and glared at Holmes. "Here," he growled, "what do you know of Hazelton?"

"More than you might think – about the strike, the massacre, and the verdict," said Holmes. "And perhaps even more about the reasons you believed your actions in pursuing Lewis Ullman to London were justified."

"Well, you seem to know all sort of things," Szabó said, settling in his chair. His tone lowered. "I guess I might as well tell you the rest. Yes, you're right, I've been on the trail of Ullman, that murdering scoundrel. It was my son Lukas that he killed – shot him in the back as he lay wounded and bleeding on the ground, helpless as a newborn baby." The man's voice broke, and his shoulders began to heave, and the violent coughing began again. It took several moments for him to regain his composure.

"Those deputies cut the miners down with less regard than if they had they been shooting bottles," he continued. "Do you know what the Sheriff said? 'A little cold lead is the only way to halt these strikers.' And that's what them deputies gave us, cold lead. Twenty-five lay dead, including Lukas, and many more shot in the back and tore up for life. They will never be able to lift a pick or shovel again."

Here he paused for a moment and took a drink of water. His face grew grim as he continued. "And wouldn't you know, the jury let them go, every damn'd one. They walked out of the court laughin' and slappin' each other on the back and forgot all about what they done. But *I* don't forget. *I* don't forget my son, murdered as he lay in the dirt bleedin', beggin' for his life.

"Yes, I resolved to get my satisfaction with this Ullman, and I told him he would never have a day's peace so long as I drew breath." He grew contemplative. "And that won't be long either, as I've got the coal disease in my lungs." Another bout of coughing followed as he tried to clear his throat.

"I learned he'd booked passage to England to escape the punishment he knew I would give him. I sold everything I owned and spent every cent I had in the world to buy a ticket on the same ship, the *Isle of Wight*. I planned to throw him overboard into the ocean on the voyage, but he hardly came out of his cabin the whole trip, and was armed when he did.

"We landed two days ago and I followed him to the Great Eastern Hotel. I knew I couldn't just walk in and shoot him like I wanted, so I came up with the idea of tricking him into drinking a brew that would drive him insane and then kill him dead. I wanted him to suffer before he died, just like he made Lucas suffer on the ground!

"I didn't have money for a hotel, so I spent my time sitting the lobby. I was able to steal a look at the registration book was when the manager went off on his duties. Then I figured out how to get it to his room without being seen."

"Which is where Mr. Larsen enters this disturbing picture," Holmes offered. The Norwegian cast a mournful look at Holmes.

"I don't know nothin' about no strike or shooting!" he pleaded. "I don't poison nobody! He tell me it a joke!"

"I don't know how you know all this," Szabó continued, "but yes, I needed a climber fast and I couldn't very well just walk around London asking for one. So, I found a mountaineering shop and asked about hiring a skilled man. When the gentleman told me he knew a Norwegian for hire, I thought, 'What a piece of luck! He will not be reading any papers in English and wouldn't know anything of the strike or the trial.' So I took this man's name and engaged him to climb into Ullman's room and deliver the bottle of spirits that had something extra added to it."

"You brought the drug with you from America?" Holmes added.

Szabó looked amazed at Holmes. "Yes. I had figured I might put it to use. And I gave him a good dose, to make sure he suffered good before he died." His face grew grim. "I told this man, 'Climb into room No. 314.' But I didn't know this man would make a mistake and go to the wrong room!" Another round of coughing exhausted Szabó and he sat back on his chair. I noted some blood flecked the corner of his mouth, which confirmed the he was in the final stages of lung disease and would almost certainly be dead before he faced a hangman.

"I went to the third floor like you said!" Larsen cried.

"But room No. 314 would be on what an American would think is the third floor," Holmes declared, "and so would a Norwegian, because they count floors as they do in the States. And so you mistakenly delivered the bottle to a man one floor below Ullman, the intended victim, who was on the European *second* floor."

Larsen hung his head. "*Ja*," he said. Then he became more engaged. "But I didn't know anyone being poisoned or killed! I think it a joke!"

"In the lobby," Holmes said to Szabó, "when you heard the dead man had been in room No. 214 and not No. 314, you realized the terrible mistake that had been made."

"Yes," Szabó confessed. "Now there was some terrible luck, and I admit I feel badly. But I still had promised this man his pay and he had my boy's watch," he said, pointing to Larsen. "I didn't need him spilling the story to the police, so I met him at The Prancing Horse as we had arranged." He looked at Waters, who remained impassive. "I thought he'd want to escape any responsibility for what he'd done and use the money to go back to Norway and that would be the end of it. I didn't think anyone could connect him to what had happened.

"As for me, I didn't care no more. I only wanted to track down Ullman and take care of him myself, but this gentleman grabbed me first," he said, jabbing a thumb at Holmes. "Now, I expect that he's got away."

"It is a bad business to take justice into your own hands," declared Waters.

"You talk about *justice!*" the old man roared. "Judge Woodward didn't care about it," Szabó spit back at him, "and my son and twenty-four more are cold and in their graves. So I guess if there's justice to be dispensed, it's up to me that's got to do it." He resettled himself in his chair. "There's not much your courts can do to me that the mines ain't done already," he declared.

Holmes motioned to Waters, who joined us outside the interrogation room.

"A bad business to be sure, Waters," Holmes said. "I think it is fairly evident that the Norwegian Larsen was an unwitting accomplice in this tragedy. Undoubtedly, he must be held accountable for his complicity in breaking into poor Mr. Flicker's room, but it seems clear there was no intent on his part. I would hope that would weigh on you as you make your recommendations to the prosecutors."

Waters regarded Holmes warily. "I don't know, Mr. Holmes, but we shall present the evidence just as it is and let the court make their decision."

"Of course," Holmes replied, adding, "Justice must be blind, but it need not be indifferent. As to Mr. Szabó, while his actions are understandable, he must face serious retribution. If he is telling the truth – and Dr. Watson believes his racking cough suggests he is – he will likely escape the noose through more natural means."

"I have no doubt, "I added. "The man has weeks left at best."

"Well, Watson, I think we've had enough of this business. Let us take advantage of this fine spring day for a brisk walk and then perhaps lunch at the Criterion?" Holmes suggested. "This was a complex and not altogether satisfying case on many fronts, and I'm happy to put the entire business behind us."

And so we did for several weeks. In late May, I rose as usual to find that Holmes had already breakfasted and departed Baker Street. He soon returned with a copy of *The Times*, which he placed before me on the table.

"The long arm of justice, Watson," he said, pointing to a small article on page four:

> *Body of American Tourist Found in Thames* [the headline announced.]
>
> *The body of Mr. Lewis Ullman of Hazelton, Pennsylvania was found Tuesday evening on the Embankment south of the houses of Parliament,"* the story read. *"Ullman had been stabbed in the heart and his body thrown into the Thames sometime in the past two days, according to police. Curiously, a lump of anthracite coal was inexplicably found lodged deeply in his throat. The investigation of his mysterious death is continuing.*

Obviously, the other Lattimer miners had found a means for extracting retribution that some might feel was warranted, but I remained dissatisfied with the resolution of the affair. "Is this justice, Holmes?" I asked. "Or is it wanton vigilantism?"

"A question to ponder, Watson," Holmes replied. "Certainly a question to ponder."

NOTES

1. "Excuse me, is it Dag?"
2. "Yes, this is Dag. Who is calling?"
3. "I'm so happy to finally find you! I've been looking for you for so long. Let me look at your face, my old friend!"
4. "Wake up!"
5. "Who are you?"
6. "Oh my God! This is terrible."

The Case of the
Suicidal Suffragist

How I wished Sherlock Holmes could have accompanied me to the Epsom Derby early in June of 1913, one of the social events of the season, made all the more appealing by the announcement that King George V and Queen Mary would be in attendance. Holmes had little interest in such pageantry, however, and was content to tend his bees in Sussex rather than attend a horse race, even one with so storied a history as the Epsom Derby.

The Derby has been run since the years of the American Revolution. This year, most eyes would be on Anmer, the King's admirable horse that would be ridden by the talented Herbert Jones, although considerable interest was focused on Craganour, the horse of Gower Ismay.

I had joined a number of friends from my club, not having any patients scheduled in my surgery for race day. Since the race would take me out of London, I called Holmes and arranged to travel from the track in Surrey to his retirement home for a leisurely weekend with my old friend. He happened to be back in England just then, having spent a great deal of the past year traveling in the United States under another name as part of a long-term investigation.

The trains down to Surrey were crowded with people in every state of dress from aristocratic finery to a more proletarian style. At Epsom, as many as five-hundred-thousand had arrived to witness the race from the viewing stands around the outer and inner perimeter of the track. After a good deal of pushing and stumbling, I found myself in an enviable position just before the "top of the stretch," where the horses would turn and make a straight dash to the finish line. The excellent location assured us the ability to see clearly the magnificent horses as they charged down the slight incline of the track at enormous speeds before having to climb on the last hundred yards, a demanding finale for any animal.

I enjoyed the camaraderie of my colleagues, several of whom flattered me with praise for my published exploits with Sherlock Holmes. They noted, with great accuracy I am afraid, that the Holmes tales had certainly brought me far greater notoriety (and money) than any activities of my medical office! However, I happily indulged their questions about Holmes, which invariably ended with murmurs of amazement at his extraordinary deductive skills.

To our right, at least a half-mile down the track at the finish line, the storied grandstand was festooned with banners and special flags marking the location of the King and Queen, whose presence was announced to great cheers. The crowd became quite animated and within a few moments, a shot proclaimed the beginning of the race. Even from our seats on the far side of the track, the sight of the massive animals, with their brightly clothed jockeys atop them, was thrilling. The horses were bunched together and threw up great amounts of dirt and dust as their hooves dug into the track. As they emerged from the cloud of debris, it was surprising that Anmer trailed badly, although there was plenty of time for his outstanding jockey to steer him around the other horses and into contention.

As the horses neared the top of the stretch, there occurred one of the most shocking events I have ever witnessed, which soon became the most important story in the country. The horses rounded the turn and began the race down the stretch to the finish line. Several passed directly in front of me, and then there was a slight space between them and the next group of horses, which included Anmer, the King's entry.

Suddenly, a solitary figure ducked underneath the rail of the infield, against which hundreds of spectators were pressed to see the horses as they raced passed. From where I stood, it was clear that it was a woman who had either been pushed under the rail or who had purposefully ducked under it. The first group of horses had passed by her and she made no effort to retreat to the security of the guard rail. Then as the second group of horses neared, she pulled a white scarf or banner from her coat and, to the horror of thousands of spectators, stepped directly in the path of the thundering horses.

The tragedy unfolded so quickly that it was difficult to recall the exact series of events. Fortunately, however, a moving picture camera filmed the scene, and so there can be no question about what transpired. In a moment, Anmer was upon the figure, raising its two front legs in a vain attempt to leap over the woman as if in a steeplechase. But the woman was far too tall for such a leap, and instead, a thousand pounds of horse traveling at perhaps thirty miles-an-hour collided with her. In a flash, the woman, Anmer, and the rider Jones were sprawled on the track like broken dolls as the remaining horses flew by on their way to the finish. The gasp of the crowd was like a muffled thunderclap! As thousands of stunned eyes watched, Anmer struggled to its feet and continued down the track, racing on pure instinct towards the finish line. Both the rider and the woman whose actions instigated the accident lay motionless on the track.

I was only a few rows from the track and reflexively, I climbed out of the stands and hastened to the rail from which the guards were staring at the carnage in the track.

"See here!" I cried, "I am a physician! Let me through!"

One of the guards came over to me.

"Are you really a physician?" he asked.

"Yes, of course," I replied. "Dr. John Watson! Let me through!"

The guard allowed me to climb under the rail and escorted me onto the track where a large crowd had already gathered about the two injured people. Far down towards the finish line, we could hear cheers for the winning horse, but we could also see a commotion in the grandstands. In a matter of seconds, I was knelling by the prostrate woman. She was perhaps thirty-five or forty, dressed almost all in black, apparently a well-to-do woman from the quality of her clothing. That the collision with the horse had inflicted grave damage was indisputable. She was unconscious and there were multiple lacerations about her head. Blood was running from her mouth and police were cradling her head. Amongst the other people congregated around her in mass confusion, a woman who was evidently a friend of the injured woman shrieked at the sight of the injuries.

"Bring a stretcher immediately!" I demanded. "This woman has been terribly injured."

I quickly ran over to Jones, who also had been hurt when Anmer rolled onto his leg.

"What happened?" the jockey asked, to no one in particular. "What happened?" he repeated. Then he asked, "Anmer. Is the horse all right?"

"Just relax," I advised. "Everything is just fine. I am a doctor. We'll get you to a hospital."

A medical team had appeared and I helped load the unconscious woman and jockey onto stretchers so they could be evacuated to a nearby hospital. The crowd was still in a tumult when I returned to my friends who pummelled me with questions about what I'd seen.

"A terrible accident," I reported. "I believe the rider has only minor injuries. He is trained to fall from a horse, of course."

"And the woman?" my friend Horace Basler asked.

I shook my head in response. "I suspect she has suffered a grievous injury, almost certainly a fractured skull and likely a brain haemorrhage," I responded. "It would be nothing short of a miracle if she survives."

"But what could she have been thinking?" asked Malcolm Polton, a fellow physician.

Again, I shook my head. "Who can possibly say?" I replied. "She may have had an objective, I suppose, or she may have been insane. Surely only someone who has lost all rationality would position themselves in front of a racing thoroughbred horse. In any event, there is little likelihood she will live to explain her motive."

The horrible incident cast a grim pall over the festivities as the stands emptied. As we through the crowd, a young man pushed his way through and accosted me.

"Say, you were down there on the track, weren't you?" he inquired. "Lyle Fitzgerald, *Daily Mirror*." He removed a small pad of paper from his pocket and a pencil from another, which he licked before continuing. "What did you see?" he asked. "What can you tell the readers?"

I regarded the impudent reporter in a censorious manner. "I am a medical man," I replied. "I do not discuss cases with the press. This was a very great tragedy."

"Oh, come on!" he quickly responded. "Just doing my job. What did you see? Did she say anything? How did she look? It seemed awfully bad from where I was."

I pushed past the young man. "As I said," I reiterated, "I do not respond to press inquiries."

From behind me, I heard one of my friends reprimand the young journalist. "Don't you know that is Dr. John Watson, the associate of none other than Sherlock Holmes?" he said. I turned and saw it was the irrepressible Basler and threw him a disapproving look.

"Dr. Watson!" the young reporter exclaimed in excitement. "That means Sherlock Holmes will be on the case, right?"

"Wrong," I responded. "Mr. Holmes is retired in Sussex, and I am finished with this interview!"

As planned, I returned to the train station and caught the next train to Sussex, where I was warmly welcomed by Sherlock Holmes. After a dinner at the nearby Tiger Inn, we returned to his charming home and I shared with him my account of the day's shocking events at the Epsom Derby.

Quite early the next morning, there was a knock on my bedroom door.

"Watson," Holmes called from the hallway outside my bedroom. "Are you now my publicity agent as well as my chronicler?"

"I have no idea what you are referencing," I responded.

"You really must see this morning's newspaper!" he answered.

"Would you mind explaining what you are reading?" I replied.

"Not at all, not at all," he said good naturedly. "Here is the headline in this morning's *Daily Mirror*. '*Sherlock Holmes to Investigate Epsom Derby Tragedy*'.

"*What?*" I exclaimed. "This is outrageous!"

"Oh, there is more," he added, reading, "'*Dr. John Watson, Mr. Holmes's close associate and biographer, attended the race and treated the injured rider and woman.*'"

I finished putting on my robe and opened the door. Holmes had the newspaper in his hand and was casually leaning against the wall.

"Holmes, I am mortified!" I declared, seizing the newspaper from his hands. "Surely you must know that I never suggested for a moment that you would in any become involved in this matter. Indeed, the only reason this reporter could identify me was because of the unwelcome remark of one of my friends."

"Watson, I didn't for a moment believe that you had volunteered me to become engaged," Holmes laughed. "I imagine this headline is about as involved in this misfortune as I am likely to become."

I quickly dressed and joined Holmes in the dining room, where a simple breakfast had been laid out by his housekeeper. As I buttered some bread and took a deep draught of strong coffee, I perused the front of *The Daily Mirror* for additional news of the previous day's calamity.

124

The unfortunate woman had been identified as Emily Davison, forty years old and a resident of London. She was an official of the Women's Social and Political Unit, the organization founded by the militant suffragette Emmeline Pankhurst to advocate for the vote for women. Like Mrs. Pankhurst, the injured woman was no stranger to militancy in pursuit of her political objectives. Indeed, she had been sent to prison multiple times for protests such as setting fire to postal boxes, climbing through the air ducts to reach the House of Commons, and hurling metal balls through windows. In 1909, she had been jailed for attempting to force her way into a room where David Lloyd George, the Chancellor of the Exchequer, was speaking. Soon thereafter, she was apprehended for chucking rocks at the Chancellor's automobile, each one wrapped in paper on which had been printed "*Rebellion against tyrants is obedience to God*".

"Quite a charming young lady," Holmes said disapprovingly. "How very American in her embrace of equal rights for all."

"Really Holmes!" I reproached. "The woman is lying near death!"

"And perhaps that was her intention," he replied. "We shall likely never know."

A knock on the door interrupted Holmes's comments, and his housekeeper entered the room. "Mr. Holmes, there's a wire here for you," she said, handing a yellow paper to my friend.

Holmes thanked her and quickly perused the telegram. "Well, Watson, I may have spoken too soon!" he said.

He handed the note to me and I read its contents.

Mr. Holmes:

I intrude on your retirement to seek your counsel, only because I have learned from The Daily Mirror *of your interest in investigating the tragic injury to our colleague, Miss Emily Davison. There are several unique questions regarding the incident that resulted in her injury that I would like to discuss with you. It is quite out of the question to raise such matters with the police. Please inform me as to your availability for a meeting in London in the next day or two.*

Very truly yours,
Emmeline Pankhurst

Holmes looked disapprovingly at me as he read of his "*interest*" in the Davison matter. "Well, what do you say, Watson?" he asked. "Should we journey to London and discuss the matter with Mrs. Pankhurst?"

"Holmes, I regret your becoming involved in this," I again apologized. "I assure you – "

He interrupted me with a wave of his hand. "The bees can manage on their own for a few days," he smiled. "Let's take up Mrs. Pankhurst on her offer. I would welcome the opportunity to meet the leader of the suffrage movement. Quite a different perspective, I suspect, from that illuminating discussion with your literary agent a year or so ago."

"I don't believe that Conan Doyle is an ardent opponent of suffrage," I answered, "but he disapproves of the more radical wing of the movement." I looked around in my briefcase and took out an envelope. "As it happens, I have brought along some recent clippings that I thought might be of interest to you, and here is a news article about Conan Doyle on this very subject."

"And what does the good doctor have to say?" Holmes inquired.

I pulled out a clipping from *The Times* of 29th April past and began to read.

> *Conan Doyle said it was necessary to differentiate between the honest constitutional suffragist, the female hooligans, and the even more contemptible class of people who supplied the latter with money to carry out their malicious monkey tricks.*

I shook my head in agreement. "Who could disagree with that proposition?" I asked. Continuing to read,

> *He believed that two years ago they might have had a chance of getting the vote, but now they would not get it in a generation.*

"Conan Doyle is quite critical of the more confrontational of the protestors," I remarked. "He speculates that their next foolhardy scheme for gaining public attention might be 'blowing up a blind man and his dog'."

Holmes snorted in response. "Or fomenting a tragic accident during a Derby," he added, "which ironically results only in the mangling of the demonstrator herself?" He reached for a briar pipe and filled it with tobacco. "Well, let us go meet Mrs. Pankhurst and perhaps she will supply us with some of the answers."

A few days later, a train to London and a cab deposited us at the home of Emmeline Pankhurst. The suffrage leader herself answered the door knock and ushered us into the tastefully decorated sitting room. Books were piled on the tables and even around the chairs, their titles focusing heavily on political and feminist matters. Mrs. Pankhurst was a dignified and still-attractive woman of sixty or so, I should say, dressed formally in a high-necked blouse and a black suit. Her graying hair was piled on her head, and her sober visage conferred a sense of calm and command.

"Thank you for coming, Mr. Holmes," she said. "And I think I can safely presume this is Dr. Watson," she added, nodding in my direction. She strode over to us and forthrightly extended her hand. Her handshake was firm and businesslike. She asked a young lady waiting by her side to bring some refreshments and gestured for us to be seated.

"I do not know whether you share your literary agent's disapproving view of the activities of the suffrage movement," she began. "I am aware of his . . . ambivalence towards our work."

"I assure you, Mrs. Pankhurst, that Sir Arthur's views on the matter of suffrage are of little interest to me and will have no bearing whatsoever on my role in this matter," Holmes responded. "I have always felt his energies were best left to ophthalmology, but he continues to promote the commercialization of my profession together with," and here, he gestured in my direction, "my 'Boswell', as Watson has been described. If I become engaged, you will have my full attention. I am interested in your suffrage movement only insofar as it is relevant to explaining the disturbing events at the Epsom Derby."

"It is not *my* suffrage movement, Mr. Holmes," Mrs. Pankhurst corrected. "It is a movement for all women, for all right-thinking people for that matter. In the Twentieth Century, it is intolerable to disenfranchise half the population, not to mention the half of the population that may well be better read, more compassionate and fair-minded, and equally hardworking as those who already enjoy the right to vote."

"Undoubtedly true," responded Holmes, his tone conveying a mild irrigation over being subjected to a speech.

"I tend to avoid discussions of politics. Murder, blackmail, and thievery are more along the lines of my personal tastes."

Mrs. Pankhurst regarded him carefully, judging whether he was mocking her. She evidently decided to allow the comment to pass.

"I have been engaged in this struggle for many years," she continued, "having devoted my life to equal rights for women."

"Most commendable," I interjected.

"It is a matter of the highest principle for me and for the W.S.P.U.."

"Excuse me," I interrupted. "The W.S.P.U.?"

"The *Women's Social and Political Union*," she explained. "We believe in 'Deeds, not words'. In fact, that is our slogan."

"And I gather from the press that those deeds include arson," Holmes said, a topic that had caused ruptures in the Pankhurst organization recently.

"Battles for basic rights sometimes necessitate extraordinary measures," she replied.

"Including interference in a Derby, perhaps?" Holmes said.

"Yes, including interference in a Derby," she said. "I will not apologise for Miss Davison's action, although I will not claim to have known in advance of her intentions. But," she grew somber, "being run down by the horse, being nearly killed – that certainly was never the intention, I am quite certain. Emily was quite practiced at what she was doing. I can only imagine the rider veered to collide with her, and I want you to look into that possibility."

Holmes shook his head. "I very much doubt that is the case," he replied. "A collision at that speed is bound to end tragically. No, a rider as experienced as Howard Jones would never have intentionally provoked a collision."

"Perhaps I did not make myself clear," Mrs. Pankhurst continued. "I believe that *is* what occurred, and I would like to engage you, and Dr. Watson, to provide the evidence so that we might take legal action against Jones and the King."

"The King?" I asked.

"It was his horse," Pankhurst replied. "We shall hold him responsible!"

Holmes stood up and picked up his hat. "Mrs. Pankhurst, I have no intention of beginning an inquiry burdened by a proscribed outcome, let alone one that implicates the Sovereign," he declared. "It is a cardinal mistake to draw a conclusion prematurely. Facts dictate the explanation, not the other way round. Watson?" he said, summoning me to my feet as well. "I am pleased to have met you, Mrs. Pankhurst," he concluded, moving towards the door.

"Do you mean that you will not take the case?" she archly asked.

"I will not take any case if there is any presumption about what I may investigate or conclude," he answered. "I would be interested in pursuing the matter on my own terms, with no restraints or preconditions."

Mrs. Pankhurst mulled over his comments for a moment and stood up herself. "Very well, Mr. Holmes," she responded. "Your way it will be. But I should not be surprised if there turned out to be more complex forces at work here than anyone suspects at the moment."

Holmes put his hat down and slumped again into the chair. "Oh, of that, I have no doubt. No doubt whatsoever."

The young girl appeared with coffee and tea and we poured ourselves steaming cups before settling back in the chairs.

"How may I help you?" the suffrage leader asked, suddenly more conciliatory. "I do wish to uncover what was behind poor Emily's rash action."

"It has been my experience that when a person acts in a way that is foreign to their nature, there is usually an explanation," said Holmes. "Of course, we don't know if that motive was honourable or not, and you must be prepared to discover aspects of Miss Davison's life that may reflect poorly or her, or on your organization, for that matter."

"I had not considered that possibility," Mrs. Pankhurst admitted. "However, I have little doubt that Emily's motivations were thoroughly honourable, however unfathomable in origin."

We quickly learned more about the activist's background. She was the rare woman to have attended Oxford, although she had not been granted a degree because of her gender. She had gravitated to the suffrage cause soon thereafter and had distinguished herself for her willingness to face arrest for engaging in confrontations with public officials and the police.

"She was sent to jail nine times," Mrs. Pankhurst declared with a sense of pride. "She was not afraid of the police or the courts. She viewed them all as part of a system designed to trample on the rights of women, and she was prepared to pay the price for her beliefs."

"Was she amongst those refusing to eat as part of their protest in jail?" I inquired.

"Most certainly. She was force fed while strong men held her in a chair. On forty-nine separate occasions! Forty-nine! I have been subjected to such abuse myself." She turned to face me. "I don't have to tell you, Doctor, that having a tube inserted into her nose and pushed into your stomach is anything but an enjoyable experience."

"Certainly not!" I agreed.

"Emily was not faint of heart, Mr. Holmes. Once at Strangeways Prison, she refused to leave her cell, and the matron flooded the cell with ice-cold water. Emily came close to drowning. And do you know what Emily did? She sued the prison and she won forty shillings! That is the price Emily was prepared to pay for equal rights. As are we all."

"Most admirable," murmured Holmes. "I am not persuaded it is the most efficacious means of achieving the ballot, but I cannot dispute the bravery required to endure such treatment. I also seem to recall Miss Davison spending several days in prison after horsewhipping a Baptist minister on the mistaken belief he was the Chancellor of the Exchequer."

"An unfortunate misidentification on her part," Mrs. Pankhurst admitted. "However, Mr. Holmes, I can assure you that politely asking Mr. Asquith has not proven especially efficacious," she said of the Prime Minister, with more than a hint of reproach in her voice. "I very much doubt that men, who have never lacked for political influence, can appreciate the humiliation and frustration felt by the women of Britain due to their legally inferior status. Please note, I said *legally* inferior."

"Not in my mind, I assure you," Holmes replied. "Not in my mind."

Mrs. Pankhurst narrowed her eyes as she stared at Holmes in an effort to assess whether he was being sincere. After a few moments, she turned to look at me.

"Unlike my friend, I have been married, and more than once," I quickly added. "I have only the very highest regard for the female sex, I assure you!"

"Marrying women does not signify a respect for them or their political rights, Dr. Watson," she reproached me.

"Let us put politics aside and focus on Miss Emily Davison," Holmes suggested. "What of her recent thinking might help explain her rash and tragic behavior at Epsom?"

"She had attended several meetings of the WSPU in recent weeks," Pankhurst began. "We have been engaged in discussions about the future of our movement."

"What about the future of your movement?" Holmes interrupted.

"Perhaps you are aware of the 'Cat and Mouse Act' that was passed just two months ago?" she responded. Both Holmes and I shook our heads. "Our refusal to eat whilst in prison has been rather bad publicity for Mr. Asquith," she continued, "and even more so the decision of the prison authorities to force feed us. The law allows for the release from prison of anyone engaged in a hunger strike – the term we use – if that person's health is threatened. But after the person has recovered, they are to be returned to prison to complete their sentence.

"Obviously, this new approach necessitates our thinking about innovative ways to protest other than hunger strikes. We have been meeting amongst ourselves and with some other protest groups to think about a new strategy."

"Which ones?" asked Holmes.

"Is that germane?"

"I will not know until you tell me," answered Holmes.

She mused about his request. "Well, frankly, Mr. Holmes, I do not know if I should be sharing such information with you."

Holmes stood up and reached for his hat. "There is no point in *my* playing cat and mouse, Mrs. Pankhurst," he reproached. "One cannot make bricks without straw, and I cannot analyse a problem without the facts. *All of* the facts. If you prefer to remain close-mouthed, that surely is your right. But I ask you to consider if the shoe were on the other foot, would your answer be satisfactory? I am, after all, working on your behalf."

Mrs. Pankhurst looked stonily at Holmes and me. "Very well, but I am relying on your discretion," she began. "Undoubtedly you are aware the Irish agitation has been gaining momentum."

"Yes, on both sides of the question unfortunately," replied Holmes. "The Home Rule bill seems to have stirred up both the Unionists who oppose a unified Catholic Ireland and the nationalists. The Irish Republican Brotherhood is a group of dangerous extremists, in my view. But I fail to understand the connection between this group and your own, except for your mutual distrust and dislike of the government."

"We suffragists do not dislike the government, Mr. Holmes. We disapprove of its policies that treat millions of British women as second-class citizens," Mrs. Pankhurst responded with a hint of disapproval. "Still, I will not deny that disparate interests may find common cause against a mutual adversary."

"In this case, that *is* the government," I clarified.

"Yes. Miss Davison had been meeting with some of the I.R.B. nationalists during the past several weeks in an effort to explore how we might coordinate efforts towards our respective goals. However, the I.R.B. has shown little interest in working together, fearing suffragism distracts from the nationalist focus of their effort." She paused to ask Holmes, "Is that significant?"

"I cannot be sure," Holmes replied. "It is one more 'brick' for me to weigh."

Our investigation began with a rail trip back to Epsom and a drive to the Epsom Cottage Hospital to which Miss Davison had been transported after the tragedy had occurred. Mrs. Pankhurst hastily wrote a note to arrange for our visit and soon, we were knocking on the door of the hospital just after five o'clock in the afternoon. Four days had passed since the incident that resulted in her hospitalization.

"We are here in conjunction with the inquiry involving Miss Emily Davison," Holmes informed the clerk sitting at a desk at the admissions office. "We have been authorised to assist in the examination and treatment of Miss Davison, whom we understand is receiving care at this hospital."

The young man looked confused. "Are you with the police?" he responded. We replied in the negative. "Let me call the manager of the hospital," he suggested.

The clerk disappeared for several moments before returning with a sober middle-aged man who introduced himself as the manager of the facility, Sheffield Grimhold.

"Are you members of the family?" he inquired.

"I am Sherlock Holmes," my friend brusquely responded. "I imagine you are familiar with my name." Grimhold seemed a bit startled by Holmes's introduction but nodded affirmatively. "And this is my colleague, Dr. Watson. We wish to see Miss Davison, as requested in this note from Mrs. Pankhurst. We understand your patient is in a very precarious state."

Grimhold looked at the note and then up at Holmes and shook his head. "Not any more she isn't, Mr. Holmes," he said. "She passed away just an hour ago from her injuries."

"Passed away?" I cried.

"The surgery could not help her," he responded. "We haven't even had the police here yet. I'm afraid they haven't given this case a very high priority."

"No police. Well, that is one piece of good news," Holmes said, drawing a quizzical look from the manager. "Would it be possible for us to examine her before the police arrive and further confuse the situation?"

"I certainly do not want any trouble," Grimhold replied. "It's just that there has been so much interest in what happened the other day at the racetrack."

"What kind of interest?" Holmes asked.

"The press," he replied. "And several Irish gentlemen called this morning as well."

"Really?" Holmes declared. "And did they have an opportunity to visit with Miss Davison?"

"Oh, no sir," he responded. "That would be strictly against the established procedures! They weren't admitted."

"Then it is all the more imperative that I view Miss Davison's remains immediately."

"I, well – all right, given as you're Sherlock Holmes and working for her friend," he responded, waving Mrs. Pankhurst's note.

He led us down to a room in which all the drapes had been drawn, which created a suitably somber atmosphere.

"Her end came quite peacefully," said Grimhold. "She never regained consciousness, and I very much doubt she was in any pain."

"Watson, would you mind?" Holmes said, turning on the room's electric lights and motioning to the bed where the body lay covered with a crisply starched white sheet. Folding back the covering, I again looked into the face of the woman I had seen for the first and only time lying on the dirt track at the Epsom Downs racetrack four days earlier. The blood had been cleaned from her face, and there were surgical scars on her scalp where some hair had been cut off. Her dark hair and wide mouth bespoke an air of elegance. She was very thin. A quick look confirmed that her neck had been broken by the force of the collision with the horse.

"Yes, dead perhaps an hour or so," I agreed, flexing her hand and wrist. "I would expect a massive hemorrhage of the brain, consistent with the collision and her fall to the track. It seems several vertebrae were severely damaged, which might have led to the failure of her respiratory system. A tragedy."

Grimhold nodded his head in agreement.

"Who else has been to see her?" Holmes asked.

"Her sister was here earlier in the day. Her brother Captain Davison as well, and several suffragists who had been at the Derby. Since they were family and close associates, we permitted them a brief visit."

"And they doubtless pinned this medal on her hospital gown?" asked Holmes, pointing to a badge affixed to the dead woman's bedclothes.

I looked at the printing on the badge. "'*Women's Social and Political Union*'," it read.

"I wonder if I might not look through her effects," Holmes said, looking about the room. "There could be a valuable piece of evidence that has been overlooked."

"I expected the police will want to see all that," Grimhold said, motioning to a table on which Miss Davison's clothing and other personal materials were neatly piled. "Please look quickly!"

Holmes's fingers pulled and pushed apart clothes, papers, and other materials. He opened her handbag and quickly looked at the contents. Every once in a while, he would utter a loud, "Hmm!" or click his tongue. Finally, he picked up a folded piece of paper and opened it. He read it quickly and returned it to the purse.

"And what is this?" Holmes asked, picking up a long scarf on which there was dirt from the racetrack as well as some printing. He held the scarf up with both hands. It was over six feet long and coloured with purple, green, and white stripes. On each end, in large block letters, were the words, "*Votes for Women*".

"That was brought in yesterday by Mr. Richard Burton, the clerk of the Epsom Derby track," Grimhold said. "It was found lying near Miss Davison on the track after the accident."

"Do we know that it was in her possession?" Holmes asked. "Might it have been placed there after the collision, to associate the accident more clearly with the suffrage cause?"

"I saw her pull that scarf from her coat just before the collision," I informed Holmes.

A knock on the door was followed by the entrance of an older man carrying a stethoscope and wearing a physicians' jacket. He looked about the room with a look of surprise on his face before waving his arms about. "What is the meaning of this?" he huskily whispered. "What are you doing in this patient's room? She cannot have visitors!"

"Visitors will do her no harm now," I said, bowing slightly in the direction of the corpse. I stepped forward, offering my hand. "I am Dr. John Watson of London, and this is my friend and colleague, Sherlock Holmes."

The physician was obviously uninterested in who we were. He moved quickly to the head of the bed and began to examine Miss Davison. After a moment, he stopped and looked at me with a pained look on his face. "I see, I see," he repeated. "I am not surprised."

"You are . . . ?" Holmes inquired.

"Mansell-Moullin," he replied, as though we should have recognized it.

"The author of *Surgery!*" I exclaimed. "A most outstanding text."

The surgeon slightly bowed in my direction. "I am the surgeon here. I operated on this woman four days ago." He placed the sheet back over her face. "A tragedy for racing and for the movement."

"You consider yourself a supporter of the suffrage movement?" Holmes inquired.

"What right-thinking person is not?" the surgeon responded. "I wish the government shared our point of view, in which case it would not have been necessary for Miss Davison to call attention to the cause by her sacrifice."

"I wonder," said Holmes, "how can you be sure that was her motive? I understand she didn't discuss her plans with her compatriots. Nor has an explanatory note been discovered. Perhaps something entirely different lies behind her action."

Dr. Mansell-Moullin shook his head. "I very much doubt that was the case," he responded. "I knew Emily through my wife, Edith, who is quite active as well. I have myself written a definitive report on the impacts of the barbarous practice of force-feeding the protestors."

"Why sacrifice her life by standing in front of a thousand-pound racehorse running thirty-five miles an hour?" Holmes responded.

"This is a woman who threw rocks in windows and endured force feedings in prison," the doctor answered.

"Yes, but those are far cries from effectively committing suicide before five-hundred-thousand people – not to mention risking the lives of riders and horses."

"Well, it certainly appears to have been suicidal to stand in front of that horse," the doctor said. "You know, she did once attempt suicide in prison."

"I was not aware of that incident," Holmes replied. He looked back at the bed. "Are there final arrangements?"

"Yes," the doctor replied. "Emily is going to be returned to London after the inquest is held. She is to be interred in Longhorsley, Northumberland following several days of ceremony attesting to her selfless sacrifice for the cause."

Holmes looked about the room one more time. "I think we have seen all there is to see here," he said. "Watson and I will remain for the inquest tomorrow. There are a number of matters which will require additional attention in the next several days to bring this matter to a conclusion."

"But surely the facts are not in dispute!" Grimhold said.

"Yes, Holmes," protested Dr. Mansell-Moullin. "Hundreds – perhaps thousands – of people saw Miss Davison duck under the rail and stand in front of Anmer. They saw the horrible collision. I fail to see how there is anything obscure about what occurred. It is a great tragedy, and senseless loss of life, but it is hardly a mystery."

Holmes looked at Grimhold and then at Mansell-Moullin. "Facts, you know, are curious things," he replied. "Some of the facts may well lead to the conclusions you have reached, gentlemen. But there are additional facts that suggest other explanations."

"Such as?" the doctor inquired.

"Such as the presence of a return ticket to London in her bag," Holmes said, holding up a piece of paper from the purse. "And this note from her sister expressing delight at their upcoming vacation together. Neither would suggest Miss Davison arrived in Epsom intending to take her own life. You see, I never draw conclusions until I have *all* the facts, and even then, I am rarely convinced that I have gathered every possible bit of evidence. On one point, however, I have no doubt whatsoever."

"And what point is that?" asked Dr. Mansell-Moullin.

"There is more here than meets the eye. I'm sure that in your surgery, you have often begun a case presuming a diagnosis only to discover something else, something even more sinister than you have anticipated, lurking hidden," Holmes suggested, and the doctor nodded. "We share that experience in common."

"What did you mean," I asked on the walk back to our hotel, "when you said something more 'sinister' was lurking in this case? Do you suspect Miss Davison was not the idealistic suffragist that has been portrayed?"

"Oh, I have no doubt her passion for the suffrage movement was sincere," he said. "But I don't think Miss Davison went to the Derby with the intention of committing suicide."

"How do you know that?" I asked.

"Because of that return ticket to London and the plans with her sister," he responded. "Those intending to commit suicide rarely make future travel plans. There are some other suggestive signs which lead me to question whether this case is as straightforward as it might appear to the undisciplined eye."

The inquest at the Epsom Police Court the following morning was a dry affair that offered little illumination about the circumstances surrounding the tragedy. Captain H. Jocelyn Davison, the dead woman's brother, offered a morose account of his sister's life, which he considered to have been utterly wasted by her irrational pursuit of a radical political objective. "Her achievements withered like Dead Sea fruit under the malignant influence of militancy," Captain Davison testified.

"I rather doubt he will be given a prominent speaking role at the memorial service," I whispered to Holmes, who grunted his agreement.

A police sergeant testified that no one had responded at the track when he had called out "Does anyone know this woman?" as Miss Davison lay crumpled on the track, although he had seen at least one woman hover briefly over the prostrate woman and then duck back into the infield area. A verdict of "Death by Misadventure" rather than "Suicide" was returned after the coroner described the fracture at the base of her skull, apparently caused by the collision with the racehorse. "It is exceedingly sad that an educated lady should sacrifice her life in so pointless a fashion," he concluded.

We departed the court building and returned to the station to await our train to London. "Wait here for me," Holmes requested as we stood on the platform. "I shall be right back." In five minutes, he had returned and we were soon aboard the train speeding back to Victoria Station. Holmes didn't show any interest in conversation during the journey but sat quietly with his eyes shut for most of the trip. I could tell he wasn't sleeping, but rather was deep in thought, and I knew better than to interrupt him during such periods of contemplation.

"I hope you don't mind that I've arranged a rendezvous at your home this evening," Holmes said as we alighted from the rail car. "If my invited guest chooses to join us, we might be able to make some quick progress on the remaining questions in this matter."

We had returned from a light dinner to my house and were settling into comfortable chairs for an after-dinner pipe when there was a knock on the door. Holmes looked at the mantel clock and nodded with satisfaction. "Eight o'clock precisely," he said. "I have no doubt many answers will be forthcoming very shortly."

"Mr. Holmes, is it?" the man said as I opened the front door, my hand instinctively resting on my service revolver in my coat pocket.

"I am Dr. Watson," I replied. "Mr. Holmes is in the sitting room."

A young man with red hair, at least six feet tall, strode across the sill and brushed past me, disappearing into the parlour. I was right on his heels in case his intentions were malevolent.

Holmes was standing by the fireplace, puffing on his briar. Looking up, he regarded our visitor for a moment before speaking.

"I presume I have the honour of addressing Mr. Liam McCorley," said Holmes.

The man looked surprised but responded, "Yes, I'm McCorley." He looked carefully at Holmes and then at me. In the better light of the room, I could see his eyes were red-rimmed, and it was evident the man had been distraught shortly before arriving. "What is it you want with me?"

"Please, be seated, Mr. McCorley," Holmes said in a welcoming tone. "Would you like something to drink? A pint, perhaps?"

The red-haired man waved off any suggestion of refreshments.

"I've read the news about Emily," he said. "What do you know of this business? How did you know of me or how to find me?" He looked around again. "Are you with the coppers, then?"

"Please sit down," Holmes repeated. "I'm not with the police and I have no interest in their becoming involved, although I cannot guarantee they will not intrude into the matter. I believe I can help ensure you aren't blamed for actions for which I strongly doubt you are responsible. But I will need your trust and your cooperation."

"I don't even know you!" he spat out. "Why should I trust an English aristocrat to care about me?"

"I assuredly am no aristocrat, and you have no particular reason to trust me save my reputation for integrity and discretion. At present, I have no reason to accuse you of wrongdoing. Unfortunately, I rather doubt the police will view the facts in the same light. I suggest we speak quickly and frankly."

McCorley eyed Holmes closely and collapsed in a chair. "Well, what do you know of Emily and me?" he asked.

"Not very much, to be truthful," Holmes said. "I do know you were acquainted, perhaps somewhat more than 'acquainted', to be perfectly truthful. I know you have a connection because of your mutual interest in suffragism, perhaps through your sister, Lucille, and that you disagreed over the levels of militancy required to achieve political reform. It is likely – no, probably more than likely – that you met Miss Davison at the Epsom Derby earlier this week, and I suspect you were as shocked as anyone by her rash action of ducking under the barricade and confronting the King's horse."

McCorley sat with his mouth slightly open for several moments after Holmes paused speaking.

"And do you know what I had for dinner last night?" he asked.

"Based on the arrangements of spots on your shirt," Holmes responded, "I would guess lamb stew, but that is really beside the point."

"Well, you're wrong about the lamb stew!" McCorley replied. "At least not last night. I didn't have any dinner, nor breakfast today. I cannot think of eating! I am distraught at the news of poor Emily, although I knew she was hurt grievously." He hesitated and covered his eyes with a large hand, rubbing them as though he could make the recent events disappear.

"Your note was in her purse advising that she meet you on the infield, at the top of the stretch run," Holmes began. "Contrary to your instructions, she had neglected to destroy it. It didn't require very much work on my part, given the other clues, to determine where you might be found and how I might get a message to you."

"And how's that?" he asked.

"I am aware of the growing connection between the British suffrage movement and some of the Irish nationalists," Holmes replied. "Of course, I don't know with which faction you are affiliated, but I felt a well-placed note to some of the London groups would find its way to you without much difficulty."

"Yes, it's true," McCorley admitted. "Emily and Lucille, my sister, had become friends in London, and when I arrived a few weeks ago, I met Mrs. Pankhurst and the others. I'm not one of the militants, Mr. Holmes. I am as much of a nationalist as anyone, and I make no apologies for that to you or to anyone else. But I take the word of my religion seriously, and I abhor violence in support of a free Ireland. Some of the suffragists thought me insufficiently committed and commenced to tutoring me to increase my level of militancy, much like they had when they formed the W.S.P.U. I spent quite a bit of time with them. I have to say it wasn't all politics and protesting and the like. I quite enjoyed their company – especially Emily's.

"Last week, she suggested we all meet at Epsom to see the races," he continued. "Lucille and Mary Richardson were coming along as well."

"And who is Mary Richardson?" Holmes interrupted.

"Oh, she's quite a disrupter," he said. "A few years ago, she saw the coppers beating up the demonstrators outside Parliament, and that was it for her. Mary said she was joining up – she called it a 'Holy Crusade' – and from then on, it was attacking police and smashing windows for the both of them. They both went to jail and got force fed. I'm sure you know that. Well, they looked on me as someone who needed a real lesson in militancy being the only way. I didn't have anything planned, and Epsom seemed like a nice diversion. I figured it would be one lecture after another, but I figured I could handle it."

"How would you describe their mood when you met them at Epsom?" I asked.

"Quite normal," he replied. "I'm not sure they ever got to the point of being jovial, if you know what I mean. Quite serious almost all the time. But I certainly didn't think Emily was thinking of taking action down there with the crowds and the King present – not to mention all those police!"

"You all planned to return to London?"

"Absolutely," he confirmed.

"Yes, I thought as much," Holmes added, looking in my direction. He turned back to McCorley. "Please continue."

"Well, there's not much to tell, I suppose," he continued. "We met at the racetrack as planned at the inside viewing area, about a half-mile from the end of the race, I suppose."

"Did you know Miss Davison's plans?" Holmes asked. "Had she confided in you?"

McCorley looked down at his feel and remained silent. After several moments, he looked up with a plaintive look on his tortured face. "I knew she was up to something, but not her exact plan. I thought maybe they were planning to march down the track after the race, or some such thing. Oh, how I wish I'd told her not to do it!" he cried, his voice catching.

"It was the scarf." Holmes said. "The '*Votes for Women*' scarf she had concealed in her jacket."

"Yes, I saw it when she reached in for some money to pay for her admission," he said. "It was a sunny day and I could see no reason for a large scarf, so I asked her why she carried it all the way from London. She patted my hand like I was a schoolboy. 'Now, don't you mind that, Liam,' she says to me. 'But we're going to create some news here today.'"

"I couldn't imagine what she was talking about, but I gave it little thought because of all the people milling about."

"She didn't seem agitated or deeply concerned?" Holmes asked.

"No, not at first," McCorley said thoughtfully. "But I will say her mood changed after that other Irishman pushed past us."

Holmes sat upright. "What other Irishman?" he asked.

"Oh, Mr. Holmes, I'd rather not say, except he is a bad character well known to Scotland Yard. Not simply a supporter of a unified and free Ireland, but one of the army's deadliest."

"The Irish Republicans," Holmes clarified.

"Oh yes. They're a nasty lot, they are, happy to use the bomb and the bullet to secure their goals," McCorley continued. "I'm all for Ireland, but not at the expense of human life."

"Did Miss Davison speak with him?" Holmes asked.

"No," McCorley said thoughtfully. "But she seemed a changed person after that – edgier, more anxious – and I didn't blame her. I asked if she wanted to leave, but she said she preferred to stay, that there were too many people and it was too late to cross the racetrack to get to the exit."

"An interesting observation from someone who only minutes later did just that, despite several horses running towards her at full gallop," Holmes added. "What happened then?"

"Well it wasn't long before they announced the race would be beginning, so naturally everyone crowded to the rail so we would have a good view of the horses as they came round the track. Emily had positioned herself with an excellent view, but I did notice something peculiar. She suddenly seemed almost indifferent to the race, and instead, she kept looking down the track towards the finish line, down by where all the pennants and flags were flying.

"Down where the King and Queen were watching the race?" Holmes asked.

McCorley nodded. "Only a minute later, the first of the horses came by in a tremendous thundering of hooves," he continued, "but Anmer – that was the King's horse – wasn't in the first batch of horses, which seemed surprising. The crowd was cheering so loudly, and everyone was pressing against the rails to get the best view. But then, I could see the horse with the King's colors rounding the bend and seeming to pick up his speed. And that's when Emily ducked down under the barrier and stepped onto the track. I still cannot believe it!"

He covered his eyes again to block out the memory. "I thought she had lost her mind! The horses were coming so fast and there was so much noise. I admit, Mr. Holmes, I froze in fear, but it was fear for her, not for me. And in that instant, she pulled the scarf from her bag and planted her feet in the turf, directly in front of Anmer. She made no effort to move out of the way, not a step!"

McCorley stopped and closed his eyes as he recalled the scene. Holmes walked over to him and put a hand on the man's shoulder.

"Steady, McCorley, steady," he said. "Take a deep breath and continue."

"It makes no sense to me, Mr. Holmes," he sobbed. "Yes, I know they are saying she tried to commit suicide once before, but she seemed perfectly normal at the race – at least until she saw that big Irishman. She certainly didn't give the impression of someone about to sacrifice herself for 'The Cause', as they say."

"What did you do after the accident?" Holmes asked. "Did you go out to the track to check on Miss Davison?"

"I started to, but Mary – that's Miss Richardson – pushed me back. 'Don't you go out there!' she said to me. 'The coppers will grab you in an instant. They're looking for the likes of you. Get out of here as fast as you can. I can handle this.' It was against my better judgment, but she was insistent, and then she disappeared under the rail and onto the track so I couldn't talk to her anymore. I figured she knew the situation better than me, and it didn't look like there was much I could do, so I disappeared into the crowd and then made my way back to London, where your note found me earlier today at the Emerald Island Pub."

Holmes stood up as he addressed McCorley. "Well, you have given me important information that I believe will help get to the bottom of all this," he said. "I appreciate your swift response to my request to come by. Meet me back here at ten o'clock this evening, and in the meantime, keep yourself well hidden. I suspect you are the target of very dangerous people."

After McCorley departed, Holmes went to the telephone and placed a call.

"Hello, this is Sherlock Holmes," he said into the receiver. "I need to speak with Mrs. Pankhurst, please." He waited a moment, and then added, "If you would please convey my request to her, I'm quite certain she will accede to my wish to speak with her." There was a short delay, and then apparently the suffrage leader was on the line.

After preliminary pleasantries and a quick updating of his activities, Holmes got to the point. "Forgive the hour, but I would like to meet with you immediately, if that would be convenient," he said. "Very good! And Mary Richardson. Yes, I would like her to be present as well. Why? Well, let's just say I think she will be able to provide some illumination to the issues. Nine o'clock? Very good, then," he concluded, hanging up the receiver.

"We have a nine o'clock appointment," he said to me. "By all means, let us assess where we are in this case."

"Some aspects of the matter seem quite clear," he declared. "Miss Davison was certainly a dedicated suffragist and not afraid to put herself at considerable risk to emphasize her political demands, as we have seen from her repeated arrests and self-starvation episodes in prison. I don't suppose, given her one known suicide attempt, that we can entirely rule out mental illness as a cause of her alarming decision at Epsom, which she must have known placed her life in peril."

"From a purely medical standpoint, I must agree," I responded. "She demonstrated what the new field of psychiatry calls 'self-destructive behaviour' on many occasions. Confronting a stampeding racehorse could well fall into such behaviour, in my opinion."

"Perhaps, but I'm not persuaded that was her intent," Holmes replied. "There are those several pieces of evidence that suggest she didn't intend to sacrifice herself at Epsom. And then there is the obvious question of why she would choose such a place to do away with herself, without apparently leaving any explanation for her action."

"There is the scarf with the '*Votes for Women*' message" I noted.

"Yes, but she could just as well have stepped in front of a streetcar or thrown herself off the Parliament clock tower," he said. "This was an especially dangerous and public act, one that I suspect was unplanned when she journeyed to Epsom."

"What do you suspect?" I asked. "Was the encounter with the other Irishman significant?"

"I don't think there is any doubt about that," he responded. "I suspect that we might well derive important information from Mary Richardson. Let us hasten to Mrs. Pankhurst's home where, I believe, the remaining facts of this case might be revealed."

We were soon ringing the bell once again at the home of Mrs. Pankhurst, who greeted us and ushered us into her parlor. Awaiting us was a woman of perhaps thirty or so with a hard glint in her eye and dark hair cut very much like that of a gentleman.

"This is Mary Richardson," said Mrs. Pankhurst, gesturing to her compatriot as we entered the room. "This is Mr. Sherlock Holmes and his associate, Dr. Watson – a medical doctor."

Miss Richardson's expression didn't change. "And what will you two gentlemen be wanting from me?" she asked in an indifferent tone.

"A pleasure," Holmes replied cheerily. We settled into chairs and Holmes turned towards Miss Richardson.

"Of course, you are under no obligation to speak with us," he said. "I have no doubt you will be given the opportunity of an interview with the police in the next few days."

"I certainly hope you don't think that is going to intimidate me!" she said in an exasperated tone. "They have interrogated me and worse for several years, and I have made clear I have no interest in cooperating with the likes of them no matter how they torture and abuse me."

"Yes, as I recall, your specific words were 'I shall be militant as long as I can stand or see. They cannot do more than kill me'," recited Holmes.

"I see you have made quite a study of me," she replied, her tone softening slightly. "Do you know what that policeman told me? He threatened to keep me till I was a skeleton and then throw me into an institution for mental wrecks!"

"No one is turning anyone into a skeleton here!" Mrs. Pankhurst interrupted.

"Believe it or not, Miss Richardson, I am personally quite sympathetic to your ultimate objective," said Holmes, "although I cannot condone your reliance on physical confrontation."

"Sometimes it is all that gets the attention of those who aren't sympathetic," she responded defiantly.

"Sometimes, but not always," Holmes countered. "For example, the other day at Epsom, I believe Miss Davison was concerned about something she learned just before the race began – something that caused her to change her own plans for the day and that, ultimately, cost her life. Something said to her by an Irishman she didn't expect to meet there."

Miss Richardson looked at Holmes intently, her jaw involuntarily working nervously.

"You see, it is clear to me that Miss Davison went to the race with the intention of creating an incident to draw attention to the suffrage cause, and undoubtedly, you were well aware of the plan. Otherwise, why would she have brought the '*Votes for Women*' scarf with her?"

"Perhaps she wished to display it at the race," said Miss Richardson.

"I think there was something more planned," Holmes countered. "She kept the scarf hidden inside her jacket until she made her way onto the track. If she wanted to display it, the time had passed once the race began. Afterwards, there would little interest in the banner because all of the attention would be directed towards the winning horse and rider.

"Moreover, she discovered only once there that the King and Queen were in attendance. If she wanted to create an incident, surely the best time was before the race since, almost certainly, their Majesties would not linger long after its conclusion. She could have walked down the infield section to the area across from the seating area and unfurled her banner. The King could hardly have missed it."

"No, she couldn't," Miss Richardson countered. "The crowd was enormous, and you couldn't just walk through the infield like that. And besides, there was a great deal of security near the King. She probably couldn't have gotten close enough for him to have seen the printing on the banner."

"So she was effectively stuck where she was, perhaps a half-mile from the person who was doubtless the object of her demonstration," Holmes said. "How inconvenient. But that hardly explains her taking so drastic an action as stepping onto the track."

"Well, that goes to show how little you know!" Miss Richardson said disapprovingly. "As it so happens, we had been practicing exactly that little manoeuvre for a week, which was the reason she went onto the track."

"What 'manoeuvre' was that?'" I inquired.

"We spent several days at a stable, practicing how one might attach the banner to a horse as it sped by, so that when it crossed the finish line, it would be carrying the '*Votes for Women*' banner," she explained. "It was Emily's idea, and she was getting quite good at it."

"And was she knocked down during these practice efforts?" Holmes pressed.

"Well, no, of course not," she replied, "she would stand to the side and stuff the banner into the saddle or the bridle."

"And she was successful in doing so?" Holmes asked.

"Yes, on several occasions, she was!" Miss Richardson answered.

"Well, then, that makes her action at Epsom even more difficult to explain," Holmes said. "It would have been one thing had she never attempted so foolhardy a stunt and was trampled in the process, but you are telling me she was practiced at it, and therefore, she knew where to stand and when to reach out to the horse as it sped by."

"And what significance to you ascribe to that observation?" asked Mrs. Pankhurst.

"The only one that is plausible," Holmes responded. "That her decision to stand in front of the King's stampeding horse was intentional!"

"Martyrdom!" commanded Miss Richardson. "She is a martyr to the cause of women's equality and suffrage."

"Perhaps," said Holmes. "What happened before she ducked under the guard rail?"

"A minute before the race started, Mr. McCorley tugged at her sleeve. He was holding a card in his hand. 'Look Emily, look what I have found slipped into my pocket!' he said with alarm. She took it to read and her entire expression changed. But then the race began and I forgot the incident until the horses came near.

"Emily had the card in her hand, and she was looking to her left, down the track to the finish line," she said.

"Towards the end of the track, and not towards the horses that were approaching from her right?" Holmes asked.

"Yes," Miss Richardson continued. "Just as the horses approached, she turned to see them. And then suddenly, she slipped under the rail and walked out into the middle of the racecourse. After the collision, I ran onto the track to comfort her," she continued.

"You undoubtedly encountered me there," I said, "as I ran onto the track to assist her."

Miss Richardson stared at me but said nothing.

"Come, Miss Richardson," said Holmes, standing and walking over to where she sat, his hand extended to her. "Let me have the card."

Miss Richardson stared at Holmes, as did Mrs. Pankhurst and myself. She said nothing, but her face hardened into a mask of defiance.

"I could simply call the police and have them charge you with withholding valuable information," he said, "although I have no desire to do so. I do not believe you were a part of a plot. Indeed, you might have been as disturbed by what was written on the card as Miss Davison herself." He walked closer to the young woman with his hand still extended. He spoke, and his voice took on a sharper tone. "The card, Miss Richardson!" he commanded. "Or I will have no alternative but to detain you until Scotland Yard arrives. I remind you, we aren't dealing with the municipal police."

The young woman pursed her lips, then reached down and opened her handbag and removed a small card. She silently read the rough writing on it and then placed it in Holmes's hand.

Holmes looked at it with a serious mien and passed it to me:

The end of the race means the end of George. Freedom for Ireland!

"Where did this come from?" Holmes demanded.

"Mr. McCorley said it must have been slipped into the pocket of his coat while we were passing through the throng. Emily was looking at it as the race began. She had it in her hand when she ducked under the rail."

"And you went onto the track to retrieve it immediately after the collision," Holmes declared.

"Yes. I didn't want that to be found on her," Miss Richardson confessed. "I was sure that whatever was to happen to the King at the end of the race would be blamed in part on the suffrage movement, perhaps by suggesting we were in collusion with the Irish Nationalists."

"You do share a common willingness to commit acts of violence," I interjected.

"To make our point, yes," she replied, "but we are not soldiers at war with the King. The I.R.B. or the I.R.A. might embrace regicide, but suffragists certainly do not! In fact, the I.R.B. doesn't even support the suffrage movement because they believe it detracts from their argument for Irish Home Rule."

"And what was McCorely's reaction to the tragedy?" Holmes asked.

"Oh, he left as swiftly as possible. I didn't even know until a day or two later how badly Emily had been injured, or that the King has been safely evacuated from the track, thank goodness."

Holmes sat on the arm of his chair, fingering the card in his hand.

"Yes, I think we have Miss Davison to thank for that," Holmes declared.

"Why do you say that?" Mrs. Pankhurst asked.

"I suspect that Miss Davison performed an act of extraordinary bravery – not simply for the suffrage movement, but for England as a whole."

He turned to the two women. "Please allow me to keep this note," he said to Miss Richardson. "If my inquiry has the outcome I expect it will, I am not going to mention that it ever found its way into your possession. I ask that you not discuss anything related to the incident with anyone but the police, should they find their way to you. I would tell them the story precisely as you have related it to me, but leave this paper out of it for now."

The two women nodded their heads in agreement, and Holmes and I returned to my rooms, where McCorley soon appeared looking anxious and furtive. He seemed grateful to find us.

"What have you learned?" he anxiously asked when we had closed the door.

"Among other things, I learned that you were not entirely straightforward with me," Holmes said reproachingly. McCorley silently looked at the floor. He withdrew the card from his pocket, and there was a gasp from McCorley.

"Where did you find *that*?" he asked as he rose from his chair, his eyes wide.

"Miss Davison had it in her hand when she was struck," Holmes said. "You have Miss Richardson to thank for retrieving it. Had it been found in Miss Davison's hand, she would surely have been connected to the Irish nationalism movement even more than the suffragists already are."

"But she wasn't I.R.B.," he protested, "and neither am I. They don't even like the suffragists! I don't know when that card came into my pocket. I assume while we were walking through the crowd."

"Yes, it undoubtedly was placed there by the Irishman you saw at the race. He surely intended that it would be found when you and Miss Richardson were questioned by the police – after the assassination of His Majesty King George!"

I stared thunderstruck at Holmes. McCorley looked at the detective seriously but without surprise.

"Mr. Holmes, you must believe, I knew nothing of any planned attack on the King," he insisted. "Nor did I have any sense of what Miss Davison would do before she ducked under the rail."

"But you showed her this card, which you had failed to mention to me."

"Yes, I found it in my pocket just as the race was commencing. She took it from my hand and asked what it meant. I saw the meaning immediately: The IRB was planning an attack on the King, presumably during the commotion after the race. I told Emily, 'My God, they mean to kill the King!' She got a horrified look on her face. I know the papers said she was smiling but it was no smile, it was a look of horror. I think she could see the danger to us all, to our movements, if such a despicable act were laid at our feet."

Holmes measured McCorley carefully. The young man seemed genuinely distraught at the thought of injury being done to King George.

"I believe Miss Davison made a split-second decision when she saw this note," Holmes said. "She had intended to attempt to place the '*Votes for Women*' scarf on Anmer's bridle, as she had practiced at the stable. But she realized that if the race were run as was planned, the King and Queen were likely to come down from the grandstand to congratulate the winning rider, and that there were assassins in the crowd waiting for just such an opportunity.

"She needed to create an incident, a much bigger incident than the symbolic one she had originally planned, to alert the

King's security people from a half-mile away that there was imminent danger and they must escort him from the track instead of visiting with the winning horse. And so instead of stepping to the side as the horse went by, she stood where the horse could not help but collide with her. That catastrophic incident that was certain to alert the King's people, a half-mile away, that danger lurked at the Epsom Derby.

"I doubt she intended to sacrifice her life for the King's safety. I would imagine she thought she might be knocked away. She kept this card in her hand in case she couldn't alert those attending to her afterwards that there was a plot against the King."

"The she is a heroine!" McCorley cried.

"Not one we can afford to celebrate in public," Holmes said. "It would be extremely difficult to prove that she didn't know about the I.R.B. plan. It might even appear she was in league with the revolutionaries. But absent holding the card, her action probably wouldn't have prompted the evacuation of the King and the Queen from Epsom Downs."

McCorley was quiet. "I suppose I am to blame," he said. "I should have brought the card to the attention of the police. But I had no time or ability to do so. I didn't even find it in my pocket till after the race had started."

"The idea of slipping the card into your pocket was to point the finger of blame at you and your colleagues in the fight for Irish independence," Holmes explained. "By discrediting you, they undoubtedly believed they would build support for their own radical movement and at the expense of the suffragists whom they dismiss as busybodies.

"I suspect there is nothing good for you here in London, Mr. McCorley," Holmes said. "I suggest you return to Ireland until this matter calms down. If no attention is turned to the plot against the King, I think you'll be safe from the police.

As to your safety from the I.R.B. – well, that, sir, is your concern and your concern alone."

McCorley stood with his hat in hand and stared at Holmes with a look of disbelief. "You're letting me go, then?" he asked with a look of relief on his face. "You're not turning me over to the police?"

"It would seem to me the most unwise thing I could do would be to sully the more reasonable wing of the Irish movement by linking all forms of nationalism to regicide," Holmes replied. "I trust you will continue to renounce the use of violence to achieve your ends. Otherwise, I will become your most tireless pursuer."

McCorley nodded several times and fled out of the room, but as Holmes feared, he didn't immediately depart from the city, and was far from safe. Two days later, there was a short report in the newspaper. "*Irish Nationalist Stabbed to Death Near London Docks*" the headline read. A small piece of cardboard was pinned to his chest on which had been written "*IRB*" in his own blood.

"A sordid group," Holmes said at breakfast as he read the account to me. "He could implicate the I.R.B. in the plot, so they had to get rid of him before he talked to the police. I'm not sympathetic with his goal of breaking apart our alliance with Ireland, but the way to fight that battle is surely through debate, not bullets, knives, and bombs. And, I believe, the same is true for Mrs. Pankhurst and her acolytes in the suffrage movement. Unfortunately, violence seems to have found McCorley despite his renunciation of direct action."

Holmes spent several days with Inspector Llewellyn at Scotland Yard, going through the information he had gathered on the I.R.B. plot against the King, although he was able to leave the connection to Miss Davison and the suffragists out of the story. Over the next several weeks, a number of arrests of I.R.A. and I.R.B. militants in London and Dublin were directly tied to the information Holmes had provided.

Miss Davison's body arrived in London to a spectacular welcome by over five-thousand women. Her coffin, inscribed with the slogan *"Fight on. God will give the victory"* was at the head of the procession that included hundreds of men supporting the right of suffrage for British women. Holmes and I did not attend the ceremony. Neither did Mrs. Pankhurst, who had been arrested that very morning under the Cat and Mouse Act.

The march proceeded from Victoria to Kings Cross, and then to St. George's Church in Bloomsbury for a service attended by members of the Church League for Women's Suffrage, and then along a parade route lined with fifty-thousand mourners, many wearing the distinctive colours of white, green, and purple of the suffrage movement. They were the same colours that had been emblazoned on the scarf Miss Davison had carried inside her jacket, onto the Epsom Derby track and then, into history.

Emily Davison
11 October 1872 – 8 June 1913

The Case of the
Duplicitous Suitor

It was just a week before Christmas, 1885, and London was resplendent with the lights and decorations of the holiday season that always brought a degree of gaiety to that bone-chilling time of the year. I had been preoccupied late by a patient: A congested child with a hacking cough and a desperate young mother fearful the lad was taking his last painful breaths. A small amount of brandy dissolved in weak tea had helped relieve the youngster's distress, and a larger amount calmed the mother. It was shortly before dawn when I climbed into my bed, still shivering from the cold, weary and longing for a few hours' rest, only to be wakened in what seemed mere moments by a loud knocking on my bedroom door.

"Awaken, Watson!" the familiar voice of Sherlock Holmes cried from the landing. "The day is fast disappearing, and a case awaits!"

A quick examination of the clock on my bedside table indicated it was just after seven, but the damage to my slumber was done. Once awakened, an old army surgeon can never return to sleep, regardless how dark it is, so I quickly conducted my ablutions, dressed, and met Holmes downstairs in the our sitting room. I noted that Mrs. Hudson had thoughtfully arranged some evergreens on the mantel above the glowing fireplace to give a touch of the season to our rooms.

Holmes acknowledged my arrival with a nod of his head and a slight smile of greeting. Despite the early hour on a Sunday morning, he was already dressed and, from the stuffy atmosphere of the room, I guessed onto his second pipe of the day. Several newspapers had already evidently been read and their contents digested, along with a breakfast on the table consisting of sausages, scones, and grilled tomatoes. I poured myself a cup of Mrs. Hudson's thankfully hot and strong coffee and eased myself into a chair by the table.

"What is so urgent as to disturb my very unsatisfactory but essential rest?" I inquired.

"Yes, I heard you go out last night," Holmes explained. "Not too challenging a case, I hope?"

"I'm surprised you don't know the precise details of it," I replied somewhat tersely, waiting for the caffeine stimulant to ratchet me more awake.

"No, I don't, and for once, I will not engage in that parlour game."

"The one in which you guess what I have been doing, or with whom, or where I have been?"

"Quite so," he replied, "but not today. I awakened you because we are due to have a distinguished visitor this morning, and I didn't think you would want to miss his arrival."

"I certainly hope he and the case he brings to your attention are worthy of my having sacrificed a decent night's sleep," I replied. "Or whatever was left of it."

Holmes looked at me understandingly and walked over to where I sat, hungrily examining the pile of bangers and tomatoes. "Perhaps this will spark some interest," he said, dropping a folded piece of paper in front of me. "What do you make of this note?"

The letter was written on heavy, high-quality cream-coloured paper. The handwriting was scrawled, barely even legible to my eyes. The engraved name atop the stationery removed all doubt as to its provenance: Collins Bookseller at 255 Piccadilly Street, in St. James.

"A most reputable book-seller," I noted.

"If you wouldn't mind, Watson, might you read the message aloud?" he requested. "It will help me to digest the contents without taxing my eyes again on that dreadful handwriting."

He threw himself into one of the other chairs by the table and speared a plump sausage with a pen knife, likely one used recently to open the envelope containing the letter now nestled in my hand.

Dear Mr. Holmes, [it began]

> *I do not make it a practice to seek the advice and counsel of men in your line of work, but an inexplicable series of events has come to my attention that I am unable to comprehend. The circumstances are quite delicate, I think, and therefore I would favour describing them to you in person at your residence later this morning, rather than include them in this letter or delay relating them to you. With your permission, then, I will arrive at your door by eight a.m. and would appreciate the benefit of your consideration of this peculiar and disturbing matter.*

The missive was signed *"Garthwaite Collins, Esq."* in the same scrawl as the text of the message itself.

"I think that's about it," I said, squinting slightly to be sure I had faithfully deciphered the perplexing penmanship of Mr. Gaithwaite Collins, Esq.

"Can you form any ideas from so curious a note?" he asked.

"Nothing beyond what he states quite clearly in the letter," I responded. "I suppose you are able to construct a grand story from it."

"Well, there is a bit that can be discerned, I think," Holmes said in response to his own question. "It seems clear the events of which the honourable Mr. Collins seeks my assistance pertain to someone other than himself, since the account has quite a secondary or detached description of the matter. Mr. Collins is a well-known merchant whose shop has provided me with some of the rare city directories I find so useful in my work. I know him to be an unmarried man, like myself, but of some advanced years, so it seems likely the matter has been brought to his attention by an acquaintance or colleagues, rather than a family member."

"That seems reasonable enough."

"Since he refers to the situation as 'delicate', I would think it most likely the person involved is a woman, probably a young woman, without parents – possibly only recently arrived in London, and perhaps a junior employee."

"How do you deduce that set of facts?"

"If the woman were young, she would surely seek the advice of her parents. If older, her husband, or more likely her lady friends, if the matter were truly 'delicate'. Since she has come to Collins, a man of sixty or more, I must assume she either has no parents or is estranged from them. Otherwise, even if the matter were urgent, she surely would reach out to them rather than turn to someone like Collins. So, she likely is young, without husband or close women friends nearby with whom to consult, and so she turns to a thoughtful and intelligent man she knows. How would she come to know him? Likely because she works at the bookstore or is a frequent client who has come to rely on him for advice about becoming acquainted with her new residence, I suspect that is the portrait of the person in need: A young woman, fairly new to London, without parents of friends and facing a disturbing situation involving a suitor that she can entrust only to someone older and yet compassionate."

"All that from this vague letter?" I pressed.

"And more, in all likelihood, but why prolong the mystery? I believe I heard footsteps on the stairs, and expect that Mrs. Hudson will imminently announce the arrival of Mr. Garthwaite Collins."

Holmes has no sooner finished speaking than Mrs. Hudson's familiar knock signaled her presence outside our rooms. "Mr. Garthwaite Collins," she announced as I opened the door and a tall, distinguished, white-haired gentleman strode through, glancing neither at our housekeeper nor me, but walking straight across the room to where Holmes stood puffing on a churchwarden.

"We have met before, Mr. Holmes," he began, offering no greeting. "At the Diogenes Club. You were visiting your brother."

Holmes nodded his head in recognition. "I recall, Mr. Collins. I believe we had a brief conversation in the Stranger's Room about the excellence of the hiking trails in the Grampian Mountains of Scotland."

"Astonishing!" cried Collins. "Believe me, I wouldn't have said the conversation was so memorable."

"Nor would I," Holmes replied coolly. "Now, I'm sure you didn't come here to discuss hiking in Scotland. Your note mentioned an urgent and 'delicate' matter. Pray, how may we be of service to you or – if I may presuppose – to the young lady who has confided the reason for her unhappiness to you?"

Collins stood with his mouth slightly open for a moment before shifting on his feet slightly. "Why, how did you know that?"

"It is, as I'm wont to say, my business to know things that others believe hidden. I merely read the inflections and suggestions in your letter to reach my conclusion."

Collins considered Holmes's explanation and then walked with a slight limp to one of the comfortable chairs near the fire and sat down. Holmes and I followed, and we all lit cigarettes as we prepared to hear the book merchant's account.

"You are quite right, Mr. Holmes," he began. "The young lady's name is Penelope Barrington, and she has been most terribly misused, I fear. Her father and I served together under General Outram during the Battle of Khushab. That was during the war with Persia."

"I am aware," Holmes murmured.

"Well, it was a nasty business, and we were in the thick of it for sure at Khushab. Many of our mates didn't make it out of there, but I did – with a bullet through my thigh. My friend, Philip Barrington, was even less lucky. He caught two rounds, one in the chest and one in his abdomen. Tore him up something terrible, but the doctors were on him in minutes and saved us both."

"I was an army physician myself," I said. "Took a Jezail bullet in my shoulder at Maiwand."

Collins glanced briefly at my shoulder and a momentary fellowship was struck between us before he continued his story. "We returned home considerably worse for wear. I became a book merchant, as you know, and have been fortunate to run a very successful establishment. Philip was less lucky. He did straightaway marry his sweetheart, Mary, and they lived happily enough for some years though without any children. Then Mary fell ill and died, leaving Philip a shattered man. A few years later, however, he was fortunate to meet a young woman – Dora – whom he wed, and within a year or two, little Penelope arrived. She was the apple of his eye for sure, and they would bring her round to the shop for me to admire from time to time.

"Ah, but time wasn't good for Philip. His injuries kept him in and out of doctors' consultancies for years, and he was fortunate that his father's good fortune in the spice trade in Indo-China kept him and his family secure and comfortable.

"Philip's luck went from bad to worse starting a year or so ago. His wife developed influenza and died suddenly last June. As if that wasn't disconcerting enough, he began complaining of all sorts of troubles and that his pain, which seemed perpetual, was steadily worsening.

"One day, he came to see me to ask that should something happen to him, would I be good enough to keep an eye on Penelope, perhaps provide her a job at my shop. Well, she was an attractive, literate, and pleasant enough young lady and I assured Philip she would be welcome if something befell him.

"Not six weeks later, he was a dead man. The old repairs in his gut had come undone, or some such thing, and he was full of infection. It was fortunate he didn't have to live long in that pain. Soon after, I received the note from Penelope, asking if I would honor her father's request. Well, 'a friend's last need' and all that, so naturally, I urged her to come down to London at her earliest convenience and I would get her settled into the book business."

"And was she an attentive employee?" asked Holmes.

"I hadn't a care or worry about her, not for a moment," Collins continued. "Oh, she was still quite sad about her father, you can understand, what with him dying so fast and in such discomfort. She had lost a bit of her bounce. But then Mr. Josephus Rexford came along, and things certainly seemed to be changing for the better."

"Josephus Rexford?" Holmes inquired. "Pray, who is he?"

"Well, I admit that is a bit of a mystery, that question," Collins said. "He came into the shop one day about six months ago looking for some books on European history, and Penelope was happy to show him our selection. He must have liked the books because he returned the next day and then the next, and each time, he would ask Penelope to join him back at the history section where they would peruse books and discuss their contents."

"And did Mr. Rexford actually purchase any books?" Holmes asked.

"Oh, yes, quite a few," Collins responded. "All sorts of books about the history and politics of Italy, Switzerland, Germany, and the like. Seemed quite knowledgeable about the subject, I might add, for we engaged in several conversations of our own whenever he visited the store."

"Can you describe him?" asked Holmes.

"Oh, quite a young gentleman," responded Collins, "or I should have never allowed him so much unescorted time with Penelope! Tall, well-dressed, perhaps in his early twenties, almost dashing. He often carries a cane with a large silver knob on the top – an affectation for someone his age, I believe. It seems to have a crest of some type, but it has always been too far away to discern any details."

"And how came he to the shop?"

"By foot, but there always seemed to be a carriage waiting for him upon his departure – a private carriage, not a cab for hire."

"And how does he speak?"

"Oh, he is very articulate – very precise in his diction, I should say."

"Any accent? Inflection? Any hint from where he might be?"

Collins paused thoughtfully, rubbing his lips with his index finger. "Now that you mention it, perhaps the slightest of accents, very faint and certainly nothing I could trace. I took him to be a well-educated young man and gave little thought to such matters. We have so many from overseas in England now."

"Did he mention his line of business?"

"Not to me, but as Penelope began spending some time with him, including in afternoon walks away from the shop, I assumed she learned more about him. I did ask. I considered my responsibility to Philip to include ensuring his daughter wasn't being taken advantage of, even by such a seemingly upstanding gentleman. But she didn't share much information with me, except to assure me that Mr. Rexford had attended Sandhurst, was quite wealthy, and engaged in private affairs of which he chose not to speak. I found the secrecy somewhat disconcerting, I must admit. One afternoon when Penelope was preoccupied with another customer, and as I found myself alone with him, I decided to do a little sleuthing of my own."

"Oh, excellent," Holmes murmured. "And what information did you uncover?"

"Well, not a great deal, to be truthful. He deflected questions about his source of income, but he assured me it was considerable and quite secure, although he declined to be more specific. As to his intentions with Penelope, he told me he intended to ask her to marry him. Well, you can imagine I was quite astonished since I knew so little about the gentleman's background, but what was there for me to do? I was neither her father nor legal guardian.

"Sure enough, several days later she fairly floated into the shop one morning, beaming with happiness and bubbling with laughter. Her glow far outshone the holiday lights that I had arranged to give the store the look of the Season.

"'Oh, Mr. Collins, I'm so fortunate!' she exclaimed. 'I'm to be married to Mr. Rexford!' She showed me a beautiful ring he had given her to commemorate the betrothal, one of several pieces of family jewelry he had apparently conferred on her, although he asked that she not wear them outside her flat until he had alerted his family of these gifts.

"I was, of course, delighted to see her so overjoyed, but I remained wary, not knowing nearly enough, in my estimation, about the man to whom she was now engaged to be married."

"Have you been introduced to his family?" Holmes asked.

"Certainly not."

"Has Penelope?"

"Not to my knowledge. I'm not even sure where his family lives, or what business they might be in. She said that many of them don't live in England. She and her betrothed intend to embark upon a trip to meet them all after their marriage."

"Well, Mr. Collins, this seems somewhat irregular, I admit, and you are certainly in an unenviable position, having some of the responsibilities of a guardian but none of the authority of a parent. You can continue to press Miss Barrington for more information. You may even insist upon a fuller explanation from Rexford himself. But I doubt you have much legal authority to demand information or act if it isn't proffered."

"Yes, I'm quite aware of the precariousness of my situation, Mr. Holmes, which is why I haven't sought legal recourse. But I have not yet told you the most singular part of this situation."

Holmes smiled gratefully, lighting another cigarette and taking a deep pull on it. The fire at the end glowed brilliantly orange as he settled back in the chair and blew out a cloud of gray smoke. "Then pray, Mr. Collins, do not keep me in anticipation," Holmes said.

"Four days ago, Penelope appeared my home after dinner. She was quite upset – even distraught, I might say."

"'Oh, Mr. Collins, he is *gone!*' she exclaimed, falling into my arms. 'Gone!'"

"Who is gone, Penelope?" I asked, anticipating the response.

"'Josephus!' she cried. 'He has left me, and intends to leave England altogether. Alone!'"

She reached into her handbag and presented me with a note.

My dear Penelope,

I despair that I should have to write these words, but I must rescind my offer of marriage to you, although it is against my wishes and my heart to do so.

Circumstances quite beyond my control have intervened and compel me to leave England and render this saddest of decisions, which will haunt me for the rest of my life. Yet duty and loyalty must rise above all else.

The reasons for my departure from this, my adopted home, will soon become clear, even as my separation from you remains painfully inevitable. I wish you to keep the gifts as evidence of my abiding deep love in hope they will allow you, in time, to remember me with affection.

Goodbye, my dearest! And I hope you will forgive this hasty and, for the moment inexplicable, departure.

J. Rexford

"The scoundrel!" I involuntarily exclaimed. "Toying with a young woman's affections!"

Holmes held up his hand and waved it from side to side.

"Let us be careful, Watson, not to jump to conclusions," he said. "There are many aspects of this matter that warrant deeper consideration." He turned to Collins. "Is there more?" he asked.

"Yes, there is," Collins replied. "A burglary!"

"No doubt at the home of Miss Barrington."

"Precisely," he confirmed. "Two days later, an intruder entered her rooms in broad daylight whilst she was at work."

"And, if I'm not presuming too much, the jewelry given her by her former suitor was stolen."

"Precisely, Mr. Holmes, as well as several other items of inconsequential value," answered Collins, "except for the engagement ring she had taken to wearing, which she now treasures as her only tangible memory of that rascal Rexford."

"I presume the burglar was nearly apprehended by the manager of the property?"

"Yes. How on earth would you know that?" Collins inquired. "He made a very hurried escape as the landlady entered the room for weekly cleaning."

"Oh, that is excellent!" Holmes replied, rubbing his hands together in what resembled glee.

"Well, I assure you that Penelope views the matter with a good deal less merriment than you," Collins said with some displeasure.

"I do not make light of these circumstances," Holmes assured him, "only that so clear a map has thoughtfully been left to lead us to an explanation for the facts as you have presented them."

"A map?" the book merchant repeated. "I must say I'm left only with questions. Who is Rexford? Was his courting of Penelope genuine or a ruse? Why has he suddenly disappeared, to the despair of the young woman he purports to love? What is this 'duty' that displaces his affection for his fiancé? And was this burglary a coincidence or related to Rexford's absconding? I must say, Mr. Holmes, I fail to see how the pieces fall together."

"Then how fortunate in that case that you have come to me," Holmes replied. "I should like to meet Miss Barrington at the earliest time. Would that be possible, say, tomorrow at your bookstore?"

"I am sure it would be," Collins replied. "She is as perplexed as I about the entire situation, and a good deal more distraught!"

The following morning, Holmes and I arrived at Collins' at ten o'clock, as we had arranged. As he had described, the entry-way was decorated Christmastime decorations creating a bright welcome to customers. We were escorted by the owner to a room in the rear where Miss Barrington awaited us. Collins hadn't exaggerated her radiant beauty that inevitably had been dimmed by recent concern. She was dabbing at her eyes with her handkerchief when we entered the room.

Introductions were made all around as we seated ourselves at a small table, and Miss Barrington turned her distraught face toward Holmes with a silent plea for assistance.

"Miss Barrington," he began, "through Mr. Collins I have learned the basic facts of your situation, but I would like to hear additional details from you directly "Can you explain to me the circumstances of how you met Mr. Rexford, the nature of your conversations, and the specific details of your engagement plans?"

"I am so grateful to you, Mr. Holmes," she began. "I know of your reputation and can appreciate that my situation must seem quite petty and unimportant compared to the types of cases that typically command your attention." She paused for a moment and turned to me. "And my gratitude goes out to you as well, Dr. Watson." I admit my heart fairly softened at such words from so charming a young woman.

"Josephus – Mr. Rexford, that is – is a good man, an honourable gentleman, of that I have no doubt."

"And yet," I interjected, "by all appearances, he has treated you most discourteously!"

"It is true, I suppose, but there must be an explanation, something that he is unable to share with me. Perhaps some terrible things he has done early in his life, or has been accused of, with which he wishes to spare me any association. Perhaps that explains his sudden departure."

"Would an honourable man have encouraged you to marry him, knowing such a black cloud hung over him?" Holmes asked. "Surely he must have realised that ignominious behavior – a criminal record, a military disgrace – "

"A past wife," I interjected.

Holmes threw a disapproving glance in my direction as shock registered on the young lady's face.

"Is there anything he shared about his life before he knew you that might have suddenly interposed itself and caused him to reconsider his promises to you?"

"Nothing!" she insisted. "I admit that, in some respects, I knew quite little about him. I don't know the precise nature of his work, only that it provided him with a generous remuneration that allowed him to live comfortably in London."

"And to proffer gifts of jewelry, I understand?" Holmes queried.

"Yes, beautiful jewelry," she confirmed. "Here is the one piece I was able to save from the intruder who pilfered my home the other day." She held out her left hand on which there was a gold ring with sparkling green emerald in a filigreed setting. "It is my only connection to him now," she said, her voice choking as the handkerchief rose again to her eyes.

Holmes's eyes stayed focused on the ring for several moments. "Do you mind?" he said, holding out his hand. She reluctantly removed the ring from her finger and handed it to the detective who examined it carefully with his hand glass. He uttered a short snort and handed the ring back to her. "And is there nothing else that he left behind? No personal items that might have indicated an intention to return to visit you?"

"He gave these cigars to me – as an 'early Christmas gift', he said." Collins brought the box to Holmes. "But they have no label indicating the manufacturer."

Holmes took the box and set it on his lap. He opened the top, which was hinged in the back, revealing a dozen cigars. Holmes picked one up and held it next to his ear, rolling it between his fingers and then sniffing it thoughtfully. He examined a small paper ring around the cigar, which appeared to be a colourful crest of some sort. Producing a small penknife from his waistcoat pocket, he cut it open with as much precision as a surgeon making his incision and separated the leaves, examining the mess of dried tobacco with his glass.

"Very good!" he declared. "I have, as you may know, made a study of tobacco ash, as Watson has recorded."

"But this tobacco hasn't been burned," Collins correctly noted.

"I usually analyze the ash because the unburned tobacco isn't available," Holmes explained. "However, when it is, as in this case, so much the better. Yes, these cigars are most instructive." He turned to Miss Barrington. "I will endeavor to determine what has occurred in hopes that knowing will give you peace of mind," he said. "But I think I can safely say you aren't responsible for any of the events that have transpired. Hopefully, in short order, I shall be able to lay all the facts before you."

Holmes and I departed the bookstore and hailed a carriage to return to Baker Street. As I was stepping into the cab, Holmes put his hand on the door. "Watson, I have several inquiries to make," he said. "I hope to return to Baker Street by five o'clock with the information I require to satisfactorily resolve this case."

I knew better than to query him about his plans, and instead nodded in agreement and departed in the cab. I watched him dash off and then gave the driver the address and settled in for the brief drive across central London. Later, I had lunch at a restaurant two blocks from our rooms and then, somewhat fatigued from the morning's activities and the heavy meal, resolved to spend a few hours catching up on some medical journals. I settled into a comfortable chair near the fire and began perusing an article on surgical treatments of club foot.

When I awoke, it was late-afternoon, the sitting room was dark, and Holmes was standing over me.

"Where have you been?" I asked.

"To the telegraph office, to begin with," he responded. "I sent a few telegrams that I thought might produce some useful answers."

"And did you receive the information you were seeking?"

"Very enlightening," he replied. He sat in his favorite chair, lit his pipe, and withdrew several telegrams which he began reviewing, scribbling some brief notes in the margins. Knowing he was connecting the pieces of the puzzle, I took my own chair and pipe and waited for him to finish his preparations.

After a half-an-hour, Holmes announced there was little else to be done until the next morning, when he expected we would be welcoming several visitors to our rooms.

"What visitors?" I inquired.

"Miss Barrington, for one," he responded. "And I expect we shall have additional guests."

"Mr. Rexford?" I inquired.

Holmes smiled thinly. "I should be very surprised if he doesn't make an appearance. But let us take ourselves to

Wimpoles. I understand they have an excellent holiday pheasant there and, I would wager, a fine wine to accompany the bird."

We passed an enjoyable hour-and-a-half at the renowned Marylebone restaurant and then a stroll back to Baker Street to walk off the rich dinner. Carolers were strolling the streets and festive residents opened their doors to offer hot cider and sweets to the singers. Back before the fire, we smoked a pipe and discussed news from the Continent before the meal and stroll began to work their effect on me and I begged off to bed.

"Our first guest arrives at ten in the morning," Holmes cheerfully called as I closed the door to the sitting room.

The next morning, we had finished our breakfast and Mrs. Hudson had cleared the dishes and set a fresh pot of tea and some lemon cakes on the table when we heard a knock on the door precisely at ten o'clock. I opened it to find our landlady, accompanied by a tall young man, fashionably dressed, carrying a silver-topped cane.

"It's Mr. Rexford come to see you, Mr. Holmes," she announced.

Holmes quickly bounded up from his chair and strode to the door. "Thank you, Mrs. Hudson." He regarded the young man standing by her side and bade him enter the room. Our visitor entered and Mrs. Hudson closed the door behind him. He quickly surveyed the room, then turned his gaze to me for a moment before focusing his attention on my friend.

"You are Sherlock Holmes, I presume?" he said, his voice clear and, as Collins had noted, with a faint hint of an accent.

"Always an error to make presumptions," the detective responded, "but in this case, yes, I am Holmes."

"Josephus Rexford," the visitor replied, removing a pair of gray calfskin gloves and extending a soft hand that looked very much like one that had successfully avoided manual labor.

Holmes regarded the extended hand for a moment, then grasped it for a brief handshake and bade Rexford to take a chair.

Our guest sat as we settled into our own chairs, then took a deep breath.

"Of course, I am aware of your reputation, Mr. Holmes," he said. "I am, however, uncertain why I should be summoned to your consulting room by the advertisement in this morning's paper." He threw down a copy of *The **Londoner-Journal,*** a German language newspaper published in London. I could see that he had circled an advertisement with a red pencil. The English translation ran:

> *Mr. Sherlock Holmes would be delighted to meet Mr. Josephus Rexford at 10 a.m. at 221B Baker Street this morning. It is worth attending the meeting before your departure.*

"I am not used to being summoned to conferences like a schoolboy," Rexford said in a somewhat irritated fashion.

"And yet, here you are!" Holmes replied flippantly.

Rexford studied my friend's face carefully. "To be frank, I could hardly pass up the opportunity to meet the famous Sherlock Holmes, even if the reason for the invitation remains vague to me, even now."

"I didn't imagine you could, Mr. Rexford," Holmes replied. "Or should I say, 'Your Highness'?"

Rexford's reaction could barely have been more startled than my own.

"I beg your pardon, sir?" he responded archly.

"Come now, do you underestimate my skills so profoundly that you did not imagine, even before you crossed my threshold, that I knew I was in the presence of Crown Prince Albert of Thurn and Taxis."

I sat upright in my chair, looking intently at Holmes and then at Rexford. Our guest betrayed no surprise. "I'm not sure I understand your implication, Mr. Holmes," he responded.

Holmes stood and walked to mantel. "Let us not be coy with each other about something so painfully evident. Discerning your identity required a minimum of effort, I assure you, and the reasons behind your duplicitous behavior regarding Miss Barrington is no less obvious to me. Would you like to make a clean breast of it, first to me and then to the young woman you have so distressed, or will you compel me to recite the facts of the case for you?"

Rexford rose halfway from his chair before settling back, his shoulders sagging slightly as he realized the pointlessness of continuing his charade.

"All right, Mr. Holmes, I shall not deny my identity any longer to you, although I'm torn about discussing the matter with Penelope. I admit my actions have been unconventional and she may well feel I have wronged her, but only because I wish to mitigate the sadness I presume the disclosure will bring her."

"With respect, sir," declared Holmes, "it is unfailingly preferable to acknowledge the truth, however unpleasant it may be, than to perpetuate a deceit, especially in matters of the heart."

Rexford, or Prince Albert, remained silent for a moment before beginning to speak. "How did you come by this knowledge, Mr. Holmes?" he asked. "I believed I had concealed my path well enough to ensure my anonymity from the most diligent of pursuers."

"And so you have, Prince Albert," replied Holmes. "All but one. You had the extreme misfortune that Mr. Collins was concerned enough about Miss Barrington that he came to see me.

"As to how I came to possess the information revealing your true identity, I assure you it was a simple matter. Mr. Collins mentioned that you had studied at Sandhurst. Together with the disclosure that you spoke with a faint accent, I inferred that you, like many at the academy, might well be in England training to assume a high-ranking position in one of the states of Europe.

"I have some very trustworthy contacts associated with Sandhurst, as you might imagine, and I was able to procure your admissions material. Rexford was a name assigned for use at the academy, but wasn't your true name." Our visitor sat silently during Holmes's remarks. "But I was unable to learn your actual identify from the directors at Sandhurst. You may applaud their honoring a pledge of confidentiality. They did tell me that you failed to complete the training program and left after just a year-and-a-half of study."

"That is true, Mr. Holmes. I was uninterested in the study of military strategy from the outset and attended only under duress. All that marching and cavalry horses and weapons – well, I had no desire to continue those studies. I withdrew and came to London where I escaped the clutches of those who had pressured me to study military affairs.

"My true interest lay in books, in literature, in the study of art and music. Not exactly what my family had in mind for me. But in London, I could live almost anonymously, visiting museums, archives and – yes – bookshops, which is where I encountered Miss Barrington. You must believe me that I had no intention whatsoever to deceive her, and certainly no intention to become involved romantically. But as you know, Mr. Holmes, the brain cannot always dictate the sentiments of the heart."

"I have been fortunate in that regard," Holmes responded, "to have maintained the superior influence of the brain. But pray, carry on."

181

"Over the past few weeks, I found myself falling hopelessly in love with Miss Barrington. We shared so many interests and perspectives! But I also felt terribly guilty. Whenever she asked about my background, from where I came, or what I had done prior to our meeting, I had no choice, Mr. Holmes and Dr. Watson, but to prevaricate." He looked to me for understanding and I couldn't help giving a supportive nod.

"I couldn't reveal my true identity even to her without jeopardizing my anonymity. Oh, I know Penelope – Miss Barrington – would never voluntarily let slip she had befriended a prince, but I couldn't take that risk. At least, not until I had planned how to proceed. But I deeply care for her, and I gave her several pieces of family jewelry to demonstrate my deep affection."

"It was through the ring Miss Barrington still wore that I discerned your connection to the House of Thurn and Taxis," said Holmes. "That, and the particular cut of the tobacco in the cigars you gave to Mr. Collins – quite distinct as the style favoured by the princes of Germany.

"As to the ring, I have made quite a study of the crests of all the royal families of Europe. I quickly recognized the distinct dual lions and crosses of your family insignia stamped onto the back of the setting – the same crest, I note, on the handle of your very fine walking stick. Given the other mysteries surrounding your courtship, I decided to place the announcement that brought you to this meeting.

"And why did you place it in *The Londoner-Journal*," I inquired.

"I presumed that a German-speaking gentleman about to depart England, undoubtedly for Germany, was likely to be reading a newspaper that would include news about developments in his home country. Fortunately, my command of German remains passable. A quick perusal of recent editions at the newspaper office yesterday afternoon revealed the brief story about the unexpected death of Prince Maximilian of Thurn and Taxis. I had no doubt I had chanced on the precipitating event."

The prince stared at Holmes in astonishment, but then collected himself and continued his account.

"By then I had resolved to ask her hand in marriage," he said, returning to his narrative, "having determined there would be little conflict with any royal duties that might arise. My role, you see, was quite incidental since my older brother, Maximilian, had succeeded our grandfather in 1871 when he was but a child."

"He succeeded your grandfather?" I asked.

"Yes. Our father had died at a young age, just thirty-five. His life had been somewhat in turmoil, in part because of the great controversy surrounding his marriage to my mother, Helene, niece of the King of Bavaria. The king objected because my grandfather, despite his title, wasn't of a royal house. So, you can understand my hesitancy in entering into a marriage that might precipitate yet another family crisis – particularly if, as I intended, we remained residents of London rather than return to Germany as I had promised. Nevertheless, my love for Penelope took precedence over such concerns, even though I was uncertain how I might marry an English commoner, live in anonymity abroad, and still honor my family responsibilities, however minor, as a prince."

"And then, you learned that those responsibilities had changed," Holmes interjected. "But wait, I hear footsteps. Unless I'm mistaken, you will have an opportunity to complete your explanation in the presence of the person who deserves to hear it most."

Holmes opened the door before Mrs. Hudson had even had the opportunity to knock and drew Miss Penelope

Barrington into the room. She gasped slightly at seeing the man she knew as "Rexford", but then ran to his side. "Josephus!" she cried. "Is it you?" She flew into his arms and buried her face in his shoulder, sobbing heavily as the prince looked awkwardly towards us. Turning to my friend, she implored, "Mr. Holmes, however did you find him?" Turning to "Rexford" she asked, "Where have you been? Why have you not communicated with me?"

Holmes drew up another chair for the distraught young woman and bade us all sit. Mrs. Hudson thoughtfully had brought fresh tea and we poured cups as we settled into our chairs.

"Miss Barrington, I'm afraid you have been ill-treated by this gentleman, although he doesn't believe he ever intended to deceive you for malicious reasons."

The young woman looked confused. "What is he saying, Josephus?" she asked.

Holmes looked sharply at the young man. "Shall I explain, or will you?" he demanded. The prince stared at his feet in embarrassment and nodded towards Holmes.

"Very well. Miss Barrington. You believe yourself to be engaged to, and in love with, Josephus Rexford. I have the unhappy duty to tell you there is no 'Josephus Rexford'. This young man, in actuality, is Crown Prince Albert I of Thurn and Taxis."

Miss Barrington looked incredulously at the man she had presumed to be her fiancé. "Is this true, Josephus?" she gasped.

The prince unhappily nodded his head without looking at her. "Yes, Penelope, what Mr. Holmes says is accurate." He looked up, his face was filled with remorse. "But I implore you to believe that I never had any intention of misleading you. I fully intended to remain in London after we married. I had no responsibilities as the head of my family and, with my brother already established as Prince, no prospects those conditions would change."

"But they did change, did they not?" Holmes insisted.

Again, the young prince nodded his head and looked at the floor.

"Yes, two weeks ago," he began. "I received a wire from Regensburg, our family seat at St. Emmeram Castle. It contained the dreadful news that my brother Maximilian had suffered heart failure and died suddenly, just as our father had at a young age. Maximilian was just twenty-three years old!" He buried his face in his hands and his shoulders heaved. In a few moments, he was able to collect himself and after wiping his eyes with his handkerchief, he continued his recitation. "The wire informed me that I was now the head of the royal family: *the Prince!* It was a designation I have never coveted, not for a moment. You must understand! But fate had intervened, to my despair. Ignoring the request to return would destroy our family's history and disgrace our position!"

"Having learned of the death of the Prince," Holmes interjected, "it hardly required much conjecture to understand that you must be next in line and had been called home, however reluctantly, to assume your familial duties."

"Why could you not tell me this?" implored the young woman. "Did you think I would love you less if I knew you were a prince? Or more?"

Prince Albert looked distraught. "My life had changed," he explained. "My responsibilities had been altered in a manner I could never have imagined when I met you. My brother should have held this position for many decades, long enough to produce sufficient heirs to ensure the role of Prince would never descend upon my shoulders. I was, you must believe me, content to live in obscurity, here, in London, with you as my wife, Penelope.

"But that possibility was irrevocably changed by Maximilian's death. I find myself the Prince, against all my wishes, with duties and family obligations I cannot abandon, even for you."

"Then take me with you!" she implored.

The Prince's face grew dark, his brow knotted as he struggled to give voice to his emotions.

"I'm obliged to marry royalty," he finally said. "It is the custom, the expectation. As Josephus Rexford, I could marry you and spend my life without anyone caring or noticing. As Prince Albert the first, it is impossible to marry a British commoner, a clerk in a bookstore – even one as worthy as you."

"You realized the jewels you had conferred on the woman you intended to be your fiancé must remain within your family and therefore had to be returned," Holmes added. "But you didn't have the courage to explain the situation to Miss Barrington."

Again, the young man hung his head.

"You are correct, Mr. Holmes. I couldn't bring myself to recount this dreadful turn of events to you," he said, turning to the young woman. The tears that had been flowing down her cheeks had stopped now, and a more determined look was on her face.

"I would have returned them, of course," she said.

"I have no doubt," Albert answered. "But I couldn't bring myself to request that you do so, particularly at this time of the year! I'm ashamed to say that I hired a man to enter your rooms to recover the jewelry whilst you were at the book shop. He was surprised during his pilfering of your rooms and in making his escape, swept up some pieces of jewelry that weren't among the heirlooms I gave you. I will certainly return them."

"But he failed to secure the ring Miss Barrington was wearing," I added, "contrary to your instructions never to wear the jewelry in public."

"Yes. I worried someone would find it strange that so valuable piece was worn by a clerk. So, I had asked Penelope to wear them only inside, at least until we were married."

The young woman reached to her left hand with her right and gave a gentle tug on the ring still on her finger. "Here is your ring, Josephus – or Albert, or whatever it is you wish to be called," she said, a measure of annoyance clearly in her voice. She reached out to hand the ring to the prince, who regarded it like an infernal device.

"No," he cried, waving it away, "I wish you to keep it. To remember me and our dreams of a life together."

Miss Barrington stood and stepped over to the Prince. She grabbed his hand and turn it palm upward, and then placed the ring in his hand.

"I have no need to be reminded of 'our dreams'," she said curtly. "If I'm unfit to stand by your side as your wife, I'm uninterested in retaining the ring or in remembering you as many more Christmases – hopefully much happier ones – pass us by. I wish you a Happy Christmas in your palace, Your Majesty, and I bid you *adieu*." Miss Barrington turned abruptly and walked across the room, opening the door and disappearing onto the landing. We listened in silence as her footsteps marked the stairs down to the street.

The Prince looked about awkwardly, then placed the ring in his pocket.

"I – ah – I – " he began hesitatingly but Holmes waved his hand dismissively.

"I don't think there is much more to say," he declared, "except to bid you a safe journey back to Thurn and Taxis." He strode to the door and opened it, gesturing to the young Prince. Albert looked about awkwardly before curtly nodding and departing. Outside, in Baker Street, we saw a carriage and fine horse waiting for him.

"A sad story, wouldn't you say?" I asked that evening as we dined at Wilton's in St. James, the restaurant decorated with candles, holly, and ribbons for the approaching holiday. "Star-crossed lovers and all that, denied a chance at happiness by a quirk death and succession to royal duties. Pity. Such a nice couple."

"Nonsense!" Holmes rejoined. "I can think of no other case in my experience that demonstrated more acutely the absurdity a system of royalty without responsibility! It is one thing to make such marriage decisions when one has a nation or an Empire to run. After all, one cannot imagine the Prince of Wales marrying a school teacher, it goes without saying. But Thurn and Taxis? Pray show me on the map of Europe the location of that nation! Surely the princehood associated with such a fantastical place is but sheer fantasy, the perpetuation of centuries of the drawing and redrawing of national boundaries that resulted in the swallowing up of innumerable inconsequential principalities. Albert will have a title, but little else. He rules no territory. He has no subjects. And yet in order to possess so meaningless a title, he is willing to abandon the woman he had come to truly love and who loved him – not for his title or nobility, but as a man."

Holmes popped an oyster in his mouth and followed it with a long drink of chilled sauvignon blanc.

"No, Watson, we have witnessed an example of the outdated micro-nationalism that I fear will someday produce a far greater number of victims than has the duplicitous suitor, Prince Albert of Thurn and Taxis. And, I might add, a man of so little character does not, in my view, deserve the affection and trust of a woman as loyal and honourable as Miss Barrington."

We finished our dinner with a delectable brandy aperitif to brace us against the December chill. Walking back to Baker Street amid the jingling of sleigh bells on the carriages bustling about, a swirl of snow had begun falling and had begun to cover the grime of London's streets by the time we arrived at our rooms.

I gave little thought to this case until I read several years later that Albert I, the 8th Prince of Thurn and Taxis, had been wed to the Archduchess Margarethe Klementine, the third daughter of the Archduke Joseph Karl of Austria, a descendent of the Holy Roman Emperor. Eventually this royal pair would have eight children – all the men, save one who joined the Benedictine monks, marrying princesses of similarly non-existent states.

As to Penelope Barrington, she happily recovered from the distress caused her by her brief engagement to the non-existent Josephus Rexford. Within the year, she was engaged and married to a young barrister who soon stood successfully for Parliament. Together they raised six children of their own and, as those who follow literature are aware, she became quite a noted poet in her own right.

The Case of the
Despicable Client

Throughout the many years of my friendship and collaboration with Sherlock Holmes, we encountered a wide variety of clients wishing to consult with the famous detective. Kings and princes, statesmen, noble families – all often crossed the threshold of our rooms at 221B Baker Street. So did jilted lovers, and the victims of theft, kidnappings, blackmail, and those accused of having committed horrendous murders. Each case in its own way served to illustrate Holmes's extraordinary intellectual gifts and analytical skills.

To be sure, there were clients who were discomforting but whom Holmes, for reasons of the intricacies of the circumstance, nevertheless found intriguing. I recall the matter of the eccentric member of the House of Lords who had smuggled a performing elephant and its pet talking parrot into England, as well as the lunatic physician of Merseyside and his abominable surgical experiments, cases upon which Holmes would rarely comment.

So, there was some precedent for the disquieting matter that compelled Holmes's urgent return to London from his home in Sussex during the spring of 1917 –

> *Arriving 2 p.m. Waterloo. Intriguing case. Despicable client. Meet me if you are interested.*
>
> *Holmes*

– the wire read. I sat in my home mulling over the meaning of the note, and then hired a cab to take me to a rendezvous with my old friend.

It was not a happy time in London. The Great War had been underway for nearly three years, with little prospect for a quick end in sight. Tens of thousands of young British men, not to mention those of other combatants, had been slaughtered like lambs on the Continent with very little military benefit accruing to either side. On the high seas, German submarines – *U*-boats – were sinking dozens of British ships at an enormous cost in food, armaments, and human life. A bright ray of hope had only recently raised our hopes with the decision, after years of neutrality, by the United States to join with the allies in active combat.

A year earlier, a calamity had unfolded in Ireland in April 1916, creating an unfortunate second front for Britain in that troubled province. The so-called "Easter Rising" had riven the island for a week, resulting in nearly five-hundred deaths, many of them innocent people uninvolved in the protests of Republicans seeking independence. Embittered sentiments were further inflamed with the execution of many of the leaders of the rebellion and another two-thousand prisoners accused of involvement had been shipped off to prisons in England. Those developments were to factor greatly in Holmes's and my activities of the next several days.

At two o'clock, Holmes's train arrived and I was delighted to greet him on the crowded platform. "Good to see you!" I cried, clapping him on the shoulder.

"And you, Watson!" he replied, gingerly touching my shoulder that had never quite fully recuperated from the nasty injury caused by a Jezail bullet in Afghanistan all those years ago. "Let us find some lunch and I'll fill you in on what I know of the matter that brings me to London."

Holmes had booked a room at the very upscale Savoy, indicating that his employer must indeed be a person of some affluence. After dropping off his bags, we soon found ourselves settled in a comfortable café in Covent Gardens, enjoying lunch as Holmes related his knowledge of the case.

"The case had its mysteries even before we dive into it," Holmes began. "I've been asked by the Home Secretary to meet with a nameless client later today to hear his appeal for assistance."

He pulled a sheet of paper from his breast pocket, unfolded it, and smoothed it out on the table before sliding it to me for my own perusal. It was a letter on official government stationery and read as follows:

My Dear Mr. Sherlock Holmes,

You would do me the great personal honour to come to London forthwith to meet with an individual in great need of your expertise and discretion. Because this matter has some significant implications for domestic security, I entreat you to consent to such an interview, although I confess that the request originates from a person you might understandably consider to be a most despicable client.

Yours very truly,
Viscount Cave, Home Secretary

"What an extraordinary request," I exclaimed. "Why would the Home Secretary presume to make such a request of you?

"I can only imagine the situation involves either the national interest or some other matter of great personal concern to the Viscount" Holmes replied. He lowered his voice even softer. "The matter, I have been assured, is nothing less than one of life and death."

"And yet you have no idea whose life or death," I observed. "Surely we will have to know more before we commit ourselves to the inquiry."

Holmes smiled at my words. "I am deeply gratified to hear you use the plural 'we' when discussing the case," he said brightly. "I wouldn't want to begin such an inquiry without my Boswell by my side."

"I hadn't even given the matter any thought," I replied. "I presumed you were soliciting my assistance, and I certainly have no intention of being left out of the affair."

We were scheduled to receive our as-yet unnamed client at four o'clock in Holmes's room at the Savoy. We were comfortably ensconced and preparing for our tea when there was a sharp rap on the door at exactly that hour. "Very precise," Holmes observed as he strode to the door, which he opened to reveal a middle-aged gentleman of perhaps fifty with wavy black hair, a manicured handlebar mustache, and a look of great anguish on his face. His clothing was meticulous and obviously of an expensive manufacture, and he carried a bowler hat and a long, black umbrella, although the day was clear with little prospect for rain. His face was one of fear mixed with great exhaustion.

"Mr. Holmes?" he inquired.

"I am Sherlock Holmes," the detective confirmed. He regarded the new arrival carefully before stepping aside and inviting our guest to join us in the sitting area of his rooms. The man seemed surprised by my presence and turned to Holmes with a look of alarm.

"I was assured that I was to meet with you alone!" he explained, looking from me to Holmes and then back to me. "The matter is highly confidential, I assure you. I'm afraid I must ask you to leave Mr. Holmes and me to our discussion," he concluded looking in my direction.

"This is Dr. Watson," Holmes explained. "He isn't only my friend and colleague, but an indispensable asset in my investigatory endeavors. I would no more consider taking a case without him than without my eyes and ears." I was touched by Holmes's endorsement of my contribution to our collaboration. "Watson is a non-negotiable partner, Mr. – ah, I didn't catch your name."

"I did not offer it – at least, not as yet," our guest explained. "I should like to explain my predicament first. If, after hearing my story, you are inclined to become engaged, I will tell you all the remaining information you wish to know."

Holmes considered this offer for a moment, then offered a thin smile and shook his head. "Come, come, Mr. J. Bruce Ismay, it will not do," he declared. "I do not accept commissions in order to play guessing games with my clients. Either lay all of the facts before Dr. Watson and me and entrust us to pursue the matter, or good day to you."

Our visitor stood glaring at Holmes, having forgotten my presence altogether. For an uncomfortable moment, he said nothing.

"Mr. Ismay may be known to you," Holmes said, turning in my direction, "as the former president of the International Mercantile Marine Company." Holmes paused as the caller shifted uneasily. "It was at his direction that his subsidiary, the White Star Line, constructed the unsinkable ship *Titanic* in the Belfast shipyard of Harland and Wolff. It was on that ill-fated ship in April 1912 that our visitor barely escaped with his life by climbing into one of the last lifeboats to depart the sinking leviathan, a bit of good fortune not shared by over fifteen-hundred fellow travelers, especially those in second and third class."

Holmes's words hung heavy in the air. Ismay made no effort to contradict him or explain his actions, which had been thoroughly documented in the investigations that followed the tragedy on the *Titanic's* maiden voyage. The shipping magnate's chin dropped to his chest, and he remained silent, awaiting additional condemnation.

"A coward," he said, his voice cracking slightly. "'J. *Brute* Ismay,' that is how Mr. Hearst refers to me in his American newspapers." He sat down wearily in one of the chairs, although Holmes hadn't invited him to do so. "Others have said worse," he added, his voice trailing off.

"And with good reason!" I interjected, drawing a rebuking stare from Holmes.

"Your actions have been thoroughly investigated on both sides of the Atlantic," Holmes declared, "including your urging Captain Smith to increase speed despite your knowledge of dangerous icebergs in the North Atlantic."

"Not to mention your decision to take a seat in a lifeboat whilst hundreds of women and children drowned!" I added, again receiving a disapproving look from Holmes.

Ismay's chin remained on his chest, and he was working his mouth quite desperately for some time before he was able to speak. "There is no charge that you can make against me, Doctor, of greater censure than that for which I've already been censured," he began. "There is not a day that passes that I don't see the faces of those desperate children and their mothers and accept that I bear some responsibility for their fate. But," he paused to clear his throat, "I did not take a seat from any of them. I did not deny anyone an opportunity of escape. My only regret now is that I survived to endure a life of disapprobation and disgrace. I only hope that I may, in some small way, compensate for the great sadness my company and my own decisions have caused."

For several moments, Ismay's words hung in the air like smoke from one of Holmes's pipes. The shipping magnate remained a picture of defeat, his head bowed and resting in his hands. Holmes had taken up a pipe and was smoking it, looking out the window at the weakening light of an April afternoon.

"Mr. Holmes, I am here to see you on a matter quite unrelated to the *Titanic* tragedy," he explained. "You are aware of last year's Uprising in Ireland? Yes, of course you are. For some time, I've made my home at Costelloe Lodge, in County Galway. The location affords me the opportunity for contemplation and fishing, which relieve my mind from the hideous memories of which I have no desire to be reminded. And I have only to follow the river a short ways to be at the sea once again, where my heart truly dwells.

"I've been fortunate to leave the *Titanic* tragedy behind me for the past several years – to go on with my life and try to move beyond the reprobation, although I know I can never escape entirely. Yet now something has occurred that is causing me great distress and which compels me to seek your assistance."

"And why should the Home Secretary be involved in soliciting my involvement?" Holmes asked with a tone of reproach in his voice.

"He is an acquaintance of some standing," Ismay acknowledged. "I had little doubt you would ignore an entreaty that came from me alone. I thought perhaps I could prevail upon him to gain me access to you. My apologies if that seems unconventional, but I'm quite distressed and need discreet assistance that, I believe, only you might provide."

He looked imploringly at Holmes, who sucked on his pipe thoughtfully before responding. "I make you no promises, Ismay," he replied, "but I will agree to listen to the facts. If they have merit, quite apart from your own personal interest, I may engage in the matter."

"That is fair enough," the magnate replied. "I assure you, I stand to gain nothing whatsoever from a resolution of this matter. My only interest is protecting a totally innocent child whose life is in danger."

"And why, may I ask, is this matter of such importance to you?"

Ismay stood and walked toward the large window overlooking the street. "I should think that would be obvious, Mr. Holmes."

"If this were a simple matter of a kidnapping and ransom payment, there would be no need for the Home Secretary to call me into the matter," observed Holmes, "You would enter into negotiations with the kidnappers, establish terms, and meet their demand. The authorities are concerned about giving in to extortionists, but it is very different when there is a deep personal involvement. Am I correct, Mr. Ismay?"

Ismay regarded Holmes and then me. "Yes, I confess there is more to this matter," he said. "It is, however, of a very personal and compromising nature that I'm not free to discuss."

"Then good day, Mr. Ismay," Holmes declared. "I wish you nothing but good luck in securing the release of the child." He took several strides toward the door, reached for the doorknob, turned it, and pulled the door inward. "It is quite impossible for me to engage myself in an inquiry when the source of the mystery is my own client!"

Ismay became distraught and walked to him. "I implore you, sir, to listen to the circumstances! Then you will be free to make whatever decision you wish concerning your engagement in this matter."

Holmes sat down in a chair facing Ismay, as did I. "Very well," he agreed. "Let me hear the facts."

"The child is nearly five years old, and has been residing in Galway with his mother," he began. "I had met the young woman – Catherine Buckley was her name – during the *Titanic* voyage, as improbable as it seems. She was traveling in second class. From time to time, I would see her as she passed by and we would share a few words, although the crew discouraged other passengers from speaking with those in first class like myself. Given my status on board, I felt I could bend the rules to show some kindness.

"At any rate, she told me she was just twenty-two years old and working to earn some money for herself so she might find a better position when she returned to County Mayo. I must say I admired her spunk and resolved to assist her once I had returned from New York . . . ." he said, his voice growing fainter and trailing off.

"Once the collision with the iceberg occurred and the rescue effort commenced, I was too distracted to consider Miss Buckley's whereabouts," he added. I saw Holmes shift in his seat, but Ismay ignored this sign of discomfort with his haughty statement. "I was engaged with Captain Smith and others in assessing the damage, and then realizing there was no hope, I went outside onto the deck to aid the crew in escorting passengers to the lifeboats.

"The list of the *Titanic* quickly became quite acute, and soon we were unable to successfully launch any more lifeboats from the rear of the ship, and so I moved up close to where the water was beginning to pour onto the deck near the first funnel. I couldn't believe the sight: the terror, the screaming. I tried to focus on moving people toward the remaining boats and collapsibles." He looked to Holmes for approval, but received none. "As the inquiries found, but there simply wasn't enough space for many on board. That was in part my responsibility, I agree. The ship lacked sufficient lifeboats for all of the passengers and crew. I do not seek to escape responsibility for the oversight.

"After helping to load and launch many of the boats, I found myself standing by Collapsible C when I heard a woman's voice pleadingly call to me. 'Mr. Ismay, can you help me?" she cried. I couldn't imagine who it might be when suddenly, from behind a pillar, the figure of Miss Buckley appeared. She was dressed in her nightclothes and a dressing gown, having evidently been roused from her bed. With nearly all the means of escaping the doomed ship already cast off, the poor girl was understandably filled with dread. I grabbed her arm and pulled her toward the Collapsible C which was preparing to be lowered.

"Get in!" I commanded, helping the crewmembers aboard the boat lift her over the gunwale as it began creaking down towards the frigid sea. In a moment, she was aboard and turned to me over her shoulder.

"'Oh, Mr. Ismay, do not abandon me!' she wailed. 'I am so alone and scared!'"

"My heart nearly broke but I knew my position ruled out my joining her in the little boat, and it continued to crank downward. I looked about and realized I was alone on the tilting deck. First Officer Murdoch had run off to supervise other rescues, I presumed. I turned back to the boat. Miss Buckley was imploring me again, and now she was joined by others on board, most of whom seemed to be of Middle Eastern extraction and unfamiliar with my name or my role. I made a decision – yes, an impulsive one. There was room in the boat, there was no one in sight to help into it and, it seemed, it was only a matter of minutes before the rushing sea would make it impossible to escape.

"So, yes, Mr. Holmes, I jumped into the boat as it was cranked down to the sea, and in doing so, I saved my life while hundreds aboard the *Titanic* lost theirs. There was nothing to be gained by remaining on the deck. The investigating commissions concluded as much, as you must know. Had I declined to climb onto the collapsible, the British inquiry concluded, I would 'merely have added one more life, namely, his own, to the number of those lost'. I shall never forget those words. And yet, I live with the shame of that decision every day, and the disdain of nearly everyone I meet.

"But I helped to rescue the poor girl who was surely lost but for my assistance," he said, sitting a bit straighter in his chair and thrusting his jaw forward, "and in my view, that was a redeeming act in the midst of great tragedy."

"Admirable, no doubt," Holmes said without much conviction. "But where does this leave us with respect to the matter which has brought you to see me today?"

"I saw Miss Buckley only briefly in New York before I returned to Ireland. She decided to remain in America and try to build a new life there. I heard only rarely from her about her life there, and I did, on occasion, wire her some money to assist with her expenses. Late last year, I received a note telling me that she had met a young Irishman recently arrived in New York and was hoping to marry him, but that he had been arrested for his role in the Uprising.

"Then, three days ago, my butler announced there was a young woman calling upon me, and I was stunned to discover it was Miss Buckley in a most terrible state of distress. She informed me there was a child, born a year or so after her arrival in New York. I did not inquire about the circumstances, of course. It took some time, but I was able to calm her to the point that she told me the boy, John, had gone missing from their flat in Galway. She had left him with a sitter as she did every day upon going to work. When she returned, neither the sitter nor the baby was at her home."

"And the sitter was the person who regularly watched the child?" Holmes asked.

"No, the regular sitter had taken ill, and this was her sister who was temporarily replacing her," Ismay relayed. "Of course, Miss Buckley is young and naïve and didn't think to confirm the identity of the alleged 'sister'. When she rang up the regular sitter, she couldn't be found either."

"Was there a note of any kind?" Holmes inquired. "Any sort of explanation?"

"None, until a day later when this note was slipped under Miss Buckley's door." He handed Holmes a sheet of paper, and the detective opened it gingerly, and laid it on the table before him.

"A cheap paper and cheaper pencil," Holmes observed. "Likely something lying about for some time – certainly not recently purchased." He caught Ismay's quizzical look and pointed to the paper. "You can see the yellowed edges where the sun has bleached the exposed portion of the page. This paper hasn't been stored in a box or drawer.

"A left-handed writer – you can tell by the slant of the lettering and the small smudging of the graphite where the cuff has been dragged across the writing. I would say the author is a young person, probably a man, literate but not terribly well educated, who works with his hands – but certainly a mechanic or some sort, and not a carpenter – and with a marked political bent."

Ismay looked quizzically at him. "How can you possibly know all that?"

"It is my business to know things," Holmes sharply replied, as he began to read the note.

Miss Buckley,

Your son is all right but won't be for long if you don't come up with £5,000 pounds by Friday evening and I'm not playing games with you so don't call the coppers or you'll never again see your boy alive. You can get the money and don't pretend you can't. So do it. OR ELSE!!! I'll be in touch with you about the money.

I.R.B.

"Hmm. The Irish Republican Brotherhood," said Holmes, identifying the revolutionary group behind the previous year's Easter Uprising. "Just four days to secure the money. Tell me, where did these fiends believe she could possibly secure such a sum? Surely they must know it would require a seamstress years to accumulate a fraction of such a large amount of money."

"I must speculate that she mentioned to someone that she knew me," Ismay said. "I have no idea if she did so inadvertently. Some of her friends must have had I.R.B. sympathies and evidently have decided to squeeze me for some money by kidnapping Miss Buckley's little boy."

"Well, why don't you just pay the money?" Holmes asked.

"Pay blackmail?" Ismay said. "Surely that wouldn't be the end of it. Both Miss Buckley and the boy would still live in perpetual danger, and I would be at constant risk of additional claims." He shook his head. "No, no. I need you to find the boy, free him from his captors, and see that these reprehensible criminals are turned over to the police!"

"You are asking quite a bit," I interjected. "This sounds like a job for the police or the military, but hardly for a retired detective!"

"It is true. I am asking a great deal, but the Home Secretary believes this incident may be tied up with the rebels and the Easter Uprising," Ismay continued. "The government doesn't want to provoke yet another series of riots by heavy-handed police action in Galway. They, and I, were hoping for a less public means of alleviating the problem, and the Home Secretary naturally thought of you."

"Return to Ireland, Mr. Ismay where I will meet you tomorrow," Holmes said after a pause. "By then, I will hopefully have devised a plan for addressing this matter."

Ismay left explicit instructions for finding Costelloe Lodge and, early the next morning, Holmes and I were on a ship heading for Galway. Holmes spent the trip with his head buried in a number of books and pamphlets that he'd acquired at the local library prior to our departure, including the full record of the British inquiry into the loss of the *Titanic*. It was a short drive from the Galway dock to Ismay's estate outside the city, where the shipping titan seemed relieved that we had safely arrived.

Costelloe Lodge was an imposing white manor house with expansive lawns and a grand view of the waterway out to the Irish Sea. Our bags were taken by two servants, and we were shown to large and comfortably furnished rooms. A day of travel had left us too weary for extended conversation and we retired after a dinner expertly prepared by Ismay's kitchen staff. After a sound night's sleep, we met Ismay for breakfast. We had just two days before the deadline set by the kidnappers, and Holmes was anxious to have any additional information concerning the case.

After breakfast, we gathered in the parlor with its large stone fireplace and windows looking out over the lush lawn. "Is there anything that you haven't yet told me about Miss Buckley or your relationship with her?" Holmes inquired. Ismay began to say something but caught himself. He shook his head.

"Please, Mr. Holmes, if you could just check to see that she is well and the boy released, I would be most grateful," he pleaded. "I'm prepared to pay what they demand. But please hurry! They sounded so desperate. I have little confidence they will refrain from harming the youngster." He appeared highly agitated, and I thought we should have just taken our leave, but Holmes stood his ground and continued to await a fuller response from the shipping man. The two men stared at each other for a long moment before Ismay collapsed into a nearby chair, his head in his hands.

"When did you first know that he was your son?" Holmes asked abruptly. Ismay gave no reply, although I started. I opened my mouth to speak, but Holmes quickly motioned me to remain silent while Ismay continued to bury his face. When he gathered himself and raised his head, it was clear that he was distraught. He stood, walked to the door of the dining room, and looked into the hall. Then he closed it tightly and returned to where Holmes and I were standing.

"I supposed I could deny it, but to what end?" he asked. "I was a fool to believe I could conceal the facts from you."

"Indeed you were," Holmes reproached him without compassion. "You summon me to Ireland in the wake of civil unrest and war on the Continent to inquire about a child you have never met, born of a woman you haven't seen in years. And you expect that I will accept that yours is merely a compassionate concern for the child or his mother?" Holmes cried contemptuously. "I had no doubt, long before I set foot on the ship yesterday, that I was being summoned to Galway to find your kidnapped child."

Ismay's face couldn't mask his dismay at Holmes's discovery. "The story that I gave you in London wasn't completely true," he began. "I had met Miss Buckley here in Galway some months before the launching of the *Titanic*. She was employed at the home of a nearby friend where she was working as a cook's assistant." Here he paused to gain courage for what followed. "She was very young, perhaps only seventeen or eighteen, and our friendship, if you could call it that, was admittedly irregular."

"I should say so!" I could not help myself from exclaiming. 'She was less than half your age, and barely a grown woman at that!"

Holmes pursed his lips and shook his head almost imperceptibly in a disapproving manner.

"I cannot contest your statement, Doctor," Ismay continued. "I had four children of my own, not to mention my wife, and had endured a great deal of pressure in my business. But I offer no excuse. It was an uncharacteristic and unfortunate act of irresponsible behaviour."

"And then, I presume, your problems multiplied at a rather dramatic rate," Holmes inquired.

"Yes," Ismay added contemplatively. "Shortly after the first of that year, 1912, Miss Buckley let me know me that she . . . ." He faltered, then regathered his courage. "She informed me that she was with child. *My* child." He grew quiet. "What could I do?" he asked. "My company, my family, my reputation all at stake. I decided to offer her the opportunity of leaving Ireland and starting fresh, with sufficient resources, in America. She expressed a great interest in doing so. I always book a cabin on the maiden voyage on my ships and was planning to do the same on the *Titanic,* which was departing in early April from Queenstown, just a few hours south of here. It wasn't difficult for me to arrange a second class cabin for Miss Buckley.

"I believed it was necessary to be discrete under the circumstances," he continued, "and I only met her on board briefly once on the tenth of April at the very beginning of the voyage. We planned to meet in New York after our arrival, where I was to provide her money to enable her to get situated and to care for the baby when it arrived.

"I confess that in the swirl of the parties and the receptions on board, I gave her little thought. I knew she had comfortable quarters and that we would have time to settle any remaining issues between us after our arrival. Once the collision occurred, I was completely focused on helping the passengers and advising the crew on the dangers to the ship, and I quite forgot about Miss Buckley until I heard her plaintive voice on the deck, near the collapsible."

Ismay paused in his story and walked to the window. He looked across the lush lawn, out at the blue water and ships leaving churned white foam in their wake. "What was I to do?" he asked. "Of course, I quickly hustled her into the collapsible before it was launched and I was preparing to return to the crew and other passengers when she called again. 'Mr. Ismay! Oh, God, do not abandon me now!'

"I was sick with dread," he said, and even now, five years later, his face reflected utter horror. "Was I to cast off the young woman carrying my own child into the sea, without offering her any protection? Without even providing for her the money I had promised to help her escape the disgrace and poverty that otherwise awaited her? I couldn't behave so reprehensively. So yes, I climbed into the collapsible myself and comforted the terrified child. The rowers moved us off far away from the dreadful sight, and soon we watched my magnificent ship rise up stern first. With that horrible, deafening roar, she broke in half, and then, amid the screams and wailing, plunged into the sea forever."

He turned away from us once again and covered his eyes with his hand to blot out the gruesome scene. After a few moments of uncomfortable silence, he continued.

"Of course, it was impossible for me to explain why I chose to enter the collapsible when all the criticism began," he said. "Was it not terrible enough that I had commissioned a ship that had . . . . " His voice broke and he stopped speaking. There was a sharp intake of breath, and he continued. "On board the *Carpathia*, I dared not pay close attention to her, lest rumors begin. My identity was known to the other survivors, and needless to say, my actions were carefully monitored. But once we arrived in New York, I was able to find her a comfortable room and, despite all of the press inquiries and official reports, I visited her several times to assure she had all she needed, including the best of medical care. Before I returned to England, I gave her £5,000 and instructed her to notify me if, in the future, she found that she needed additional funds to support herself and the child."

"And did you, in fact, hear from Miss Buckley after your return to London?" Holmes inquired.

"Yes, toward the end of the year, I received a letter explaining that the child had been born – a boy – and that she was well," Ismay reported. "She named him 'John', which is my given name, but one that few know and none else use. She sent me this photo as well." He reached into his desk and pulled out a small picture of an infant.

"And since?" Holmes asked.

Ismay shook his head. "Not a word until a week ago when she suddenly appeared at my door with the ransom note. I had no idea she was back in Ireland, let alone living so close by. She was naturally distraught and seeking my assistance. What could I do but to use whatever resources I had available to assist her?

"Of course, there was no question of going to the local authorities. I spoke to the Home Secretary, an old friend, and explained I desperately needed the most confidential of services. He was totally discreet, of course, and was kind enough to put me in touch with you, sir. I entreat you to do your best to find the culprits and save the boy." His voice caught again. "My son," he corrected himself. He looked to Holmes and then to me. "Will you help me?" he asked mournfully.

Shortly before noon, Holmes and I were in one of Ismay's comfortable motorcars on our way to Miss Buckley's address in Galway, a small two-room apartment above a locksmith's shop just off Quay Street. A knock on the door was answered by a young woman who couldn't have been more than twenty-five, but whose face showed strain and fatigue. Her brown hair fell in ringlets below her shoulders, and she wore a dark green dress with a cream-colored blouse.

"Can I help you?" she asked.

"We have come at the request of Mr. Ismay," my companion replied.

At the mention of the name, the young woman started. "What?" she said. "I thought he'd be coming himself."

"That would not have been possible," Holmes responded. "But we are here to aid you. May we come in?"

She cautiously opened the door to the small room and we entered. It was dark but tidy, and there was a small table with several chairs and a small sofa in the room.

"My name is Sherlock Holmes. Perhaps you have heard of me?" he asked as he surveyed the room, but the young woman gave no sign of recognition. "This is my friend and associate, Dr. Watson." Again, no sign of familiarity. "I take it that you are Miss Catherine Buckley?"

She nodded her head affirmatively but made no suggestion that we sit. "Why are you here?" she asked.

"I am a detective – a private detective," Holmes began. "I very much want to help you find your son and return him safely to you."

Miss Buckley considered his words. "Have you brought the money, then?" she inquired. "For the men who have him?"

Holmes looked at her and surveyed the small room. "I'm prepared to deliver the ransom once the boy is returned."

"Oh, but they are demanding the money, Mr. Holmes, *before* they will release my boy."

Holmes shook his head. "I'm afraid that is quite impossible," he responded. "I must know that he's unharmed and restored to you first. Otherwise, we might well lose the money and the boy together."

Miss Buckley considered Holmes's words and paused before speaking again. "Do you know the identity of the boy's father?" she inquired hesitatingly.

"I know all of the details on that subject, as well as what transpired on board the *Titanic* and in New York," he responded. "Why did you return to Ireland?"

Miss Buckley eyed him cautiously. "Why is that important?"

"Well, you hadn't been in touch with Mr. Ismay for five years, and then suddenly you reached out to him with a report that you had returned to Galway and your child has been kidnapped," Holmes continued. "I'm naturally curious about your decision to return from America, and why you didn't send a message to Mr. Ismay earlier."

Miss Buckley suddenly became agitated. "I didn't contact him for the same reasons I'm not interested in speaking with you!" she cried. "It's none of your bloody business what I do! I've had a hard enough time thanks to Mr. J. Bruce Ismay, and if I need money to protect my son, then I will do what I need to get it, and not be treated like a witness in the dock, thank you please!" She strode over to the door which she opened. "Good afternoon!"

Holmes and I walked down the two flights of stairs to Quay Street and found a café just down the street for tea. We sat silently as the throngs passed by on their way home from work or the market while the tea steeped in its small green pot. Finally, I couldn't hold my tongue any longer.

"So what do you make of Miss Buckley?"

"What indeed?" he repeated. "A curiously well-ordered flat, don't you agree?"

"I saw nothing there that seemed especially out of place," I responded.

"Yes, that is exactly right," said Holmes. He sprang to his feet, nearly knocking over the small table and our tea-pot. "I shall meet you at Costelloe House later. Be cautious. There is evil afoot." In a moment, he had disappeared into the crowd and was gone.

"Where is Holmes?" asked Ismay when the car dropped me at his front door an hour later.

"Is he not back yet?" I responded. "Well, I'm unsure then."

"Did you see her?" Ismay asked.

"I should say that we did – a most charming young lady!" I added facetiously. "She asked for the ransom money and then fairly threw us out when Holmes declined to give it to her!"

"What!" he exclaimed. "I cannot imagine what prompted such a response. She has never taken such a tone with me."

"You have seen little of her in recent years," I noted. "Perhaps her personality changed with the sinking of the ship, or with motherhood, or as a result of this dreadful kidnapping. But she was unappreciative of Holmes's offer to assist her in locating your young son."

Holmes returned after I had already retired for the night, and I had hoped to hear about the preceding night's activities during breakfast the next morning. Instead, an envelope was delivered to me when I arrived in the sun-drenched breakfast room. A brief note included an apology for his late evening and early departure, but he would telephone later in the morning if possible. I busied myself with a game of croquet on the lawn. At eleven o'clock, Ismay's butler found me to announce there was a telephone call awaiting me, and I followed him to the library.

"Watson," the familiar voice declared.

"Are you all right?" I asked. "What have you been up to? Have you been in touch with Miss Buckley again?"

"Listen carefully," he interrupted. "I want you to come to Galway immediately. Bring Ismay with you, and also £10,000 – the price has doubled." He provided me with an address, which I jotted down in my notebook. "But don't drive in one of his fancy automobiles," he added, "and do not use a chauffeur."

"Why?" I inquired.

"Because, my friend, I have every hope that you will survive this trip, and perhaps I will as well," Holmes said. "However, arriving amid the accoutrements of the landed gentry would quite likely diminish our chances of ever seeing London again. Goodbye."

I hung up the receiver and thought about Holmes's words. Although they were shocking, I could have sworn, knowing him as I do, that there was a hint of humor in that most serious admonition.

I relayed Holmes's request to Ismay and he quickly summoned one of the ordinary cars used for running errands to be driven to the front of the house. Having slipped my service revolver into my pocket along with the money in a brown envelope, I jumped in beside Ismay and he took off along the coastal road towards Galway. As we neared the city, one could still see the impact of the previous year's Uprising: Burned buildings and walls shattered by the salvos from the *HMS Gloucester* that had been stationed in Galway Bay during the rebellion. Fortunately, since the release of the Galway rebels in December, the mood in the city had remained largely subdued.

Our route took us across the River Corrib, then through several twisting streets to a working class area of the city. A number of pubs were bustling even though it was early afternoon, and I couldn't help but speculate whether any of the rough-looking men ambling about had, just a year before, been among those in the Irish Republican Brigade that had taken up arms against His Majesty's Government.

We found the address on Churchyard Street and knocked on the heavy wooden door. There was the sound of some shuffling inside, and then a gruff voice.

"Who's that?" a disembodied man's voice demanded.

"This is Dr. John Watson," I replied. "I have been instructed to come to this address by Mr. Sherlock Holmes. If he is in there, I insist that you open this door immediately and admit me!"

"*You* insist," the voice derisively repeated. There was the sound of the lock being worked from the inside and the door opened slightly enough for the man to peer at me, although I was unable to make out anything of his appearance because of the dark interior. "And who's that with you?"

Ismay began to answer, but I cut him off, not knowing to whom I was speaking.

"You just open that door and admit us," I responded. "Mr. Sherlock Holmes has asked that this gentleman accompany me. I'm concerned only with my friend's security. I assure you this man does not represent the police." I added a falsehood, but one I felt warranted under the circumstances. "And we are not armed."

A blood-chilling cackle emanated from behind the door. "Hah! You aren't the police!" he mocked. "You aren't armed!" I could hear the jangle of the chain as he removed the lock from the door and it swung open. "Right this way, Doctor," the man said, stepping aside so we could enter the building.

The passageway leading into the sitting room was darkened and smelled of stale cigarette smoke. We entered a room in which four men sat around a table, upon which a partially-filled bottle of whiskey and several glasses were placed. The men all were roughly dressed and some needed shaves. Most wore caps that partially concealed their faces. Little light filtered into the small room from the broken shutters outside the grimy windows. None spoke as Ismay and I entered the room.

"Where is Mr. Holmes?" I declared, attempting to sound as authoritative as possible. "I'll not engage in any discussion with any of you until I know he is safe." With that, I drew out my service revolver carefully so as not to present a threat but to let the men know I was indeed armed and prepared to defend myself.

"Come, come, Watson, our situation isn't nearly perilous enough to require a display of firearms!" said a familiar voice coming from the vicinity of the table.

"What?" I cried, expecting to see my friend tied up on the floor in a darkened corner. "Holmes? Where have they put you?"

One of the men at the table stood up. "I'm here, Watson," the man said. In the faint light of the room, I could now see the familiar form of Sherlock Holmes, dressed in workingman's clothing, a cheap cloth cap pulled down on his head, and a cigarette in his hand. "I decided that it would be safer conducting my inquiries in their neighborhood if dressed like one of the locals. It didn't take long for these men to find me."

I replaced my pistol in my jacket and briskly walked to him and grasped his arms with both of my hands. "It is you!" I exclaimed, barely recognizing him through the disguise. "Are you safe?"

"Well, 'safe' is a relative term, but for the moment, I believe that we are free from danger – at least my colleagues here so assure me," he said. "Ismay, you and Watson should sit down so we may discuss the business at hand – some of which I suspect will come as a surprise to you."

I had quite forgotten entirely about Ismay, who had shrunk into the shadows, evidently hoping not to be seen, but at Holmes's words he slowly walked forward and warily regarded the men around the table. Holmes motioned me to a chair and I sat, as did he. Ismay seemed more dubious about doing so, but under the stares of everyone else in the room, he tentatively joined us.

"Thanks to information provided by Miss Buckley and this rudimentary costume, I was able to meet these gentlemen," Holmes began. "Their names of are of no importance. And for the record, I have made clear my unequivocal disapproval of their political objectives and their violent tactics." There was a slight stirring amongst the others but no one raised any objection. "Similarly, these men have no particular interest in doing harm to us, and therefore, we are free to engage in conversation to see if we might resolve those matters which remain between us."

He pointed to the others in the room. "These are Republicans," he explained by way of introduction. "They are members of the I.R.B. that launched the Rebellion, and they tell me they remain as committed to their cause as they were the day they took up their positions at the Moyode Castle."

He paused for dramatic effect, to make sure no one would misinterpret his sentiments for our hosts or the motivations of his actions. "Yet I long ago learned an unpleasant lesson in life: Fulfilling one's duties sometimes involves interaction with disreputable men that one might otherwise choose to avoid. Such is the situation in this current matter."

Holmes walked around the table to stand over Ismay.

"I was retained to find and recover a child, the son of Miss Catherine Buckley of Galway, and *your* son, as well, Mr. Ismay."

Ismay abruptly pushed his chair away from the table stood up. "I have no intention of discussing such matters with the likes of these . . . '*gentlemen*', as you call them!" he insisted, shaking his fist. "You have no power over me!" he cried, pointing to the seated men who showed not the slightest sense of alarm over his outburst. "You can prove nothing! How dare you make these accusations and threats against me!"

"All that's true enough," said the tall, red-haired man who had led us into the room. "And you are free to go anytime you like." Ismay took a step towards the door. "But I would remind you, Mr. Ismay, that both your son and your reputation *are* very much within our power. And I will tell you without hesitation, if you walk out that door, you will never again regain whatever standing you might still retain or wish to have, either with your family or in society." He made a disapproving sound with his mouth. "Tsk, tsk. My, my, a prominent capitalist like you, knocking up a poor young Irish girl, shuttling her off to New York on your grand new steamship, paying her off so's she would keep quiet and just disappear. Such damnable behavior, Mr. Ismay!" The last words were spoken with ill-concealed contempt.

"You disgraceful traitor and blackmailer!" Ismay spat out. "Why, I could summon the police and have the lot of you thrown into prison before the sun sets, and you would rot there until you tell me the whereabouts of the lad."

"Undoubtedly you could," the man responded, "but if that was the wise course, don't you think Mr. Holmes here might have done exactly what you say?"

Ismay considered the man's words and returned to the table, slumping down in the chair. "You have no proof of anything you have said," he responded, regaining his combative bluster. "It is all your words against mine. Miss Buckley would never sanction such criminal behavior as you have taken against me."

A door at the far end of the room opened and a young woman walked in, her arm tightly held by another of the Irish band. "But my words *do* add some weight to the matter," she said. Ismay stared at her for a long while, his eyes searching to see her better in the thin light and smoke that hung in the room.

"Catherine? Is it you?" he called. "I cannot be sure."

"Oh yes, Mr. Ismay, it is I!" the young woman cried.

"And these devils have captured you as well as the boy?" he cried.

"Shortly after I wrote that note, there was a knock on my door," she explained. "These men," she pointed to the ruffians sitting around the table, "insisted that I come with them, if I wanted to see young John again. And so I am here. I didn't mean to engage you in this business, you must believe, and I never thought that I'd see you again after you returned from New York. I'm so sorry for the inconvenience I've caused, but as you can see, I had nowhere else to turn except to you, the boy's father, for assistance."

At that, she began to cry the most plaintive sobs I've ever heard. Only the cruelest of men could have witnessed such a scene and not felt the deepest sympathy for her plight, beginning with her disgrace at the hands of J. Bruce Ismay.

"Don't let them hurt our son!" she shrieked, causing the hairs on the back of my neck to stand erect. "Save him! Save him!" She collapsed on the floor and lay there without movement. I rushed to her side and gathered her head in my hands. "She is breathing," I cried reassuringly. "Whiskey! Bring me that whiskey!"

One of the men rushed towards the girl and myself and I grabbed the bottle from his hands. Gently opening her mouth, I poured a small amount of the liquid down her throat. She gave a sharp cough and her eyes fluttered open. As I handed the bottle back to her compatriot, her hand flew up and grabbed it. She took a lengthy drink of the whiskey before seeming to pass into unconsciousness.

The men all looked around the table at each other and, eventually, all eyes settled on Ismay, who again was standing, his stunned face pointed towards the young woman sprawled before him on the floor. "What is it you want?" he asked, turning to the ringleader of the Republicans. "Money?"

"Yes, money," he replied. "And quite a bit of it. I should say the £10,000 should be sufficient."

"£10,000!" Ismay exclaimed. "That is quite a bit of money!"

"Not to the likes of you," replied the leader.

"How can I be confident that will be the end of it?" he asked. "How do I know you'll release the boy and his mother, and that you will not return in a month or a year with demands for more and more?"

Here Holmes interjected. "Mr. Ismay, I had exactly the same concern, which is why I initially rejected the offer. I told these men that I couldn't do business with criminals and treasonous ruffians." Again, the men in the room stirred. "But we have reached an agreement, and it is my experience that even among thieves, a man's word is his bond. They have assured me that if the ransom is paid, no harm will come to the boy and you will never hear his name again."

"And Miss Buckley?" he insisted.

"We have no need to hold her against her will," the leader said. "Ten-thousand pounds, Mr. Ismay, and your reputation, or what remains of it, will not be further sullied by us, and the boy and his mother are no longer your concern."

Ismay walked around the table to where I remained on the floor holding Miss Buckley's head cradled in my arm. "Catherine," Ismay said gently, "can you assure me you will be safe if I comply with these demands?"

The young woman weakly nodded. "They have sworn an oath to me, Mr. Ismay," she said. "They may be rebels, but they wouldn't lie before the Holy Father. I'm so sorry to have caused this trouble, but you may rest assured, this will be the end of it."

Ismay stood up and walked back to the table. "Not a penny can be used for weapons," he insisted. "I know you believe that you might have prevailed in the insurrection had the twenty-thousand German rifles come through. But I'll not be party to rearming the I.R.B. to again take up arms against the Crown."

"Our need right now isn't weapons, Mr. Ismay," the leader said. "Your King is doing nothing about the disease and hunger amongst our children here in Galway. That is what we desperately need your money for – to feed starving children and get them some medicine so sickness doesn't do what the British Army could not."

Ismay looked to the young woman on the floor.

"Do you need my assistance, Catherine?" he asked.

"No, I will be fine once this business is ended," she replied. "You have nothing to be concerned about on my account."

"And the boy," his voice caught. "My son."

"He will never even know your name," she assured.

Ismay turned back to Holmes. "All right," he said. "I'm uneasy with this arrangement, but I acknowledge my responsibilities. If I have your assurance, Mr. Holmes, as well as these men, than my funds will not be used to purchase so much as a single bullet, I can accept these terms. But there can never be mention of my having provided money to those who took up arms against the King." He nodded to me and I removed the envelope from my jacket and handed it to Holmes. "I will wait while you count it," Ismay said.

"That isn't necessary, Mr. Ismay," he replied, handing the envelope to the red-haired man. "You are a man of your word. And for the record, I believe your account of what happened on the *Titanic,* and that your decision to join Miss Buckley in the lifeboat was motivated by concern for her well-being and not your own. But that opinion, like the facts of this transaction, will never be discussed by anyone in this room again."

"I hardly know what to say," Ismay replied, turning to the leader of the group. "I wouldn't have believed rebels – well, that you would display such honor towards me." With that, he stood and looked around the room. "Will you be joining me?" he asked Holmes and me.

"We will remain here and catch the next ship back to England, if you don't mind," Holmes replied. "I would appreciate your sending us any items left at Costelloe Lodge, as well as my fee for resolving this matter."

"Name your price!" Ismay cried.

"My price is standard," said Holmes, "but given the peculiar nature of this matter, I shall be required to make some adjustments."

"Consider it done!" Ismay declared. "Goodbye, Catherine. Remember, you need only to call upon me if you need assistance." He shook hands with Holmes and me, and then hesitatingly, offered his hand to the leader, who grasped it as well. Without a further word, he turned and walked out the door into the bustle of the Galway markets.

Soon, Holmes and I were sitting on deck chairs as we steamed our way along the coast of Ireland, on our way back to Portsmouth, heading eventually for Holmes's residence in Sussex. Holmes had kept his thoughts to himself during the two days we remained in Galway, during which I presumed he was assuring the promises extracted from the rebels were fully honored. I was determined to wait for him to initiate a discussion of what certainly had become one of our more unusual adventures.

"Perhaps not one of the cases you will record," Holmes finally said as the English coast came into view. "But certainly one with a number of unique features. I don't suppose you will find many other examples of my directing substantial amounts of cash to aid insurrectionists!"

"At the request of the Home Secretary!" I reminded him.

Holmes smiled. "Watson, perhaps you should have been a barrister rather than a physician," he said. "I shall keep that point in mind if I find myself in the dock over this little escapade."

He lit a cigarette and turned his eyes from the coastline to face me. "I suppose you will want an explanation of what transpired," he offered.

"I'm practically bursting with questions," I admitted. "How did you find that group of terrorists? What has become of little John? How came Miss Buckley to that cramped room in Galway?"

"The key to this adventure, Watson, isn't understanding those portions of the story we have assembled, but rather revealing those that are concealed from us," he began. "And in this case, a great deal has been concealed.

"On the surface, the story seemed plausible. Ismay is a wealthy and prominent man who, finding himself burdened in mid-life with a career, children, and a wife, all making demands upon him, falls prey to a familiar weakness of the upper classes. He became infatuated with a poor but appealing young woman – Miss Buckley – with a result that could easily destroy his career and home. With the imminent sailing of his new steamship, the *Titanic*, it was an easy matter to convince Miss Buckley to start life over in America, with a promise of a generous settlement for her and the child. A berth is secured for her, the *Titanic* sails off to New York, and the problem, it would seem, is resolved.

"Except that fate intervened and Ismay and Miss Buckley arrived in New York under very different circumstances. Nevertheless, the arrangement remains intact. Ismay settles a handsome sum upon her, she invents a story of a husband lost at sea, and Ismay returns to his estate at Costelloe Lodge, his embarrassment over his treatment of Miss Buckley overwhelmed by the enormity of the loss of the *Titanic*, the inquiries, and the ruination of his reputation.

"The world moved on, the Great War began, and suddenly the fifteen-hundred souls lost on the *Titanic* seemed almost a trifle compared to the tens-of-thousands perishing in the forests and trenches of France and on the sea as a result of the *U*-boats. Ismay was engulfed in business activities and had quite put Miss Buckley and their son out of his mind, although he kept a photograph of the child that she had sent to him locked in his desk.

"Then his past caught up to him. Miss Buckley was back in Ireland, he learned, when she suddenly appeared at Costello Lodge with the ransom note. He realized that his name and reputation, which he had spent five years rebuilding, were again at risk, not only because of Miss Buckley's resurfacing, but because a connection might be made to the Irish Republican Brotherhood, which had apparently kidnapped her young child."

"But why would the I.R.B. seize her son?" I asked. "Surely they couldn't believe that a seamstress had access to the kind of ransom they were demanding."

"Miss Buckley is a young and naïve woman," Holmes said. "Somewhere along the line, I concluded, she had revealed her relationship with Ismay. Not surprisingly, that information made its way to the I.R.B. network, which realized that in this innocent young lady they had found a very lucrative source of much-needed revenue.

"The day after we arrived, I dressed in those somewhat proletarian clothes in which you found me and went to Galway to see her and to explore portions of her story. As I had anticipated, much additional information came tumbling out once I hinted at the possible criminal penalties which she might expect if she refused to cooperate. My first question to her had to do with the young boy who had been kidnapped."

"What is the mystery about him?" I asked.

"I felt there were holes in Miss Buckley's story," Holmes answered. "Do you remember my commenting on the tidiness of her apartment? I thought that her housekeeping exemplary, given the presence of a four or five year old boy who inevitably would create a good deal of clutter for an exasperated mother. And yet there was no evidence of a child's presence at all. Not a shoe, not a toy – and importantly – not even a photograph, although there were photos of others, presumably family members, as well as one of Miss Buckley with a most handsome young man.

"I immediately drew the only conclusion the facts would support: There was no child."

My eyes must have bulged at Holmes's disclosure. "No child?" I exclaimed. "Then there could have been no kidnapping."

"Indubitably," he answered. "A young mother will sacrifice many comforts for herself, but a child must have clothing and toys. And no mother with any means would fail to have a photograph of her child prominently displayed. Nevertheless, I played along with her game to uncover the true motive for her attempted extortion. I asked her to contact the kidnappers without revealing my identity and to arrange a meeting, as I was prepared to deliver the entire ransom to them. She quickly did so, and within an hour, I found myself in that small, dark lair surrounded by a band of Irish nationalists.

"I came right to the point. 'I know there is no child and therefore there is no kidnapping,' I informed them. The men looked menacingly at Miss Buckley but I waved them off. 'Miss Buckley has played her role in this melodrama with great aplomb,' I assured. 'But it is no good to continue the masquerade. I'm no inexperienced village constable. You invented – or rather, resurrected – the child to serve your political motives. I could walk out of here right now and inform the police. The outcome, I fear, would be unpleasant for all of you.'

"One of the men took a step threateningly towards me. I removed the small pistol I had hidden in my jacket and pointed it at his heart. 'I wouldn't recommend your coming any closer,' I warned. 'I said I *could* walk out of here, but undoubtedly that would result in much bloodshed and loss of life, of which I have no interest in being an instigator. I prefer to learn the details of how this little plot unfolded, although I suspect I already understand much of the story.'

"The men and Miss Buckley remained mute.

"'All right, suppose I tell it to you then,' I said, turning to Miss Buckley who appeared astonished at the sudden developments. 'You let me know where I go wrong – although I rather doubt that will be the case.

"'I expect that there indeed was a child born of your liaison with Ismay, but that this child was given up for adoption or didn't survive," I began. Miss Buckley uttered a small gasp and sunk into a chair, burying her head in her arms upon the table. After several moments, she regained her composure. She acknowledged that her son had been born in New York in 1912 but fell desperately ill during his first month. The photograph of him, a copy of which she had sent to Ismay, was her only remembrance of his brief time with her. Just eighteen years old and already mourning a child, she was incapable of managing her grief. She appealed to Ismay for additional money, explaining that living expenses for her and the boy were much higher than she had anticipated. She doubted he would send the money if it was just for her, so she needed to perpetuate the existence of the child. He sent her additional money which tided her over until she collected herself and found work as a seamstress."

"How came she to return to Ireland," I asked, "and why the invention of the kidnapping story?"

"Late last year, still eking out a living in New York, she had met a young Irishman named Liam Mellows who had recently fled Galway after the Uprising, in which he had played a leading role. It was his photo with Miss Buckley that I noticed in her flat. They quickly became involved with one another, during which time he indoctrinated her with the ideology of the Nationalists. But soon he was arrested by the authorities and held in the Tombs prison, awaiting extradition back to Ireland. He was able to give her some money, however, and the name of close friends in Galway who would look after her. He urged her to leave immediately, lest she be suspected of being an accomplice and imprisoned as well.

"Returning to Galway infused with the Republican spirit, Miss Buckley contacted Mellows' colleagues and armed with the information she provided about her relationship with Ismay, they concocted the scheme of inventing a child and kidnapping to secure a substantial sum from him. They knew that Ismay's conscience, not to mention his fears of his secret being revealed, made it highly likely that he would comply with the ransom demand."

"But what if he demanded proof that there was a child?" I asked.

"I doubt they felt it was likely that Ismay would ask for proof," Holmes said. "After all, he knew the child had been born and had no reason to suspect he wasn't with Miss Buckley and in good health. If such a demand was made, in any event, there is no shortage of Irish five-year-olds who could be produced as evidence of his existence.

"The I.R.B. made one mistake," he continued. "They couldn't have known that Ismay would contact his friend, the Home Secretary, who would enlist me in this matter. They might have concluded involvement of the regular police was unlikely to uncover their scheme, but they didn't consider what a private consulting detective might uncover."

"Let alone Sherlock Holmes," I added.

Holmes smiled. "The holes in their arrangement were as evident to me as if they had written and signed a full confession.

"'So, Mr. Holmes,' their leader said. 'You have us dead to rights, and you have a pistol as well. We could kill you right here, but you would kill some of us in the process, and we are not murderers. We are patriots.'"

"I chose not to debate the political point under the circumstances, but I couldn't deny that I was in a delicate situation. 'I cannot be a party to underwriting treasonous activities, particularly with the nation at war,' I insisted.

"'Well, *we* aren't at war anymore,' he responded. 'But our children are starving. Our old folks can't get their medicine. Our young women are dying in childbirth because we can't afford doctors. We are in a desperate way, and your government in London is happy to see us starve and die. Is it a wonder the people rose up?'

"I considered his words and believed them to be honest," Holmes continued. "Miss Buckley, who had herself lost her child to illness, stood by with tears running down her thin face, obviously a willing accomplice to the entire affair," Holmes paused and looked at me. "I have no sympathy for revolutionaries, Watson, but neither do I countenance the slow strangulation of the Irish.

"It struck me that perhaps an arrangement might be made that would satisfy all parties," he continued. "I could relieve Ismay's fear of disclosure for a munificent sum that he would barely miss. It would help relieve the suffering of a poor and desperate group of our countrymen, perhaps earning a measure of trust that the government has thus far been unable to secure.

"'I will make you a proposition,' I offered their leader. 'The money you seek in return for several promises.'

"'Name them,' the leader cautiously responded.

"'I need assurances that there will be no further financial or other demands made on Ismay,' I said. 'He must not be the subject of continual extortion and threats of exposure. And I need your firm pledge that every shilling provided to you will be reserved for food and medicine. Not a penny for munitions, or I will disclose your activities to the authorities in such a way that I can guarantee the lot of you will end your days on the gallows or prison.'"

"Holmes," I inquired. "Is that honorable? Is that being square with your client, Ismay? Is it proper from the standpoint of the Crown?"

"I will not contest the sentiments behind your questions, Watson," said Holmes. "In the strictest sense, I'm aiding in the deception of a rather despicable client, and for that, I do not apologize. Despite his support for Miss Buckley and their son, he bore full responsibility for the actions that necessitated her flight to America. It is a matter of some justice that he should pay a significant sum to assuage the pain and discomfort she has endured by his disgraceful behavior.

"As to financially supporting the I.R.B., that decision troubles me more, but we live in a world where war and slaughter seem commonplace. I can justify steering some of

Ismay's vast fortune to helping the impoverished and embittered of Ireland. Perhaps in doing so, we can wean them of their affinity for Germany, and help to re-establish their secure place in our Empire."

With that, Holmes closed his eyes and appeared to drift off to sleep, leaving me in both literally and philosophically troubled waters, sailing back to a nation at war, perhaps even now in the crosshairs of a *U*-boat. Yet I was on the verge of dozing myself when Holmes's voice startled me.

"Oh, by the way, Watson, the I.R.B. had only requested £5,000," he said looking at me and then closing his eyes again. "I decided that ten-thousand sounded more appropriate. And can't we all benefit from some greater measure of generosity in these troubled days?"

The Curious Case of
President Harding

Part I – Things Come in Threes

"Have you ever noticed," I asked Sherlock Holmes as we sat overlooking the magnificent cliffs of Sussex, "that things come in threes?"

Holmes stifled a yawn. "Really?" he responded in a bored tone. "I was not aware." He looked up from *The Police Gazetteer*, which, even in retirement, consumed several minutes of every day at his home in Sussex. "Nor can I imagine that the aphorism has any basis in fact."

"Well, The Holy Trinity, for example," I offered, regretting immediately having offered a theological example would make little impression, given Holmes's skepticism of all things ecclesiastical in nature. He predictably sniffed his indifference. "The primary colors, then. The Brontë sisters!"

"Watson, you might just as well say 'Good things come in twelves' and cite the number of inches on a ruler – or the days in the Christmas song," he added. "Certainly, there is no significance to such an observation if one is focused purely on facts, not sentimentality or coincidence."

After more than four decades of friendship and collaboration, I was well aware when my words were unlikely to influence Holmes, and I decided to abandon the discussion and focus instead on the brilliant white of the Dover seashore.

"Ah, this is magnificent," I said. "The sea, the blue of the Channel, the white cliffs. What a welcome change from the congestion and bustle of London. You have made a very wise choice in selecting the south for your retirement home."

"Yes, my bees keep me quite busy," he replied. "And yet, there are times when the lure of London – the challenge of a perplexing case, the intelligence of a conniving criminal – all exert a very strong nostalgia."

"Why, Holmes!" I cried. "You are a sentimentalist after all!"

"No, but there are aspects of the chase that even the intricacies of the apiary cannot replace," he admitted.

"Possibly you should think of a diversion," I suggested. "A trip? Perhaps a return visit to America. I would be pleased to accompany you on such a journey: New York, Boston, Washington. If we are to consider such an excursion, I say, we should get on with it." I tapped the cane I used for steadying myself. "We aren't getting any younger."

"No, America is too far a journey at this point," Holmes said, shaking his head. "Perhaps the Continent would be rejuvenating. But no, not across the Atlantic. I could not bear how stultifying such a trip there would inevitably be."

And yet just three weeks later, at the beginning of August 1923, Holmes and I could be found sunning ourselves on the deck of *HMS Olympic*, bound for New York, enjoying a whisky-and-soda as well as the brisk salt air. "A perfectly relaxing way to spend several days, don't you think?" I inquired. "We'd better have another one of these," I said, raising my nearly empty glass as a steward walked by. "We certainly won't be enjoying a good stiff drink in the States, what with this silly Prohibition they've implemented!"

We landed in New York on 5th August, but there was none of the gaiety one typically associates with ship arrivals to greet us. "Good Lord!" I cried, "Look there!" The sign displayed on the newspaper seller's kiosk proclaimed in bold, six-inch high letters, "*Harding Dead, Body Being Brought to Washington, Burial To Be In Ohio*". All about us on the quay, peoples' heads were buried in the open newspapers as they read about the shocking development.

I hurried to buy one of the papers and together we scanned the story as we rode in a clattering automobile to our hotel. Harding, who had been elected in a landslide not even three years earlier, had been engaged in a cross-country trip that included a visit to the territory of Alaska. It had been reported that there had been some concerns about his health and state of mind of late. While in Alaska, he had referred to being in Nebraska, and had teetered while behind his podium. His physicians had ministered to him when he arrived in San Francisco, the last stop on his journey.

"*Death, apparently balked by medical science, struck suddenly and with no warning, at 7:30,*" the newspaper account read. "*The President had been believed definitely on the road to recovery from ptomaine poisoning, acute indigestion, and a pneumonic affection which followed them.*" Evidently Mrs. Harding had been reading to him by his bedside in the Palace Hotel. He had bade his wife to continue when he suddenly threw his hand up over his head and convulsed. "*Then the President stiffened and as suddenly dropped back limply,*" the story continued. His wife, who had in an instant passed from being the nation's First Lady to that of a widow, was quoted as resolutely stating, "*I am not going to break down.*"

"What do you make of it?" Holmes asked. "Does anything about this narrative strike you as unusual or suspicious?"

I thought for a moment. Despite some concerns about Harding's health following his bout with the flu, he hadn't appeared to be at risk of dying. Indeed, the scandal sheets had been filled with allegations of chronic promiscuity that, if true, would surely qualify Mr. Harding as America's most virile leader ever. And yet, here he was dead at the age of only fifty-seven, thousands of miles from home, in a hotel room.

"I cannot say without more facts," I responded. Holmes smiled at my utilization of one of his own axioms: Never form conclusions without facts. As a medical man myself, it did appear strange for an energetic man to be cut down so quickly, but then again, there were millions of people who had suffered just such unexpected deaths from the recent influenza pandemic.

We hired a Negro porter to gather up our bags and arrange for a taxicab to our hotel, the Ritz Carlton, where we were shown to our room, which afforded us a magnificent view of the city. We were in the midst of unpacking our trunks when there was a sharp knock on the door. I opened the door to find a serious-looking young man with two companions standing behind him.

"Thank you," I said before he could speak, "but we have just arrived and do not have time just yet for tea. If you don't mind, could you return in perhaps a half-hour?"

The young man coughed uncomfortably. "Excuse me, but are you Mr. Sherlock Holmes from England?" he asked.

"I am Dr. John Watson," I replied. "Mr. Holmes's friend."

"Ah, Dr. Watson," the young man said, brightening somewhat and extending his hand, which I shook. "Mr. Holmes's scribe! A real honor to meet you. I've read your adventures in *Lippincott's*. Most entertaining!" He paused. "However, I wonder if I might speak with Mr. Holmes."

"We have just arrived by steamer and are quite fatigued," I answered. "Mr. Holmes is on a private holiday, and – "

"On, forgive me," he said smiling. "I am not merely an acolyte! My card," he said, presenting a small white business card embellished with a small shield.

"'*Jonathan Radner*'," it read. "I'm a member of the United States Secret Service," he explained. Noting my confused look, he added, "Our organization has as its primary mission the safeguarding of the President."

"Ah, I see," I responded, looking at the card carefully. I looked up into Mr. Radner's face. "And what may I tell Mr. Holmes you would like to discuss with him?" I queried.

Suddenly, Holmes appeared at my side and the Secret Service man swallowed hard and bit his lower lip in awe.

"I think it is perfectly self-evident, Watson," Holmes responded. "These gentlemen want to talk with me about the possible assassination of the President of the United States."

Radner's expression was one of complete shock. "But . . . but how could you have guessed that, Mr. Holmes?" he sputtered.

"I never guess, Mr. Radner," Holmes archly responded, inviting him into the room. "I would have thought you would know as much from reading Watson's little essays." He motioned Radner to one of the chairs in the sitting area and sat in the other one himself while I perched on the edge of a bed. Radner's companions closed the door, remaining in the hallway. "Tell me how I may be of service."

Radner's face grew grim. "What I'm about to tell you, Mr. Holmes," he began, "requires the strictest of confidence. Disclosure of unproven suppositions could have the most calamitous implications for the United States government. May I have your assurance of complete confidentiality?"

"Mr. Radner, you are far from the first client of mine with connections to the highest levels of his government," Holmes assured. "I have counted kings and prime ministers amongst my clients. I ensure them the very same level of confidentiality I give a secretary whose fiancé has gone missing – that is, complete discretion."

"Very well," Radner answered. "And I do want to assure you that the government is prepared to pay you a handsome fee if you can shed light on this cataclysmic situation."

Holmes waved his hand. "My fees are fixed, except when I choose to forgo them altogether," he insisted. "Pray, how may I be of service?"

Radner studied Holmes carefully, as if attempting to assess the trustworthiness and intellect of the actual person rather than the larger-than-life subject of my accounts. Holmes was now considerably older than the incomparable sleuth recorded in *The Adventures*, *The Memoirs,* and other stories as illustrated by Mr. Paget. What hair he retained was grayer but still combed backwards. His face, still thin, was more lined, but his aquiline nose remained just as prominent and his eyes burned with an intensity undimmed from those days in Baker Street.

"Our country has just suffered a great calamity," Radner began. "The President – " His voice caught, and he took a moment to calm himself. "Our President is dead. Dead! He was taken ill in San Francisco where he died."

"So we have read in the newspaper," Holmes noted, adding his condolences. "And what was his condition on this journey? Was he healthy? Vigorous?"

"To tell you the truth, Mr. Holmes, the President hadn't been well," Radner admitted. "He had a bad case of influenza earlier in the year and had remained quite fatigued and weakened."

"So we gathered from the press accounts. And his habits?" Holmes pressed.

"President Harding indulged in heavy drinking and heavy smoking," Radner admitted somewhat sheepishly.

"And in several other vices, I understand," Holmes added, making it clear he would abide no withholding of pertinent information.

"It is true," the officer agreed. "He stopped drinking, or so he said, but he wouldn't give up his tobacco."

"And what do the doctors say was the cause of death?" Holmes asked.

"Perhaps apoplexy, perhaps a heart attack," Radner answered. "Perhaps a combination of factors. There was some thought he might have eaten something that disagreed with him – possibly tainted seafood – and the doctors purged him to reduce the effects."

Holmes sat upright. "Then they haven't ruled out poisoning as a cause?" he asked.

Radner regarded Holmes closely. "I believe they are focused on natural causes, Mr. Holmes."

"And yet you have come to see me, Mr. Radner," said Holmes, "which tells me you have suspicions that you are cautious about sharing with the regular police."

"Sir," he said, adding a small cough and looking over his shoulder at me, "let me be honest with you. Some of us suspect that the President was murdered."

"Yes, so I concluded when you announced your employer," said Holmes. "If you accepted without question that the President had died of natural causes, surely you would have had no reason to interrupt my holiday in New York, so you must harbor suspicions as to who might be behind this devilry."

Radner remained quiet for a long moment. "Mr. Holmes, I must admit I have no evidence of foul play. But it seems to me prudent to make inquiries surrounding his rapid decline, and those are questions I cannot pursue in my official position with the government." He paused and looked at Holmes. "Might I persuade you to take on this case? There is no promise of official recognition or even public acknowledgement of your efforts, and there might well be some resistance from the Harding family and those in his administration to a public discussion of this topic. But history must have answers, Mr. Holmes!"

Holmes looked hard at the young man. "Very well," he said, "let us see where this journey takes us."

'I think the first step must take us to Washington, D.C.," Radner suggested. "Most of the individuals you'll want to speak with are going to be there. We've already begun that process, and I can fill you in on the train. One is leaving in an hour-and-a-half."

Fortunately, we had barely begun to unpack, and within a few moments, the three of us were on the way to Pennsylvania Station, the enormous *Beaux Arts* edifice in mid-town Manhattan. The ride through the streets of New York was fascinating – columns of stone, glass, and concrete soared overhead, leaving much of the street in shadow. Throngs of people, automobiles, buses, and an occasional horse-drawn wagon clogged the streets. The smells, costumes, and languages of dozens of cultures assaulted one's senses as we strode from our cab up the stairs and into the magnificent station.

Within a half-hour, we were nestled into our private compartment as the train pulled out of the station, traversed the Hudson River, and crossed into New Jersey and then southward. There was little time, however, to consider the countryside as it rushed past.

"This is Agent Withers and Agent McCloskey," Radner said, motioning to his two companions. "They've been in touch with the President's – I mean, the *late* President's – party in San Fran. Jack, whatcha have?"

The agent identified as Withers hunched forward to speak in a low voice, "Harding certainly wasn't well," he began. "He was complainin' to the agents up in Alaska. Then once he got to Washington – that's Washington State, not D.C. – " he clarified for Holmes and me, " – he was really gettin' bad. By time he got to 'Frisco on the 29th, he had a fever, so the doc gave him some medicine, but it didn't seem to do no good." I saw Holmes wince at the American grammar, but he said nothing. "Well, yesterday, about 7:30 in the evening, his wife was reading to him and – poof! – out he went! Never knew what hit him."

"Doesn't it seem odd that he was strong enough to recover from a flu that killed millions of people in recent years, and yet succumbed so suddenly?" Holmes inquired.

"Oh, yes, Mr. Holmes," Withers agreed. "He had quite a time of it in January."

"I wonder," Holmes said aloud. After a few moments, he looked up at Radner and Withers. "Mr. Coolidge becomes President now, is that right?"

"He's already President," Radner responded. "Sworn in by his own father, a justice of the peace, up in Vermont."

"And who else is on the obvious list?" Holmes asked.

The agents looked at each other in confusion. "What 'list' would that be?" said Withers.

"Why, the list of who might benefit from the President's sudden and unanticipated demise," Holmes replied. The agents looked at him as though he had begun to speak in a foreign language.

"Benefit?" Withers asked incredulously.

"Whenever a crime occurs – and I consider an unanticipated death a potential crime – I invariably ask who stands to benefit," said Holmes. The agents looked skeptical. "Who had a motive? In this case, surely there are a great many people who stand to benefit immeasurably by the death of President Harding. Of course, I don't mean Mr. Coolidge necessarily, but colleagues, political rivals, or foreign despots."

The Secret Service agents stammered, pledging to assemble a list of possible beneficiaries of the President's death.

"And the autopsy results, once the *post mortem* is completed," Holmes continued. "I would like for Dr. Watson and me to examine them at the earliest opportunity," he explained, nodding in my direction.

Agent Withers coughed and said, "I'm afraid that won't be possible, Mr. Holmes. There was no autopsy. Mrs. Harding strictly forbade it. Our agents spoke with Dr. Ray Wilbur of Stanford who was with the President when he expired. He confirmed the First Lady wouldn't hear of a *post mortem* examination. In fact, the President's body was embalmed within an hour after he died."

I drew Holmes from the compartment, out of earshot of the agents. "Do you seriously suspect foul play?"

"Facts are more valued than suspicions," he said, "and in this very significant case, a great deal of effort appears to have been made to obliterate any evidence of the actual cause of death.

"It is curious, is it not – such a drastic turn in the President's health," Holmes said after we'd returned to the cluster of agents. "Not what one might expect in the case of a middle-aged man whose health is so carefully attended and guarded."

"Well, perhaps not as curious as you might think, Mr. Holmes," Radner said. "Our presidents endure a great deal of stress, and it isn't unusual for their health to suffer. Why, President Harding's predecessor, Mr. Wilson, suffered a severe stroke just a few years ago that very nearly killed him, and he was just sixty-two! And he still was thinking of running again for a third term!"

"And T.R. had a stroke earlier that year, and he was just sixty!" added Withers. "That's Theodore Roosevelt. Teddy wasn't President any more of course, but he was sure thinking of running again in 1920."

"Things come in threes," Holmes turned to me and murmured, barely loud enough to be heard.

"What's that you say, Mr. Holmes?" asked Radner.

Holmes ignored his question and grew quiet. He turned in his seat and looked out the window as the rolling fields passed by. I waved off the agents, knowing that Holmes had entered his cerebral stage, analyzing information in ways that could not be replicated by the average brain. Several minutes later, he motioned for me to lean in.

"Watson, doesn't this strike you as curious?" he asked softly.

"That three men should suffer strokes?" I responded.

"That three men who all served as President – all of an age when they should have been physically robust – that all three should suffer the same deadly attack," he said. "Wilson survived, it's true, but he could barely function during his last year or so as President and has been an invalid ever since, if memory serves me correctly. The agents just told us that Roosevelt and Wilson both were planning to run in 1920, and Harding most certainly intended to seek another term in 1924, one must presume. All were stricken a year in advance of the coming election, ending their candidacies. Doesn't that strike you as, at a minimum, *coincidental*?" Holmes grew quiet again, and I dared say nothing while his mind considered his own observations.

After a few moments, I dared to offer an observation. "I will admit the coincidence seems striking," I said. "But are you suggesting a plot against these three presidents? And who would wish to harm three completely different men?"

"Someone who also wished to be President," he reasoned, "and who wished to eliminate the opposition." Holmes sat back in his seat and leaned towards me. "If I'm not mistaken, you are the one who recently noted that 'things happen in threes'."

"Yes, but Harding wasn't stricken in 1919 or 1920, but three years later, so if someone was plotting to affect the 1920 election, they would seem to have missed their mark," I suggested. "Harding didn't become a target until this year – 1923 – although he, too, had been running in 1920."

"True enough," Holmes acknowledged. "And yet . . . ."

The impact of Holmes's words rang in my ears. Could he possibly be serious? He was proposing a conspiracy so monstrous that it hardly seemed plausible – three Presidents, each the victim of a plot designed to clear a path to the White House, with two of them in office at the time of the attack? And how would such an outrageous scheme be carried out?

"What do you want to do?" I asked.

"*We*, Watson, *we*," he replied, "for I will certainly need medical skills beyond my own capability to uncover this plot, if there is such a plot at all. For the moment, however, we must share some information with Mr. Radner – but not *too* much, for if there is a conspiracy of some type, it may well be orchestrated out of the Secret Service itself!"

Holmes asked Radner to confer without the other agents, who soon stood outside and guarded the sliding doorway, which Radner had closed behind them. "Did you have a thought, Mr. Holmes?" he asked.

"If you have read Watson's little stories about my methods," he said, "you are aware that I cannot reach conclusions without facts. I will need more information. I want to find more about President Harding's medical condition, including any medications and procedures to which he was subjected over the past two weeks. I also require the names of all those who were in close contact with him over the past week including his staff, his family, hotel employees, and medical attendants."

Radner's eyes opened wide when he heard this last statement. "What's that? Those traveling with him? Why is that a matter of concern?" he asked with alarm. "No one goes near the President without the approval of the Secret Service!"

"Yes, precisely," Holmes responded. He sought to deflect Radner's sudden concern about the need for information. "I simply wish," he explained, "to investigate whether anyone who was close to the President might have observed changes in his health or demeanor in the days leading up to the tragic event, you understand."

Holmes's explanation seemed to reduce Radner's distress. "I can get you that information," he explained. "We will be in Washington soon, and I'll have a discussion with the White House physicians."

Radner made some notes in a little book he carried with him. We rode along in silence until we arrived at Washington's Union Station, a massive building just a few city blocks from the U.S. Capitol. When we arrived, Radner slipped away and made a quick telephone call.

As we emerged from the station, we could see the gleaming dome of the Capitol building, topped by a statue, towering over the bustling city. A black automobile was waiting for us and we were hustled into the rear seat. In just a few moments were on our way to the Treasury Building, where the Secret Service offices were located. Black bunting had quickly been hung in windows and over the entry ways of many of the buildings lining our route. Many of the passing vehicles had their headlights illuminated in honor of the late President.

"Will the materials concerning the President's health be available for my review at your office?" Holmes asked.

"To the extent that we have them, yes," he replied. "I've asked that they be brought over from the White House, which is just across the street from the Treasury."

"And I will need to examine the President's body when it arrives," Holmes informed him.

"Oh, I'm not sure that can be arranged," Radner said, furrowing his forehead.

"Please turn the car around," Holmes said, addressing the driver, who ignored the request. "Driver! Turn the car around!" Holmes commanded again although the driver showed no sign whatsoever of following the instruction.

"What are you doing?" asked Radner.

"I have no intention to commence an investigation with one hand tied behind my back," Holmes said. "I must insist that I have full access to the President's remains to conduct an examination."

Radner's face froze. "I . . . I don't think that will be possible, Mr. Holmes," he stuttered. "There will be so much security. And Mrs. Harding is being very protective of her husband," he added.

"I appreciate the deep shock that the passing of the President must have caused his widow and the nation, but my concern is quite apart from such considerations," said Holmes. "I have imposed these same conditions on Scotland Yard detectives and village constables: Either I conduct the inquiry as I choose, and without a scintilla of interference, or I shall return to my holiday. The choice, sir, is entirely up to you."

Radner considered Holmes's statement and gave a quick nod of consent.

The car deposited us at the rear entrance of the Treasury Department and we passed by a statue of Alexander Hamilton, the first Secretary, as we entered the building. Inside, we were met by a white haired gentleman of perhaps sixty wearing heavy glasses and a somber mien. Radner immediately took him aside and they conferred for a few moments before returning to us – Radner having no doubt explained Holmes's conditions.

"Mr. Holmes, this is Director William Moran of the Secret Service," Radner said. Moran shook Holmes's hand. "And Dr. Watson," Radner added as I also shook hands with the director. Moran looked closely at both of us. "Glad to meet you," he said. "Come on to my office and let's talk."

As Holmes and I settled into leather chairs in the director's office, Moran thanked Radner and the others who had escorted us from New York, closed the door, and settled behind his large desk. "Coffee?" he asked us, but we declined. He already had a steaming cup on his desk and he took a sip before speaking.

"Been here six years," he said, pointing to the array of autographed photographs on the wood-paneled walls. He pointed out one of an ascetic-looking man in spectacles. "He appointed me in 1917," he continued. "Woodrow Wilson. Hell of a guy." I was startled by his irreverent reference to the former President. "This guy – " he said, jerking his thumb to the autographed photo of the late President Harding. "A different kind of man."

"Yes. The Teapot Dome matter," Holmes added.

"I see you follow the news on this side of the Atlantic," he said appreciatively.

"We do have newspapers in England," Holmes responded with a smile, "and from time to time they will report events in our former colonies, particularly scandals involving the President and his Cabinet. I must say that I'm curious as to how you knew of our presence in the States."

Moran looked carefully at my friend for a long moment, then slapped the desk with his large hand. "Okay, Mr. Holmes, let's put our cards on the table, what do you say?" he asked. 'We have our ways of knowing things."

"As do I, Mr. Moran," responded Holmes. "For example, I know of your familial connection to Colonel Sebastian Moran – I believe a great-uncle – whom I was compelled to send to the gallows some years ago for his collaboration with Professor Moriarty."

I recalled the air gun attempt on Holmes following his return from exile after disposing of Professor Moriarty at the Reichenbach Falls. "Are you truly related to that Colonel Moran?" I asked.

"I regret to say I am," Moran said, "although the two halves of the family had little to do with each other after my father left England. I learned of his criminal activities long after his encounter with you, Mr. Holmes. Anyhow, no hard feelings! I'm glad to meet you, and maybe you can be of assistance."

"I should like to believe that I might be," Holmes responded. "Why don't you tell me what you know, what you suspect, and what service I might provide to you and the Secret Service?"

"On its face, this would seem to be a cut-and-dried tragedy," Moran began. "The President wasn't well. He'd had the flu and other health problems. Drank a lot. Smoked a lot. Caroused a lot. Had been treated for neurasthenia for years."

Holmes looked to me. "A serious nervous condition," I explained.

"Yes. He was hospitalized a few times in the 1890's for depression," Moran continued, "although it wasn't widely discussed, of course. Part of the idea for his trip out to Alaska and California was to get him away from some of the stress – let him see some wide, open parts of the country, breathe some fresh air. But he wasn't feeling so good for most of the trip, and then he arrived in San Francisco, and – well, you know the rest."

"How unfortunate that there was no *post mortem* examination to clarify the cause of death," Holmes said.

"Yes, that is true," said Moran with a weary sigh. "The Duchess wouldn't hear of it."

"The Duchess?" I questioned.

"Mrs. Harding," Moran explained. "Very much in charge. Screened most of his mail and readings. Told him how to dress. Lots of people think she was the reason he got into politics instead of sticking with publishing a newspaper in Ohio. He never much liked it."

"The newspaper business?" I asked.

"No, politics," Moran replied. "Too many people with their hands out and in his pockets. Not really what he enjoyed. And the inquiries – perhaps you have heard of the scandal at the Veterans' Bureau? There is more to come on that front, I fear. Those oil leases out at Teapot Dome. And then," he hesitated, "there is the problem of Mrs. Carrie Phillips and Miss Nan Britton. " He took a deep breath. "Did you know Mrs. Phillips and her husband were blackmailing him during the 1920 election over his old letters? And she was a German agent during the war, involved with a senator! It was quite a great burden for any man, let alone one with a weak heart."

Holmes took in this full report with his hands on his chest and his index fingers peaked and touching his lips. "I am impressed that he found time to govern a nation," Holmes said. "You have described a complex and troubled man, but more importantly, a man who might have multiple people who would gain financially, politically, or emotionally from his death." He paused for a moment. "How utterly convenient that he died when he did – at least for someone."

"It is for that reason that I entreated you to come to Washington and look into the matter," Moran said. "It may well be there is nothing to the rumors that are beginning to circulate already – of a plot, or revenge, or an effort to silence Harding. Or," he paused, "there may well be something there. As you have noted, there was motive, and it seems likely with all this traveling and various people coming and going in the official party and at receptions and meals that someone may have taken the opportunity to accelerate the pace of the President's demise a bit quicker than nature might have intended."

"Was it thought he would stand for re-election next year?" Holmes asked.

"Oh, yes," Moran answered. "Not that he loved the job. In fact, he told the historian Nicholas Murray Butler, 'I am not fit for this office and should never have been here,' but that consideration alone discourages few men from seeking the presidency. Even if he preferred to retire, there is little doubt that his wife would have pressed him to run again. She quite enjoyed the power and prestige of being First Lady."

"And does she have as colorful a background as the President?" asked Holmes.

"Well, sir, not as recently, so far as we know. But before she married Mr. Harding – well, that was another matter," Moran admitted. "A marriage – we think – when she was little more than a girl, a drunkard for a husband (if he truly was her husband by law), a child, a divorce (if there had been a marriage), a fair amount of running around. Not the typical preparation for a First Lady! She became an active suffragette, concerned about the rights of Negroes, very devoted to her husband despite his . . . " Moran paused. ". . . *indiscretions.*"

"She sounds perfectly fascinating," Holmes said. "Let me ask how you are investigating the President's death."

"To tell you the truth, my hands are a bit tied," Moran admitted. "We have a Bureau of Investigation at Justice, run by William Burns. You've probably heard of his detective agency." Holmes nodded his familiarity with the firm. "They tend to think of such matters as their responsibility. Touchy about their jurisdiction."

"I see some things are similar on both sides of the Atlantic! Shall we speak with Mr. Burns?"

"We can try," Moran said, standing up to signal the end of the meeting. "Come around about ten tomorrow and we'll go see Burns together. Oh, the train with the President and First Lady aboard arrives tomorrow, so there will doubtless be some official activities which I'll need to attend during the day."

"Very well, but please keep in mind I still want to see the late President's remains," Holmes declared. "Even at this late stage, there may be suggestive clues if there was, in fact, any wrongdoing."

Holmes and I left the Treasury Department and strolled along Pennsylvania Avenue, enjoying an excellent view of the massive White House that serves as he President's official residence and working office. We took in some local sights before arriving at the Willard Hotel, one of the capital city's finest which had been refurbished after a fire the previous year. Our trunks had been sent on ahead while we met in Moran's office. After a brief rest, we took dinner up the street at the Old Ebbitt Grill, the oldest restaurant in the city.

"An odd situation, don't you think?" asked Holmes. "Why we were brought into it? There is no allegation of wrong-doing. There may be a shortage of clues, but there is certainly no shortage of people and agencies to investigate what meager ones exist. There are law enforcement officials not only in Washington and San Francisco, but the Secret Service, and this Burns fellow as well. So why engage me?"

I thought about Holmes's question as we began our meal of grilled oysters and roast beef. "I can only imagine the coincidence of Sherlock Holmes being in America at so propitious a moment intrigued them," I said. "You are the disinterested party. You neither guard the President nor investigate crimes involving his administration. You have no particular stake in this issue or its outcome, whereas the reputations of Moran or Burns, and likely others, might well be affected by the outcome of the case should they attempt to close the matter too quickly."

"Exactly," he said. "I believe you have hit on it. I am the proverbial 'honest broker' – not because here are not sufficient American investigators, but because none of them trusts the other to conduct a fair and thorough inquiry. Well, if a dispassionate inquiry is what they want, that is what they shall have, and let the chips falls where they may!"

Part II – The Facts of the Case

In the morning, Holmes and I breakfasted at the Willard and waited for the car that would take us a few blocks to the Justice Department. The newspapers were filled with little but accounts of the tragedy that had occurred in San Francisco, the arrival of President Coolidge in the city, and the train bearing Harding's body, which was scheduled to arrive in the city that evening. There would be a short laying-in at the White House and then a brief funeral at the Capitol the following day. Harding's casket would then be placed on the train and taken to Marion, Ohio for another funeral and internment. As a result of this tight schedule, Holmes's opportunity for examining the body would be extremely limited if, which seemed unlikely, he was able to do so at all.

Moran and Radner arrived promptly at 9:30 and we were soon deposited at building that housed the Bureau of Investigation. Promptly at ten o'clock, we were shown into the director's office. Burns, a burly man with a great mustache, was about sixty years old. He came around from his desk to greet us. He extended his hand to Moran first, uttering a gruff, "Hello, Bill," while eyeing Holmes and me suspiciously. Moran reciprocated the terse greeting and turned to us.

"This is Sherlock Holmes and his associate, Dr. John Watson," he said by way of introduction. Burns nodded, continuing to look us up and down. "You surely know of his great reputation."

"I've read the penny stories," Burns said dismissively.

"And I have heard of *you* mentioned as the 'Sherlock Holmes of America'," Holmes offered, receiving no response.

"They're here to explore some matters related to the President's passing," Moran continued. There was a loud and derisive snort from Burns. "I have promised them that their presence here will remain strictly clandestine," Moran continued, ignoring Burns's reaction. "Neither they nor we have any benefit to be gained by knowing that a British detective has been summoned to assist in our investigations."

Burns walked back around to his desk, signaled us to be seated, and then sat down heavily into his chair with a grunt. A two-inch stub of a rancid-smelling cigar lazily burned in an ashtray, the thin line of blue smoke spiraling upwards and spreading out into the room. He picked up the cigar and took a long pull on it, the end brightening to a fierce orange glow. "I have no problem keeping your presence a secret, 'cause I don't know what you're doing here in the first place, Mr. Holmes. I think we have the situation well in hand," he added confidently.

"I have no reason to believe anything to the contrary," Holmes answered. "I might mention that I did not seek to intervene in this matter. We were on holiday . . . ."

Burns interrupted him brusquely. "Look, Holmes, Moran here provides security for the President and that's fine," he said with a dismissive tone. "You can check with the Garfield and McKinley families about how well the Secret Service carries out its duties." Moran shifted uncomfortably in his seat at the mention of two Presidents who had been assassinated since the Secret Service was formed in the aftermath of the assassination of Abraham Lincoln nearly sixty years earlier. "But I run a criminal investigation bureau here, not a babysitting service."

"Knock it off, Bill," Moran said sharply. "We don't need to air our rivalries in front of Mr. Holmes and Dr. Watson."

"There hasn't been a crime that anyone's alleged, Holmes, so my shop ain't involved," Burns continued, ignoring Moran's protest. "I suggest you and Dr. Watson head back to New York and enjoy your vacation, and let me worry about people breaking the law in this country. In the meantime," he said with determination, "if it's all the same to you, I will have a few of my boys keeping an eye on you – just to be sure nothing happens to our guests from England."

Moran began to say something but Holmes was instantly on his feet. "I couldn't agree with you more, Director Burns," Holmes said. "If there has been no crime, there surely is no need for my involvement and, as you say, this is detracting from a rare holiday. Good day, Mr. Burns," he concluded, picking up his hat and turning to leave. I rose as well and was right behind him when he stopped and pivoted to look back at Burns.

"Ah, one last point," he said. "I understand the President died at 7:30 and was embalmed an hour later. The next morning, his body was on a train back to Washington."

"Yeah, that's true."

"I have a question about the *post mortem* examination."

"There was no *post mortem* examination."

"Yes, that is my question."

We left Burns with a pinched mouth and exited the building. The heat was quite stifling outside and we decided to walk back toward the Treasury Department, stopping at a café on the way for something cool to drink. Choosing a table at some distance from the nearest patron, we discussed our next moves in hushed voices.

249

"The President's remains will arrive at the White House at about eleven on the seventh," Moran said. "I'll be able to arrange your entry to the White House and, with any luck, a short time for you to examine the body. I suspect it will be kept in the East Room, the large public room on the first floor. But we'll have to act very quickly because the plan is for a service at the Capitol, and then removal back to Ohio."

Holmes nodded his head in agreement. "Then I will meet you at our hotel at nine o'clock tomorrow evening," he said, "which should give us time to gain entry and devise a plan once inside the building. In the meantime, I have some additional research I would like to conduct."

"I can have you driven down to the Library of Congress, if you like," Moran offered as we left the café.

"No, my research must take place in *your* records," Holmes said.

"*My* records?" Moran replied aghast. "What might you be searching for that would be in the files of the Secret Service?"

"I would prefer not to say at this point, if you don't mind," he responded, "but I'm considering every possibility, and based on what I've learned so far, some matters definitely warrant additional scrutiny. I presume that your records will reveal the identity of everyone who had access to the President at various times of the day and evening."

"Unquestionably. We monitor every person who comes into proximity of the President or his wife. That includes those who prepare meals, lay out clothing, or provide security services."

"And all of those records remain in your office, I presume? Good! I shall have a most productive afternoon."

We were just arriving at the Treasury Building and Moran agreeably took Holmes and me down to his records office. "This is the safest place to examine my records," he said. "I'll be sure that all of the wires and memos from the last few days are brought down to you. In the meanwhile, please feel free to use any one of these desks. I am sure Miss Miller will be pleased to provide you with any materials you may require." He introduced us to the young woman he'd mentioned who served as a clerk in the records office.

We settled into our seats at a large desk, once Moran had departed to return to his own office in order to prepare for the arrival of Coolidge. Within minutes, a sheaf of papers – the cables from those attending Harding in San Francisco – appeared on our desk, and Holmes began to thumb through them, reading quickly as his eyes flashed across page after page of the memos. He withdrew a pad of paper and pencil from his attaché case, looked up to the ceiling, and then turned to me.

"Suppose you wanted to poison someone already in somewhat compromised health," he asked. "It would have to look sufficiently natural so as not to raise alarms, especially if the victim were a powerful and prominent individual. What would be your candidates for such a crime?"

Holmes knew as much about poisons as I – likely far more given his criminal researches – but I was willing to play along with his game. "Well, I might think of *Cicuta maculate* or perhaps *Ricinus communis*," I speculated. "But see here! Do you seriously thinking Harding was poisoned?"

"Oh, I have little doubt about it," Holmes replied distractedly. "Yes, those are most certainly effective choices, but not in this case. *Cicuta maculate*, or hemlock, would surely cause symptoms uncharacteristic of what has been reported to have afflicted Mr. Harding."

"True. Convulsions and cramping, although he had complained of stomach pains," I offered.

"As to *Ricinus communis*, yes, castor is a deadly plant, but again, it would have induced very noticeable symptoms that the physicians haven't mentioned in these cables," he countered.

"Well, let me see. There is *Abrus precatorius*, the inappropriately named 'Rosary Pea', extremely deadly in small doses and difficult to detect."

"Yes, a possible candidate, especially as it can cause organ failure, but it isn't especially fast acting."

"Well, what about *Atropa belladonna*?" I asked. "In the proper dosage, it can paralyze the organs of the body, including the heart, which could create the semblance of a coronary thrombosis or a stroke."

"Yes," Holmes said in a half-dreamy way, indicating the idea had occurred to him as well. "Belladonna. 'Deadly nightshade', as it is more commonly known. Certainly a possibility, although one would have to have access to it." He became quiet as he pored over cable after cable, passing them along to me as well. They seemed to recapitulate the account we'd already heard: The President complaining of feeling poorly, a number of treatments administered by the physicians, and then a sudden worsening of the condition and death.

"Watson, I shall be consumed by some of this work for the rest of the day. I wonder if you might be willing to pay a visit to the National Botanic Garden, which is located near the Capitol, and then meet me back at the Willard for dinner by six."

"Are you sure that I cannot be of assistance to you here?" I inquired. "It seems a waste of my time to be looking at flowers."

"I will be fine and properly focused on these materials," he replied. "But I need you to examine their collection of plants carefully."

"What am I looking for?" I asked.

"Why, any of the poisonous plants that we've been discussing. Few grow in this climate, and unless acquired in a powdered form, which would easily be traceable from the chemist, a Botanic Garden might prove a ready source for all sorts of lethal flowers, roots, and berries."

I didn't like the idea of leaving Holmes alone, but as it seemed his desire, I gathered my things and walked out of the building, turning to the right to follow the broad expanse of Pennsylvania Avenue as it jogged around the Treasury and continued to the end of the boulevard, where the gleaming white Capitol building sat atop a low-rising Hill overlooking the city. It was a stroll of nearly a mile, I should think, and I was fairly dripping with perspiration by the time I arrived at the base of the hill leading up to the Capitol. There I found the glass building that served as the Botanic Garden and went inside. The high degree of humidity maintained for the benefit of the tropical vegetation unfortunately made the interior of the building even more uncomfortable than the out-of-doors, but at least I was afforded some relief from the brutal sun.

I browsed amongst the orchids and palms and every variety of plant in between, it seemed, but I didn't see a section devoted to the dangerous varieties I was seeking. Soon, however, an official looking chap in a uniform passed me and I hailed him. He wore a small piece of black crepe pinned to his chest to signify, I presumed, his mourning for the late President.

"Good afternoon, sir. May I be of assistance?" he asked.

"Yes, my good man. I need some advice."

"Ah, a visitor from England, I take it? What can I do for you?"

"Yes, London," I replied. "I wonder if you might have any plants here that might fall into the category of 'dangerous'," I asked.

"A 'dangerous' plant?" he repeated, barely suppressing a smile. Then he became serious. "Ah, you mean something that's poisonous to eat, or that could hurt your skin? Something like that?"

"Yes, precisely. Do you have any examples of such plants?"

"I do, yes sir, I do," he responded. "Let's just go over here." He wound his way through the broad green leaves and bright flowers that engulfed the building and stopped in a section of low-lying plants. "Here you are, sir. One deadlier than the next! Don't be touching them please. I wouldn't be wanting something to happen to you like what happened to our Mr. Harding!"

"What on Earth do you mean by that?" I asked. "Was he poisoned?"

The guide blanched. "Oh, no! I only meant his sudden death. I surely don't think . . . Why, who would do such a thing?" he asked. He turned away and examined his plants for a moment.

"Have you by any chance an example of *Atropa belladonna*? I inquired.

"I certainly do," he responded, pointing to a plant with small, broad leave and purple flowers with five-petals. Many of the branches had small, purple berries on them as well.

I fairly flew out of the Botanical Garden and hailed a cab to take me back up to the Treasury Department where Holmes was working, but as we pulled up, I saw my friend emerging from the great stone building. "Holmes!" I cried. He glanced up with a look of satisfaction on his face.

"Hello. Did you have a productive visit to the garden?"

"Deadly nightshade!" I cried. "Here in the capital!"

Holmes brought his hand up to his face and raised his index finger to his lips, signaling that my outburst had clearly piqued the interest of Miss Miller, who had also exited the building and started down the step in a different direction.

"Wait until we're in the hotel."

Departing Moran's office, the two trackers following us at a discrete distance, we crossed the street and hurried to the Willard and up to our room. Holmes peered down onto the street and then drew the curtains against the late afternoon sun. "Now, tell me what you learned," he entreated.

I related the events of my trip to the Botanic Garden, my discussion with the guide, and the discovery of the deadly nightshade bush. "I should think that it would have been child's play to secure a sample of the poisonous berries," I offered.

"Excellent!" Holmes said. "A bit of luck there, I should say. Now, let us have a nice quiet dinner." We went to the hotel restaurant and ate a delicious meal, strolling afterwards along the broad boulevards of the city. Washington was clearly a growing metropolis, and the new official buildings contrasted markedly with many rooming houses and shops that clearly dated from the turn-of-the-century. It was difficult to gauge the typical gaiety of Washingtonians, however, since a subdued atmosphere had descended upon the residents following the President's passing.

The next day was spent with Holmes again reviewing papers at the Secret Service office while I gathered information about the train carrying Harding's body, which was due to arrive at 10:30 pm. I met Holmes at a local restaurant for dinner at six and we enjoyed a hearty meal. By nine, we were waiting in the hotel lobby when Moran appeared alone. Lurking near the door, however, were the same two men we had noticed earlier, and Holmes discretely pointed them out to Moran.

"Yes, I recognized them when I came in," he said. "They're Bureau people. Come with me." He grabbed

Holmes's arm and hustled us quickly back into the lobby, then through the restaurant and into the kitchen. Rushing down a corridor, we emerged into the sticky night air on the opposite side of the building from the entrance where the Bureau men had been lurking, and we were quickly swallowed up into the night.

There were hordes of people lining the route from the White House down towards Union Station, where Harding's train would soon be arriving. As we looked down the avenue, we could see that black bunting and crepe had been hung on many storefronts and decked the trolleys and carriages that ferried people down towards the station. We, however, moved in the opposite direction, towards the side entrance to the White House near the Treasury Building. Moran showed his credentials to the officer at the guardhouse, who snapped to attention when he read the name. "Yessir, Chief Moran," he barked, and then cast a sideways look at Holmes and me.

"These are the special security men I am bringing to prepare for Mr. Coolidge," he explained. "They haven't had time for their credentials to be prepared, but they are with me." The guard obediently nodded his approval and we passed onto the grounds of the looming white mansion. We walked quickly to the rear entrance where Moran repeated his masquerade, and within moments we were inside, passing by the library and several other well-appointed rooms, past portraits of former Presidents and first ladies. I couldn't help feeling a sense of awe at being in such an historic place, but Holmes gave no indication of curiosity or excitement.

Moran opened a door, above which was written "Secret Service", and we walked into a small office with a desk and several chairs. "This is my White House office," Moran explained. "We're going to park ourselves right here till I get a call that the train is in, and then we'll make our move." Within a half-hour, the telephone on his desk rang and he picked it up, spoke briefly, and replaced the receiver. "The train is here," he reported. "They'll be arriving at the White House in about five minutes. It's time to go."

We walked up a back stairway and found ourselves at the broad transept that connected the State Dining Room on the west side of the building to the East Room, where there was feverish activity. Crepe was prodigiously hung in the doorways and up the bannisters to the private residence on the second floor, and in the center of the East Room was a platform covered in black cloth.

"The Lincoln catafalque," Moran explained softly. The platform had been hastily constructed in 1865 to hold the remains of the assassinated sixteenth President, and since then had been used to hold the caskets of other Presidents and dignitaries.

We walked to the foyer of the mansion where a number of guards and dignitaries were awaiting the arrival of the President's remains. Within moments, the large black hearse arrived with a phalanx of other vehicles and the doors to the White House were swung open. A group of soldiers entered carrying the President's coffin, which was covered by an American flag, followed by Mrs. Harding who was dressed entirely in black. The group proceeded to the East Room and the coffin was placed on the catafalque. The military escorts quickly dispersed, leaving only a few men to watch over the scene. When most of the others had filed out, the widow, who appeared quite stolid, approached the coffin for a few moments of private reflection. When she stepped back, she was engulfed by a small group of well-wishers, some of whom also made their way to the flag-enshrouded coffin to pay their respects.

This scene continued for about a half-an-hour in near silence, and then the guests were escorted out of the East Room, as we remained by a little-used entry door at the top of the stairs we had ascended from Moran's basement office. I had barely noticed that Mrs. Harding had departed as well, leaving only four military guards standing at each end of the coffin. Suddenly, after the bustle of the preceding hour, the room seemed still and eerily quiet. The lights throughout the first floor were dimmed and the entire White House itself seemed in a state of quiet mourning.

Moran signaled to us that it was time to make our move. He stepped into the East Room, drawing the attention of the guards, two of whom turned towards us.

"Who are you, sir?" one asked.

Moran had his identification card with him, as well as a badge of some kind identifying him as the Chief of the Secret Service. "These are my mortuary assistants," he said, motioning to Holmes and myself. "We must confirm the President's body has been properly preserved. Until he is safety interred, under federal law, I am personally responsible for his safety and care."

"Well, I hardly think his safety is a major concern under the circumstances," said one of the guards suspiciously.

Moran leveled a disapproving eye at him. "Unless you would like me to report your insubordination to your commanding officer," he said with a firm voice, "you should hold your tongue, soldier, and let me do my job! Now, we are going to take a brief moment to evaluate President Harding, and then we'll get out of here." He spoke the words without a hint of conditionality, as though he was giving a direct order that the guards dare not countermand. Indeed, the lead guard looked around at his colleagues, and then gave a short nod to Moran.

The flag was removed and Moran, Holmes, and I went to the casket and raised the portion of the lid over the late President's head. A chemical odor escaped from the coffin but quickly dissipated. Moran shone the light from his torch into the coffin and illuminated what was incontrovertibly the well-preserved face of the late President.

"Who goes there?" shouted Moran suddenly and he spun around towards the main doors that opened onto the transept. I had heard nothing, but like the guards, I reflexively turned. Two of the guards followed Moran to the door, but there was no one present. "Must've been one of those White House rats they're always complaining to me about," he said. He returned and asked if we were nearly finished.

"Yes, all done here," said Holmes in a most credible American accent. He reached up for the lid and brought it down with a gentle thump. "No doubt, Director Moran, that's him. And a first-class embalming, I might add. I guess we can head home now." We thanked the guards for their indulgence and made our way towards the empty foyer.

We were nearly to the door when Holmes stopped abruptly, his chin slightly elevated. "Do you smell it?" he asked anxiously.

"Smell what?" Moran asked. I admit that I detected no odor, but Holmes's sense of smell was remarkably acute.

"Something is burning. Upstairs," he said, casting an eye towards the staircase that rose from the first to the second level of the building where the First Family resided. "Most certainly."

"A fireplace?" I suggested.

"In August, and in this stifling heat?" Holmes responded. "I think that most curious." He thought for a moment. "Moran, Watson – you must both leave so that our departure is clearly noted by the guards. Hopefully they will overlook the absence of one of your number. But I am remaining. There is something foul afoot, I have no doubt, but you must leave it to me to determine what it is. I shall return to the Willard later tonight, assuming I am not apprehended here, and hopefully will be able to give you a full report at that time."

Moran looked quizzically at Holmes. "I don't know," he said. "That's not even close to being authorized. Leaving you alone in the White House?"

"Your mission is to protect the President," Holmes reminded him. "Well, the President is now Mr. Coolidge, and he isn't here, so you aren't violating your duties."

Moran looked dubious, but he shook his head. "Only because it's you, Mr. Holmes," he said. "But I sure would appreciate it if you could avoid being apprehended."

"That is my own fervent hope as well," Holmes said. "And by the way," he said handing Moran a thin stick with a swap of cotton on the end, "have your chemists analyze this sample I took from Harding's mouth when you so admirably distracted the guards, as I had requested. Please see if they can find any traces of chemicals on it."

Moran accepted the swab uncomfortably and, with a considerable amount of trepidation, I said goodbye to Holmes. Moran and I then returned to the basement and exited into the White House garden. It was a beautiful if muggy evening, and the flowers and trees were lush and the air filled with the scent of nature. It was a welcome contrast to the somber scene we had just left in the East Room, and as we departed the grounds, I couldn't help but cast my eyes backward towards the illuminated mansion and think of my friend still inside.

Part III – The Man with the Green Hat

Moran and I dropped the swab at his office with instructions for the laboratory assistants to analyze its contents as quickly as possible. Then we walked down F Street into the downtown, saying nothing of what we had just done or what Holmes might be engaged in doing at the moment. My thoughts were swirling – here we were in Washington, the President had died, and we had been summoned to ascertain whether the reports of a natural death were accurate or if something far more nefarious might be at work. My plan for a summer holiday to give Holmes the chance to inconspicuously visit the United States for a restful vacation couldn't possibly have gone more off track!

My agitation must have been evident. "Could you use something to calm your nerves?" Moran asked, raising an eyebrow.

"I certainly could," I replied, "except that you Yankees have gone and imposed Prohibition. If we were in London right now," I explained, "we would be having a pint or two at The Donkey and His Keeper."

"Well, we don't have pubs here, but we do have something that might help," said the agent. We walked into a narrow alley and up to the rear door of a shop that fronted on G Street. Moran knocked three times, then twice more, and the door opened a crack.

"I've come to see the man with the green hat," he said. There was a grunt of recognition from inside. The door opened slightly and a middle-aged man peered out through the crack and looked us up and down.

"Ah, it's you," he said to Moran without mentioning his name. There was the sound of a chain being removed, and the man said, "Come right in and enjoy." We walked down a set of stairs and Moran pushed open another door and we found ourselves in a well-appointed pub, or bar, as the Americans say, with men and women drinking what certainly appeared to be prohibited beverages while a Negro woman sang gently to a small group of accompanists.

"But I thought – " I began.

"There are laws," Moran said, "and there are laws, Doctor."

"Who is this man in the green hat?" I asked, looking around for the colorful headwear.

Moran laughed. "Oh, a very highly regarded bootlegger who supplies the White House, Congress, and just about every other powerful figure here in Washington," he replied. He looked around. "I come here rather more frequently than I should, I suppose. That's why I was quickly admitted."

We sat down at a small table somewhat away from other patrons, and shortly I was enjoying the first welcome spirits I had tasted since the steamship.

"There's plenty of government folks here, including quite a number of congressmen and senators, who voted for Prohibition. Lawyers from the Justice Department. That man over there – " he subtly jutted his thumb toward a rotund gentleman. " – is one of the city commissioners."

He assumed a more somber demeanor. "Our late friend back there in the box – " he motioned over his shoulder towards the White House " – he was known to indulge quite a bit when he was a senator, but then his wife got him elected President against his wishes, and he had to give up the speakeasys, though I think he had a pretty good stash up in his personal quarters for his card games. A least that was the rumor."

"An indulgent man," I noted.

Moran looked hard at me. "Booze wasn't all of it," he said. He lowered his voice. "Carrie Phillips. Nan Britton." He rolled his eyes.

"Yes, those names were mentioned earlier, but I admit to not recognizing them," I confessed.

"Well, let's just say Warren Harding had a roving eye," Moran said, "and there was quite a gleam in it when he spotted an attractive young woman."

"Was Mrs. Harding aware of his carrying on?" I asked.

"Ha!" Moran laughed, causing a few heads to turn in our direction. "She would've been the last person to know if she wasn't! But she had what she wanted – respectability – which wasn't bad for where she came from. Her husband as President. It's made a former piano teacher one of the most well-known and influential women in the world." He moved closer to me and put his face next to mine. "Tell me, – what's Mr. Holmes doing? Do you have any idea?"

"I presume," I responded, "finding out the source of that smoke. You know what they say, don't you. Where there's smoke – "

"There's fire" the slightly tipsy Moran finished the expression.

It was well after midnight when I heard the key opening the lock of our sitting room at the Willard Hotel and I started awake. I had intended to wait for Holmes, but the overstuffed chair had proven too comfortable and I must have drifted off to sleep. The overhead light clicked on and Holmes walked into the room, accompanied by two men I would have guessed were in their thirties.

"My apologies at disturbing you, Watson," he said, "but my escorts insisted upon returning me to these quarters." The two men we had spotted watching us over the past two days were on either side of Holmes with their arms holding each of his. They looked decidedly unfriendly and officious.

"Just be sure you remember, Mr. Holmes," one of them said. "The first train in the morning." He looked around the room and at me. "No calls. No leaving the room," he said. "No talking over the telephone," he added, leaning down and pulling the wire out from the wall. "On second thought, I'll take this with me." The two men looked around the room again, paying little attention to me. "I suggest you grab some sleep. It's been a long night."

With that, they turned and walked out, closing the door behind them. Holmes watched them go and then turned to me.

"Well, I think we can consider ourselves very fortunate," he said as he took off his jacket.

"Why do you say that?" I inquired.

"Because we will spend the night in this very comfortable hotel, and we shall enjoy a hearty breakfast in the morning before our train to New York. And that is a decidedly better prospect than the alternative that presented itself only a short time ago."

"And what was that?" I asked.

"I believe the exact quote was, 'Twenty years in Leavenworth'."

Part IV – Holmes's Account

"I was always convinced there was more to this case than was originally presented to us," Holmes began as he lit a cigarette and settled into a chair. It was after one in the morning, but neither of us felt tired now, and it was impossible to consider sleeping before I had the full account of Holmes's adventures after I'd left him in the White House. "Frankly, as my ideas coalesced this afternoon, I doubted my own reasoning, but the facts, Watson! The facts! They became incontrovertible. And they all led to one conclusion."

"Was Harding murdered?" I asked. "Was he the victim of an assassination conspiracy?"

Holmes leaned back in his chair and took a long pull on his cigarette, inhaling deeply and sending a blue stream towards the fan rotating in the centre of the room. "Yes," he responded wearily. "Yes, he was. But his murder is not the most consequential or even the most remarkable part of this story," he added. "Nor is it the only portion that must remain confidential. Yes, Watson, I must entreat you to refrain from committing what I am about to tell you to writing."

"For how long a time?" I asked.

"I am afraid I must ask that this never become an *'Adventure of Sherlock Holmes'*," he replied. He looked at me intently and tilted his head, as if to seek assent. I paused before responding.

"It is never my intent to violate a trust or disclose material related to national security," I said, hedging my promise.

A sharp laugh escaped from his lips as Holmes's face broke into a smile, the lines around his eyes crinkling into deep folds as his mouth formed a smile. "Washington must agree with you, Watson," he said. "You have been here but three days, and that evasive answer indicates that you are showing true signs of becoming a politician! That is not an answer, but let us trust your judgment. When you have heard this tale, I suspect you will understand the necessity of confidentiality.

"It was the smoke, Watson, the *smoke* in the White House that convinced me swift action was required," he began. "After you and Moran departed, I flew up the stairs and, as silently as I could, and began checking the rooms on the second floor for the source of the smoke. The third room I looked into contained a sight as startling as any I have seen over our forty-plus years of knowing one another.

"There was a roaring fire in the hearth, which was producing the only light in the room, as well as the odor I had detected as we had left the East Room. Stacks of papers and notebooks were piled up in front of the fireplace. A woman dressed in black sat on the floor near the papers, briefly looked at each document for a moment before throwing it into the flames, where it quickly burst into brilliant orange and was consumed. Standing several feet away in the darkened room was a man who silently watched as the woman intently reviewed the materials. Neither heard me enter.

"'Are you going to burn it all, Mrs. Harding?' I asked.

"The former First Lady, whose husband lay in a casket one floor below, looked up and was about to scream, but she could see me holding up my hands. The man was also startled and quickly opened his jacket and withdrew a revolver, which he menacingly pointed at me. They regarded me for a moment, and then the woman stood erectly and smoothed her dress. She motioned to the man to lower his pistol, which he did. 'May I ask who you are, sir, and why are you trespassing in my house at this hour,' she asked, 'and why I should not immediately summon the police?'

"'I do not think calling for the police would be in either of our best interests, Mrs. Harding,' I replied, casting an eye towards the armed guard. 'And I presume you would be Mr. Clayton Graham of the Bureau of Investigation.' I walked closer towards her. 'My name is Sherlock Holmes. Perhaps you have heard of me?'

"She took several steps towards me and looked at me carefully, as if to confirm my identify. She is a woman in her mid-sixties, with graying hair piled on her head, wearing rimless eyeglasses and a serious mien. She is most commanding in appearance, but clearly didn't appreciate my presence."

"'Yes, I have heard of you, Mr. Holmes, and I heard that you had appeared in this city at the most unhappy of times for me and for our grieving nation.'

"'Also a most inconvenient time, I might add,' I responded. 'No doubt that report originated with Mr. Burns at the Bureau of Investigation, your ally – and your supervisor,' I added, looking to Graham. She nodded her assent after a moment, but Graham remained rigid.

"She took a deep breath and looked about the ornate room with rich furnishings and portraits on the wall. The fireplace was of elaborately carved marble and the rugs very fine Persian. She turned on several electric lights and I could see the richly furnished room, as well as the face of her young guard who had returned his firearm to his pocket. 'Clayton, why don't you wait for me outside?' she said. 'I have no doubt I'm quite safe here with Mr. Holmes.' The young man looked disapprovingly at me, but followed her instructions and left the room, closing the door behind him.

"'This is the Treaty Room, Mr. Holmes. Did you know that?' she asked. I shook my head negatively. 'Before Mr. Roosevelt built the new wing with the President's office, this was used by my husband's predecessors – Lincoln, Grant, McKinley,' she mused. 'Since then, it has been the President's private study – for Roosevelt, that uncontrollable child who stumbled into office. And Wilson, that insufferable, priggish racist!' She paused. 'I loathed him for his indifference to the plight of our Negro citizens.' She paused again. 'And Harding, my husband.' She turned to face the desk, from whose open drawers she evidently had removed the papers she had been busily feeding into the inferno. She stood and walked back to the pile of papers and threw more into the fireplace without looking at their contents, and then returned to her chair.

"'I understand this was also a favourite room of my late husband for his trysts with Nan Britton in recent years.' she added. She turned away from me and walked to a large sofa. 'Come, Mr. Holmes, why don't you sit down and tell me what you think you know of all this business, and I might as well fill in any of the blank spots.' She sat down and patted the sofa next to her. 'I promise not to bite you.'

"'It is not your bite nor your bark that worries me,' I replied. 'But there is more than good reason to be wary of you, isn't there? You see, I have spent the last two days looking at a great deal of material about you and your husband, the late President, and I spent much of the evening putting the pieces together. It is a complicated story and one that, I suspect, you would not want publicized.'

"'Suppose I tell you four names,' I suggested, 'and one word, and then you can decide if I am on the right track.' " Her tired eyes searched my face in the darkened room as the fire burned down – a wisp of gray smoke escaped from the flue and spread through the room like a London fog. 'Clayton Graham, Roosevelt, Wilson, and Harding, and belladonna.'

"Her eyes opened wide and she sat forward in her chair. Her mouth moved slightly, as if she were uttering a silent exclamation. She licked her bottom lip and sat back in the chair.

"'All right, Mr. Holmes, I can see your reputation is well-earned,' she said. 'I can tell you the story, but I suppose you will tell me the ending. I would ask that the facts go no further than the two of us, but I doubt you would make such an agreement.' I shook my head silently. 'Very well, very well.' She paused, and this is the tale she told me . . . ."

Part V – Mrs. Harding's Story

"I married Mr. Harding in 1891," she said, "but it was not my first marriage. Many people are not aware of my earlier marriage when I was just nineteen, to a young man named Pete deWolfe. It was an impetuous decision, but I was frantic to escape from my father, an uncivil and even violent man. Although he had begun life as a hardware salesman, my father had proven adept at business and by the time I was a young woman, he had become quite prosperous. Not surprisingly, he didn't approve of his daughter even socializing with a common laborer. The thought of marriage was utterly out of the question.

"When I found that I was to have a child, Peter and I agreed that we didn't want the baby born out of wedlock, and so we eloped to escape my father's disapproval. Eight months later, my son, Marshall, was born – a strong and healthy baby

– but my life was far from an easy one. Within just two years, my husband had become a drunk and abandoned us. After I divorced him, I couldn't support Marshall. He went to live with my father, who refused to allow me to live under his roof.

"A decade later, I married Mr. Harding, the publisher of *The Marion Star*, in whom I saw great promise. He and I worked closely together to make the newspaper a success, and he also began to dabble in local politics as an ally of Governor Foraker and Senator Hanna, which led to his election to the State Senate in 1899. Although he was a reluctant politician, he proved quite adept at speaking and greeting crowds, and he developed an admirable following.

"We didn't have children of our own, and so we put all of our energies into the paper and then into building Mr. Harding's political career. He was doing quite well – he was elected lieutenant-governor in 1904 – but then there was a bitter public disagreement with Mr. Roosevelt, who had become President after our Ohio native, Mr. McKinley, was murdered. That quarrel helped contribute to Mr. Harding's defeat for governor in 1908, and many thought his political career was over. But not I, Mr. Holmes. Not I!

"As you may know, Mr. Roosevelt soured on President Taft, whom he had essentially appointed his successor, and in 1912, he challenged Mr. Taft for the Republican nomination. Taft won, but T.R. ran as an independent – he called himself a 'Bull Moose', and his antics cost Mr. Taft and the Republicans the presidency. That insufferable little southern schoolteacher Woodrow Wilson was elected." She gave an involuntary shudder.

"As fate would have it, Mr. Harding won election to the Senate just two years later, and embarked on a career that I had determined would eventually place him in the White House. After the death of my son soon after the election, I had no other distractions and no goal on Earth higher than for my husband to become President. I resolved I would let nothing stand in the way of achieving that ambition. Nothing! Did you know that Madame Marcia, the Washington astrologer, predicted that Warren would become President! Yes, she did, and that he would die suddenly, perhaps by poisoning!

"And yet two obstacles jeopardized our reaching that goal in 1920. One was that horrible Mr. Roosevelt, who had been traipsing all over South America doing who knows what since he had nearly destroyed the Republican Party. And the other was that bigot and liar Wilson, who had been re-elected in 1916. You know, he had campaigned on the slogan 'He Kept Us Out of War', but as soon as he was re-elected, he could not wait to send our boys to die in the trenches in France. And his new wife, Edith, wanted him to run for a *third* term – could you imagine such a thing?

"Those were the men who stood between my husband and the White House! Horrible men.

"That could not be allowed! One man had tried to derail Warren's political career and then nearly ruined the Republican Party. The other had caused tens of thousands of deaths by lying to the American people. I resolved I would do anything to ensure they never had the chance to run again and keep my Warren from his destiny.

"You mentioned Clayton Graham, Mr. Holmes, which tells me you have untangled much of the story. Your reputation is well-deserved.

"Yes, Mr. Graham was an Ohio native, an orphan, whom Mr. Harding and I came to love like a son during our early years in Washington, and we helped him find a job at the Bureau of Investigation and work his way up quickly. Mr. Harding was always happy to help him along with a favourable word to the right superior at the Justice Department, and I think it's fair to say that as much as we regarded Clayton as the son we had never had, he regarded us as substitute parents. Clayton had no less ambition for the senator than I, and we often discussed – just the two of us – how to further Mr. Harding's fortunes.

"When Roosevelt began making comments about running in 1920, we were very concerned. Yes, he remained popular with some of the party faithful, but he was hated by others – like us, who blamed him for Taft's defeat. And he was a very sick man, from illnesses contracted during his adventures in South America. He had been hospitalized late in 1918 – did you know that? Why, he might not even survive a term as President! When Clayton was assigned to provide protection to him during January of 1919, we considered that it might be best for our party, and for the country, to ensure Teddy's candidacy went no further than his own ambition.

"I was the one whose ambition would not be denied! Madam Marcia had described me as 'a dominant, willful, tenacious person with a great desire to rule'. I remembered her prediction, and I became determined to see it through!"

Holmes paused in relating Mrs. Harding's account. "Of course," he said to me, "by this point, it had occurred to me that the lady was quite mad."

I nodded my head in agreement.

"That is when the idea came to me," she continued. "Surely there must be a substance available without going to a pharmacy that might help Mr. Roosevelt on his way to his greatest glory before he could make good his intention to run for President again. It did not require much research to discover the remarkable qualities of deadly nightshade or, as you called it just now, bellandonna. Of course, that plant isn't native to Washington, but it was a simple matter for Clayton to acquire a sample from the Botanic Garden and to take it to

Oyster Bay during his assignment to guard Roosevelt. A bit of the berry crushed into his drink and Mr. Roosevelt was no more. They called it a stroke – a blood clot in his lung."

The enormity of what Mrs. Harding had just admitted to Holmes took my breath away. I looked carefully into his eyes to see if he doubted what she had confessed, but Holmes's eyes were resolute and his face grim. He continued his account of her story.

"Mr. Wilson still remained a formidable foe in 1920, should he break with precedent and run for a third term. Having taken our first step with Roosevelt, executing a plan to ensure that Mr. Wilson ended his presidency in 1921 was, in my view, merely a 'next step' in our efforts to place Mr. Harding in the White House. What great fortune occurred in October of 1919 when the President journeyed westward to promote his ludicrous League of Nations and Clayton was assigned to aid in the security plans.

"Once again, Clayton made a visit to the Botanic Garden and acquired an additional sample of the nightshade which had proven so effective with Mr. Roosevelt. Wilson was exhausted and not in the best of health, so Clayton gave him perhaps a smaller dose than he should have when they were in a hotel in Pueblo, but the effect was quite stark. Like Roosevelt, he suffered a stroke, but Wilson survived, though terribly disabled. However, any discussion of his seeking a third term was ended and the route for my Warren to win election was that much clearer."

I couldn't believe my ears. The former First Lady of the United States, whose own husband had died of a stroke just a week before, had admitted to Holmes her role in eliminating two of her husband's most feared rivals in the 1920 election which had resulted in Harding's election. Suddenly, however, the awful conclusion of the story dawned on me.

"No!" I cried. "You cannot be serious. It isn't possible that such devilry exists!"

Holmes said nothing, but gazed out the window. Even at this late hour, there remained traffic and crowds on Pennsylvania Avenue as the capital prepared to mark the departure of the funeral train for Ohio in just a few hours. He reached for another cigarette and the flare of the match lit up his face. I don't believe I ever saw it so drained of energy, so filled with a sense of tragedy, as in that hotel room.

Mrs. Harding continued her narrative. "Well, as you know, Senator Harding did win the election in 1920. In fact, he not only won it, but he won the biggest victory in history. In history! And do you know what was especially pleasing? He defeated the cousin of that Teddy Roosevelt – Franklin – who was the Democrats' vice-presidential candidate!

"But, Mr. Holmes, the presidency was not what he had expected. Not at all. He was unhappy with the demands of the job, as he had told Nicholas Murray Butler, the president of Columbia University. Isn't that so sad? And then his supposed friends were creating such embarrassments, like Mr. Fall selling those oil leases on the federal land at Teapot Dome. It seemed that these scandals might even complicate his efforts to win a second term in 1924, assuming I could persuade the President to run (although I am quite sure I could have done so).

"But then, reports began to reach me that Warren's enemies were organizing against him. If Warren didn't step aside, he learned, the newspapers would run stories about my first marriage, my divorce, about Marshall dying from alcoholism, about whether I had even been married to Pete at all. His rivals began to circulate rumors about my husband and his relationships with those other women – even about producing a bastard daughter with that whore Nan Britton!"

At this disclosure, she dabbed at her eyes and took several moments to settle herself. She suddenly looked very old and very exhausted despite the alarming admissions she was making.

"And then there was the rumor that he really was a Negro, or at least that he had some Negro ancestors," she said. "You know, we have been very supportive of the Negroes – we really were, not like that horrible Mr. Wilson. But in this country, Mr. Holmes, there mere suggestion of having black blood would instantly disqualify any person from being elected President, and it will always be that way."

"So, three terrible rumors – about my marriage and divorce, about those trollops and a bastard child, and his alleged Negro ancestry."

Hmm, I thought, as we had discussed – things do come in threes!

"He was so miserable and depressed," she continued, "and his health began to fail. I could see it happening in January, when he got the flu, and I thought I would lose him then. The doctors advised us to take a trip out West, to California and Alaska, in hopes it might revive his weakened state of mind that had necessitated several hospitalizations when he was a publisher. Did you know that, Mr. Holmes? Another story we didn't want to see promoted!

"So we went on the trip – seven-thousand miles by train and ship – and yes, some of it was magnificent, but I could see the toll is was taking on him. Once we arrived in San Francisco, I knew the end was near, and I didn't want him to suffer. At my request, Clayton had brought with him a small amount of the nightshade in the event it might be needed. The doctors had just about worn him out with their purges and medicines. I felt I could help him go to his rest and avoid all the embarrassment and humiliation that would follow him back to Washington and through the next campaign.

"Don't you see, Mr. Holmes? It was better to end it this way, on *our* terms, free from the mortification his enemies would cause, tainting his legacy forever. And so, yes, I did give him a little nightshade in his milk as he was resting, and he went to sleep forever. Although that horrid Mrs. Johnson, the owner of the Palace, nearly ruined everything by insisting the police test the milk remaining in the glass! But I put a stop to that! I grabbed the glass and poured the residue down the drain!"

* * * * *

The room was quiet as Holmes ended his account of Mrs. Harding's unspeakable actions. It took several minutes before I could collect my thoughts.

"And the Bureau agent, Graham?" I asked.

"He would surely deny involvement, even if Mrs. Harding would accuse him, which she never would," Holmes responded. "She is obviously insane and has been for some time, perhaps stemming from the death of her son. Moreover, I have little doubt Director Burns might well have become aware of this plot and might have been persuaded to conceal the role of one of his agents so that he wouldn't be implicated in the premature deaths – to put it obliquely – of three American Presidents. Such a disclosure would hardly enhance his stature as the director of the Bureau of Investigations."

"What are you going to do?" I asked in amazement, the full weight of the incredible story sinking in.

"Mrs. Harding offered me one more piece of information that she believes is relevant," he said. "She is dying of kidney disease. Indeed, she has been suffering from it for many years, and now her doctors say she will be dead within a year." He took a deep pull on yet another cigarette, the orange tip burning furiously in the near dark of the room. "I suppose I must weigh the merits and drawbacks of revealing all I've been told against the terrible impact disclosure would surely impose on a people already bereft at the loss of their President.

"And to what end? Mr. Graham undoubtedly is a good enough investigator to have covered his tracks sufficiently. The Washington police would never be able to incontrovertibly connect him to these tragic events. The real perpetrator, the President's widow, would seem an implausible conspirator, and she appears likely to pay with her life long before a trial and sentence could be executed.

"Moreover, I don't think that I, as a foreigner, should be so deeply involved in disclosing a plot so heinous that it could have profound political implications for the Americans. No, Watson, I believe this is a case that will not only go unsolved but unrecorded, if you don't mind. Certainly I will inform our colleague, Mr. Moran, of my findings, but I strongly suspect he'll come to the same conclusion. The Americans have endured enough. We cannot serve the ends of justice by tightening the hand of guilt around the treacherous Mrs. Harding."

We used the few remaining hours of the night for a brief and, in my case, fitful sleep. Rising early, we ate our breakfast under the careful gaze of the Bureau agents. We were joined by Moran, whom Holmes quietly informed of his astonishing adventure in the White House the previous night. I doubt I have ever seen a man as shocked as was the Secret Service director as Holmes spun out his account of the sinister actions of Harding's widow and her Bureau of Investigations accomplice.

"Good Lord!" the astonished director cried. "She has accomplished as much as Booth, Czolgosz, and Guiteau combined! I will have to give all this some thought, of course, but I understand your hesitation to publicize Mrs. Harding's confession," he said. "But I have no choice but to bring your findings to the attention of President Coolidge. He'll have to make whatever decision he thinks warranted with respect to Mrs. Harding, Graham, and perhaps even Burns." He shook his head. "It's almost impossible to believe, Mr. Holmes. Let me ask you: Do you think it's all true, or has Mrs. Harding simply been confounded by her emotions upon losing her husband?"

"I believe her story, although I don't recall one I would so prefer to have never heard," Holmes said quietly. "Has your laboratory confirmed a trace of belladonna on the swab I inserted into Harding's mouth as he lay in the East Room of the White House?" The director nodded tersely. "Yes, I thought so. Your diversion of the guards was most effective."

Moran rode with us to Union Station to await our train back to New York. There was a great crowd around the station waiting to bid farewell to the late President, for the train bearing the late President and his family and friends was soon due to depart as well. Indeed, as we waited to board our train, the automobiles carrying both the President's coffin and Mrs. Harding arrived.

A respectful silence fell over the crowd as she disembarked and turned to enter the station. As she walked past us, the widow caught Holmes's eye and they locked stares for a long moment. Then she was caught up in the rush of police and dignitaries and swept along to the crepe-draped train that would carry Warren Harding back to Ohio and his final rest.

Epilogue

"Do you remember mentioning how things have a way of happening in threes?" Holmes asked as we settled into our compartment for the ride to New York. "Well, that thought crossed my mind when I realized the unnaturally brief time span in which three presidents, all competing for the office in 1920, suffered strokes that left two dead and one an invalid incapable of running for office.

"True, it might be a coincidence, but experience has taught me that coincidences deserve, at a minimum, further investigation – especially when they involve unanticipated deaths and coveted positions.

"My research into the Secret Service's records of the death of Roosevelt and incapacitation of Wilson in 1919 revealed one point that immediately jumped out at me: In both cases," Holmes noted, "one particular Bureau of Investigations agent – Clayton Graham – was assigned to the potential victim. I asked Moran for a list of those in San Francisco with Harding just before he was fatally stricken, and again, Mr. Graham's name appeared on the manifest of names." He shook his head. "That was simply too coincidental, and it made me think that there must have been a conspiracy at work.

"But one point complicated my theory, and that was that Graham was nowhere near Mr. Harding for two days before the President's death. He certainly might have administered the poison earlier in the trip, which might have explained the

278

President's confusing symptoms in Alaska and when he first arrived back in San Francisco. But he was then not close enough to Harding to slip the nightshade into food or drink.

"Indeed, while he was bedridden in the Palace Hotel, only Mrs. Harding never had left his side, right up until the time he expired. And that caused a sudden and dismaying thought: Might his *wife* rather than Graham have administered the poison that caused President's death?

"But why would she have been an accomplice in the deaths of Roosevelt and Wilson?" I asked.

"Because, as she admitted to me, those two men stood between her husband and the office *she* intended that he occupy," Holmes said. "As to the relationship between the First Lady and Graham, I cannot be sure, but I would not be surprised if Dr. Freud would hypothesize that she viewed him as a substitute for her lost son and he, in turn, viewed her as a substitute mother he sought only to please.

"He became her agent, acquiring the belladonna berries and administering it to Roosevelt and Wilson, and then providing her the dose needed to kill her own husband," he concluded.

"And her motivation for doing so?" I asked.

"The dishonesty in the administration, the tawdry relationships, and the ignominy that would be her husband's certain legacy" Holmes answered. "Disclosure would surely have ruined a life of privilege that Mrs. Harding had carefully constructed from the tatters of her earlier marriage, if there even had been one. No, far better to have Harding depart as the martyr of a bereaved nation than the humiliated President driven from office in disgrace."

As Holmes had anticipated, his account of Mrs. Harding's confession was never made public, until now. As Holmes requested, my agreement with Cox and Company ensures that this story will remain confidential until 2020.

While they did not face trials, a judgment of another kind awaited the two key figures in the case, neither of whom survived 1924. Mrs. Harding was not exaggerating the hopelessness of her own medical condition. Shortly after returning to Ohio, she had fallen gravely ill with inoperable kidney disease and she died just weeks after Mr. Coolidge was elected to a full term as President in November 1924. As to Graham, he didn't live long enough to disclose whatever he knew of the crimes, if he could have been persuaded. Assigned by Burns to a group of special agents enforcing Washington's prohibition law, he was shot in the back in January – presumably by accident, by a fellow agent during a raid on a speakeasy associated with "the man in the green hat" on Capitol Hill, only weeks after Holmes and I had returned to London. In February, Mrs. Harding's last victim, Woodrow Wilson, the former President who had suffered grievously since his stroke in 1919, died as well.

Of the others with knowledge of the great plot, Moran has continued to serve as director of the Secret Service. But I suspect word of Graham's treachery made its way to Coolidge, raising questions about the Bureau of Investigation's chief, Burns, the so-called "Sherlock Holmes of America". Both he and the Attorney General under whom he served, a Harding crony named Harry Daugherty, were soon implicated in the massive Teapot Dome scandal and were removed from office in 1924. The new Bureau of Investigation chief – a young, former librarian named J. Edgar Hoover – appears likely to be an interim replacement until a more experienced director can be appointed.

The only other people who know the story surrounding President Harding's sudden death are Holmes and myself. He was soon back tending his bees in Sussex and I returned to my writing desk in London, where this startling account of our adventure in America has been finally recorded for future readers to contemplate.

www.ingramcontent.com/pod-product-compliance
Lightning Source LLC
Chambersburg PA
CBHW051247260626
47162CB00002B/656